True Colors

Krysten Lindsay Hager

Clean Reads
ALL STORY. NO GUILT.

www.CleanReads.com

To my grandparents—
Frank, Lillian, and Ione, who always believed in me

One

Every day I walked down the sidewalk to school and wished I was one of those interesting girls who ran up with exciting news. They were always yelling, way before they got to their group of friends so everyone could hear, about how they got asked out, or their parents were taking them on some amazing vacation or something. I'd prefer my news to be more like, "Guess what? I'm going to be in a music video!" Or maybe, "Guess who's going to be in a movie?" But nothing, *nada*, never any news to share. Well, once a stray cat had kittens in my garage, but it was more annoying than anything since it smelled like cat pee in there for months after my mom found homes for them all. I couldn't even say, "Ooh, guess who got a kitty?" since my mom said I couldn't keep one because the poor thing would get lost in my mess of a room and starve.

Still, just once I'd like to be the interesting one instead of the girl who didn't get invited to things because people "forgot" about her. Instead, I was the girl picked last in gym class (like today) and who couldn't even get noticed there when I tried to get hit during dodge ball so I could sit down.

"Okay, hit the showers," Coach Daly said.

I hadn't done anything to cause me to break a sweat, so I didn't need a shower. I pulled my ponytail holder out of my hair and hoped for the best. My pale blond hair, which behaved so well last weekend when no one saw it, now looked and felt like a broom. The more I tried to fix it, the more it felt like hay. I tried putting in a dab of styling crème, but it just made it greasy. I didn't know how my hair managed to have a dry texture while looking oily at the same time, but it did.

I gave up on my hair and went to get dressed. I tugged on my khaki pants and navy sweater, which made up my glorious Hillcrest Academy uniform, (it was just my luck my school picked colors which made me look like a dead goldfish), grabbed my bag, and went to join the rest of my class lined up to go to the cafeteria. I was almost fourteen and yet had to walk to the lunchroom in a straight line like Madeline from the storybook. Stupid Hillcrest.

Lunch was my favorite part of the day. For one, it meant the school day was half over. I went through the lunch line and grabbed a ham sandwich, some chips, and a bottle of water and went to join my two best friends, Ericka Maines and Tori Robins. The lunchroom was always extra noisy on Fridays because everybody was talking about their plans for the weekend. Sometimes Ericka, Tori, and I went to a movie, but we didn't do much else. Tori and I liked to go shopping, but Ericka's parents thought hanging out at the mall would "morally corrupt" Ericka, blah, blah, blah. And they about had a stroke when she wanted to get a social media page. So I was surprised when Ericka said we should all go to the mall tomorrow.

"Landry, they're having modeling tryouts to be on the *American Ingénue* show," Ericka said, showing me the ad she had torn out of the *Grand Rapids Press*. "The *Ingénue* judges are trying to find local teens to compete on their reality show."

I watched every second of the last show. Talisa Milan won and got a Little Rose cosmetics contract and was on this month's cover of *Bright and Lively* magazine. She was also a host on *Hot Videos Now*, a music video show. Melani Parkington, the runner-up, was the new spokesperson for Bouncy Hair conditioner. You were almost guaranteed to be famous if you made it to the final round of the contest.

"First you have to win in your city, and then your state, and then the regional competition," Tori read. "Then you get to the tough part of the competition where they vote off someone new each week on national TV."

"It's an amazing opportunity to get discovered," Ericka said, checking out her reflection in her spoon.

"Yeah, except for the fact the judges are known to be brutal when they're honest. Like when they told Melani her gorgeous face was too pinched, her forehead was too low, and her eyebrows were too high," I said. "They also told one girl she was pretty, but her lips looked like she had walked into a sliding glass door."

"Well, they did," Ericka said shrugging. "The newspaper says the first fifty girls who try out got a free *American Ingénue* tote bag and Little Rose makeup samples."

They were holding auditions at the Perry Mall, which was the smallest mall in Grand Rapids. There weren't a lot of stores there, so you usually just saw old people mall walking around there. Still, it had a decent bookstore and a cute clothing store, so I said I'd go watch while they tried out.

"No, we're all trying out," Ericka said, grabbing the ad back from me. She said her mother thought she'd be a "natural" for the show since she always got the lead in the school plays. However, Ericka was usually the only one who tried out for the lead. Everyone else felt too stupid singing on stage in front of the whole school. Besides, you had to stay after school to rehearse, and I liked to go home and watch my favorite soap opera, *As the Days Roll On*.

"There's no way I'm trying out," I said. "They always make the girl stand on a platform while they tell her everything that's wrong with her. Melani's gorgeous, and they tore her apart. Besides, I don't look anything like those girls on the show."

I didn't even buy makeup at the Little Rose cosmetics counter because I hated having the salespeople stare at my face to determine whether I was a summer gladiola or a spring daffodil.

"You're tall," Tori said. "Remember one judge wanted to kick Melani out for being too short."

"Yeah, you're practically the tallest girl in school," Ericka said.

I was hoping Tori and Ericka would say I was so beyond gorgeous I was destined to be a model. Instead, they pointed out I was freakishly tall. Of course there was no use arguing with Ericka — especially when she had Tori on her side. It seemed like it was always two against one, and I was always the one left out. Maybe I'd at least get a tote bag and some free makeup out of it.

"I'm going to wear my black mini skirt, and my sister said I could borrow her high-heeled sandals. I think my legs look even longer in heels," Ericka said.

I didn't say anything, but I hoped Ericka changed her mind. Her legs weren't her best feature. I mean, my legs were skinny, but I had heard people say she looked like a flamingo on stilts when she wore a skirt. She always bragged about her amazing Molly Sims legs, but last year she wore a short skirt to sing "O Holy Night" during the holiday pageant. As soon as she started to sing, Kyle Eiton said, "Ericka looks and sounds like a little fawn that got kicked in the gut."

Ericka found out about it and was mad, but Tori and I told her he was just kidding. He was right though. I wouldn't even notice those sorts of things if Ericka wasn't always pointing out my flaws. Sometimes it seemed like her mission in life was to make sure I knew my hair looked like crap.

A lot of girls at school were talking about trying out, but most of the girls at Hillcrest were jocks. Yasmin McCarty, the most popular girl in our class with one thousand-three people on her social media friends list, could win a modeling competition, but she would never enter because it would be beneath her to stand in line and wait to be judged on her looks. She was always saying modeling and stuff was so superficial, but she was also the same girl who walked around school pretending she was freezing so the teachers would let her wear her designer hoodie over her uniform.

I dunno, maybe some girls just knew they were hot and didn't need some TV show to confirm it. I loved watching the show, but the thought of going up there to be judged on how I looked scared me. I was afraid of the judges but even more afraid of Ericka. I knew she'd get mad at me if I didn't try out. So while some girls were secure enough not to need strangers to tell them they were pretty, I spent the whole day trying to figure out the right outfit for my audition (and my dad wondered why my math grades sucked). I mentally went through my closet, and nothing seemed right. My clothes said American Couch Potato, not *American Ingénue*.

I went to math class still trying to decide on an outfit. Thalia Zimmer started reading the answer key, and I realized I forgot to stop at my locker to get my homework before class. I went up to Ms. Ashcroft's desk holding my stomach.

"Ms. Ashcroft? Can—" I stopped as she raised her eyebrows. "*May* I have a bathroom pass?"

"Are you sure you need to go, Miss Albright?" she asked, looking at me over her glasses.

It was pretty risky of her because if I was sick I could puke on her floor and the janitor would have to throw pink sawdust on it and it would sit there, soaking all day, but hey, it was her call.

I nodded putting on my "brave little trouper fighting through the pain" face. She sighed and pulled out the laminated bathroom pass. Earlier in the year she tried to limit our bathroom trips by saying we only got five passes a semester, but several parents called to ask her if an increase in bladder infections was worth the extra class time. If the angry parent calls hadn't worked, I had planned to mention to my dad, who was a doctor, I was afraid to drink anything from seven-fifteen till two-fifteen each day in case I needed to use the toilet.

I raced to my locker and got my homework. I slid it under my sweater so she wouldn't notice me holding it when I walked back into class. As long as I had the pass I went to the bathroom and stopped at the drinking fountain before I headed back to class. Ms. Ashcroft didn't even bother to ask me if I was feeling better. I swear I could die on her floor and she would just move me aside with her foot, lecture the students about not getting distracted by my decomposing corpse, and continue on with her lesson.

When Ms. Ashcroft got up from her desk, I carefully slid my homework out from under my sweater. Math took forever, but I didn't mind because it was my daydreaming time. Nothing was expected of me as long as I pretended to be working on the problems.

After school, I tore my closet apart looking for an outfit. I got so desperate I asked my mom for help when she got home from work.

"You're going to a modeling audition at the mall?" she asked, looking up from the carrot she was chopping. "You know you'll have to go up in front of people to try out, right?"

"Maybe I'll just say I'm sick," I said, popping a piece of carrot in my mouth.

"I didn't mean you can't be a model, honey, it's just... well, you hide whenever you see a camera," she said. "How are you going to get up in front of all those people?"

I told her I didn't have a chance of getting picked anyway. The producers wanted girls with great hair. I just didn't want to trip or anything because the show did an embarrassing moments segment right before they announced the winner.

"I don't want to talk you out of it. I just want to make sure you know what you're getting into. You could wear the plaid kilt grandma got you. You look adorable in it," Mom said.

Models were supposed to be "exotic" and "gorgeous," not "adorable." I was trying to get chosen to be a super-model, not to sell grape juice. It was true the kilt was the nicest thing I owned.

We were supposed to wear heels to the tryout, so I borrowed a pair of my mom's strappy black heels and practiced walking in my room. My right ankle kept wanting to cave in, and I think one of my legs might be shorter than the other since my right foot seemed to drag behind me. I just didn't have a fierce runway walk.

"How about wearing my navy pumps. The heels are a little lower, and your toes won't squish out the sides," Mom said.

"No, it's hopeless. I'm just going to call Ericka and pretend I have the flu, and if she gets mad—"

"Just try the pumps," she said. I put her shoes on and practiced walking in the hallway. The pumps didn't make me wobble from side to side, and I didn't look half bad. Even Mom looked impressed.

Ericka's mother picked me up at nine o'clock the next morning. The competition didn't start until eleven, but Ericka wanted to get there early in case there was a huge line. I always had to sit in the front seat of Mrs. Maines's SUV because even though Tori and I lived on the same street, Ericka always picked up Tori first. I think it was so they could sit together in the back. Ericka had spent extra time curling her hair, but it looked more like the "before" picture in a Bouncy Hair conditioner ad. I had put on makeup and curled my hair, but any illusions of being the next *American Ingénue* died when I saw my reflection in the van's visor mirror. The curl had fallen out of my hair, and I had a foundation streak on my chin. I scrubbed at the peach colored smear and wondered why I thought I could be a model in the first place.

It had only been an hour since I washed my hair, and already, my bangs looked greasy and I swore my chin was breaking out the closer we got to the mall. I thought about pretending to get explosive diarrhea (nobody would accuse me of lying if I admitted to something super gross), but I knew Ericka would get mad at me if I backed out now. Tori was super quiet, so I asked her if she was nervous, too. She looked like she was going to puke, but she straightened her back and said she was fine.

There was already a line when we got to the *American Ingénue* table. The organizers made us wait the full time before they had us fill out forms. Then some lady, who smelled like cinnamon and cigarettes, took a picture of each of us and gave us stickers with numbers on them.

"Great, I got unlucky thirteen," Tori said. "Anyone wanna trade? Landry?"

I had number twelve, and I offered to trade with her since I knew I wouldn't get picked anyway. Besides, I didn't even know if I wanted to be chosen. I hated being singled out. I wouldn't even yell "Bingo" when we played in social studies. Ericka pulled out a compact and started pushing her finger against her eyelashes.

"Did you get something in your eye?" I asked.

"Duh, I'm trying to curl my lashes," she said. "It opens up your eyes."

Ericka wasn't allowed to wear eye makeup, but her mom had gotten her some medicated foundation to cover up her blemishes. Her makeup looked caked on as it tried to cover up her bumpy complexion. She was allowed to wear nail polish, although for some reason it was al-

ways chipped around the edges. It was weird, but I didn't
think I'd ever seen her wearing fresh polish. Tori wasn't
into makeup, but she already had rosy cheeks and lips
and pretty gray eyes, so she didn't need much. However,
I had skin the color of a dead goldfish, and my eyes were
pretty uninteresting as far as blue eyes go. My mom said
I was lucky to have such light blonde hair, but if you
asked me, it was way too pale. Ericka called it "albino
blonde." I looked like I needed a blood transfusion without blush, and mascara kept me from looking like a new-
born baby chicken.

"Okay, I need numbers one through twenty to line
up," the cinnamon/cigarette lady said, gesturing towards
a big velvet curtain. More girls had begun showing up,
and now the line stretched all the way down to the Mr.
Fluffy Muffin Man counter. The Perry Mall probably
hadn't seen so many people since they had "free donut
day." I asked the woman in charge when we got our tote
bags. I did not get there two hours early to go home
without a tote bag. She snapped her gum, and she said
we could pick them up after our turn on the runway.

"What runway?" I asked. Tori pointed out they had
cleared some tables off in front of the curtain to make a
platform. I walked to the front and looked out from behind
the curtain. The tables were now part of a runway, and
there were folding chairs set up for the audience to watch.
It was just mall walkers and parents, but they were still
people who were going to watch me walk... in heels. The
competition was for girls between the ages of thirteen and
seventeen, but it felt like Ericka, Tori, and I were the
youngest ones there. I only saw a couple of girls from
school, and the lineup looked more like something you'd see
on a music video set. All the girls were gorgeous, and they
had these curvy womanly bodies. I looked like a skinny little kid next to them. The first girl walked out, and I heard
the judges say she "owned the runway," and, "walked like a
gazelle." I was starting to feel ill. I wasn't sure which way it

was going to come, but I knew I had to find a bathroom —
fast. I started to get out of line when Ericka grabbed my
wrist.

"It's almost time," she said. A tiny bit of spit flew out
of her mouth and hit my cheek.

I wasn't sure why she was so intent on me going
through with it, but she had a death grip on my arm, so I
didn't have much of a choice. Her number was called and
she walked out to the stage. One of the other girls said
she walked like a kid with sand bucket stilts on her feet,
but she came back with a smirk on her face like she
knew she'd get chosen.

"They said they had never seen such long legs," she
said.

Tori was next.

"She walks like a gorilla at feeding time," said the girl
behind me. I went next, and I tried to focus on not tripping
over my feet. My mom's pumps had a rubber sole on the
bottom, which probably wasn't the brightest idea seeing as
my shoes were making squeaking noises as I walked. I was
so nervous I couldn't stop smiling as I walked. I looked like
the plastic clown who blows up balloons with its mouth at
the Pizza Palace. When I got to the end of the runway, I
tried to cross my feet to turn like the other girls had, but I
over rotated and ended up doing a full spin which made my
kilt fan out and gave the mall walkers a view of my blue
underpants. I tried to act like it was intentional and did an
extra turn. One of the judges put her hand up to stop me,
and I held my breath as she started to speak.

"Nice improvisation," she said. "You looked like you
were enjoying yourself. Thank you, we'll let you know."

I hoped it meant they thought I twirled like an idiot
on purpose. Oh well, I didn't fall. I just hoped my panties
didn't show too much. At least it was the good pair. I felt
pretty good about myself... until I went backstage and
Ericka said, "Real models don't smile." I didn't know any

better. I was just lucky I didn't wet myself or fall off the stupid runway.

We went back to the registration area and got our free tote bags and makeup samples, which were just little smears of blush, lipstick, and eye shadow on tiny cards. What a waste. There wasn't enough lipstick on the card to put on a doll. I was hoping we'd get to shop for a little while, but Mrs. Maines wanted to leave right away. I was home by two o'clock and spent the rest of the day reading my old copies of *Teen Vogue* and trying to picture myself on the cover. Somehow I just couldn't see myself on the cover of any magazine. At least I had something interesting to write about on my blog. Mine were always so boring the only person who bothered to comment on them (or even read them) was my dad. Nothing makes you look cooler than having "Way to go, kiddo! Love, Dad" in your comment section.

I had pretty much given up on any hope of having a modeling career until Sunday night when the phone rang. A woman named Celine Myeski called and asked for me. She said "Congratulations," and I thought I won free muffins from the Mr. Fluffy Muffin Man stand because I always enter their "Win Free Muffins for a Month" contest, but she was calling about the *Ingénue* tryouts.

"You've been chosen to advance to the next round in the competition. The next segment will take place in Lansing," Mrs. Myeski said. She told me there would also be an ad in the local newspaper with the Grand Rapids finalists' pictures.

"A lot of agents and managers participate in this competition, so even if you don't get picked for the show, there's still a good chance you might find an agent," she said. She needed to talk to one of my parents to make sure I could continue in the competition, so I put my mom on the phone and I ran to get the cell phone. Tori wasn't home when I called, so I tried Ericka next.

"Guess what? I got a call from the show, and they're moving me on to the next level! Isn't it amazing?"

"Seriously? *You* made it?" Ericka asked. "I hope they don't call me. I would hate to have to go through more stupid auditions. I mean, I just wanted a tote bag, ya know?"

I wanted to point out she had been the one who had dragged me to the mall in the first place.

"The next round is in Lansing, and I'm—"

"—Landry, my mom needs to use the phone," she said and hung up.

My mom came into the room. "Mrs. Myeski said we would get a discount on the hotel room since you're part of the show. If you want to go then I guess I could take off work the day before and we could drive to Lansing."

I think Mom expected me to start jumping up and down, but instead I headed to the bathroom. I was going to have to bring some extra strength stomach stuff when I went to Lansing. I wasn't sure if I wanted to do it. It would be a lot easier to say, "My mom wouldn't let me go," and have everybody wonder what could have happened than for me to go and fail... or worse, fall flat on my face on TV.

"Hon," my mom said through the door. "Mrs. Myeski said if you advanced again then the next show would be in Detroit, and it would be televised in Michigan. If you move on again, then they'll fly you out to New York and you get to be on national television."

Anyone who watched *American Ingénue* knew they didn't show the whole tryout process on TV, but they did show clips — like somebody falling or tripping or acting stuck up. I knew the chances of me making it past this round weren't good, but there was this little voice in the back of my head which made me wonder, *What if this was my big chance?*

Two

~~~~~~

The next day I got up and, for the first time ever, I felt excited about going to school. For once I could be one of those girls who walked up the path at school and said, "Guess what?" and everybody would crowd around *me* for a change as I told them I was moving on to the next round of *Ingénue* tryouts. Of course it was all shot in the butt when I saw myself in the mirror. I looked more like the "before" picture in *Allure* than a model. My hair went flat after I attempted to curl it, and my skin managed to be both oily and peeling at the same time. Plus, my gross uniform colors didn't help matters. Meanwhile, those colors always made the two most popular girls at Hillcrest, Yasmin and Arianna, look like tanned goddesses. I tried putting moisturizer on my dry spots, but it just made me look greasy all over. I put powder on, but it made my skin look orange, so I had to rewash my stupid face again which, of course, made my dry spots drier.

"Landry, you've got to get moving in the morning," Mom said as she swerved the car to dodge a trashcan in the street. "Ms. Ashcroft already gave you a warning and she's going to be on my neck if you're late to homeroom again."

Mom gave me her new Franciszka T jacket to wear so I wouldn't freeze when we went outside at lunch. I made it to homeroom before the final bell. In English class I found

17

out everybody had already heard about my audition. I
wanted to tell people myself, but I guess Ericka had beaten
me to it. I also found out another girl from Hillcrest, Devon
Abrams, had been chosen for the competition, too. My English teacher, Mrs. Kharrazi, dropped musty smelling pa-
perbacks of *The Call of the Wild* onto our desks. I hated
reading old stuff. I didn't understand why we couldn't read
something new and fun. I mean, how did dogs in the wil-
derness relate to my life? I guess it could be useful if I got
stranded in Alaska or something, but it was not one of the
places on my dream vacation list. I'd rather go somewhere
warm where I could lie out and go shopping.

"Landry, please read the next section," Mrs. Kharrazi said. My face got warm when I realized I had no idea
which page we were on. She let me stutter for a second
before calling on someone else. After class, Mrs. Kharrazi
stopped me to ask if everything was all right. Most
teachers would just humiliate you if you messed up in
class, but Mrs. Kharrazi always told us we could come to
her if we had a problem.

"I have this modeling audition coming up, and I'm
kinda nervous," I said.

"I'm sure you'll do fine, but don't put too much importance on a career based on appearance. You're a good
writer. In fact, the short story you wrote last week was
one of the best I've seen. I'd like to enter it in the Michigan Young Pens essay contest," she said.

I could be a model *and* an author. I'd impress even
myself. I couldn't wait until lunch to tell Tori and Ericka.

"What do you guys think I should wear to the audition?" I asked, sitting down at our usual table. "It's an
overnight trip, you know."

"You're actually going?" Ericka asked as she pushed
her bushy copper hair out of her face.

"Well, yeah. Mrs. Myeski said if I move on to the
next round then I might have a chance of getting signed
with a modeling agent."

"Models are always sick because they're so skinny and they have to get implants," Ericka said.

I casually folded my arms over my flat chest and glanced over at Tori, but she didn't say anything. She just sat there chewing on the ends of her light brown hair. I knew Tori had wanted to get chosen for the modeling competition because she had to be the best in everything. She and Ericka were always competing for grades. Ericka was super annoying last week when she was the only one in the class who got a hundred percent on the history test.

After lunch, we always went outside and sat in the courtyard. A lot of people played soccer or kickball on the grassy part, but we usually just sat on the benches and talked. It was cold out so I put on my mom's silver jacket.

"Landry, I love your jacket," Ashanti Russell said, walking over to us. A bunch of people had already told me they liked it, but neither of my best friends said anything about it. Ericka went crazy over Tori's hair thing yesterday, but my jacket didn't even get a second glance. Kyle Eiton walked over to us, and Ericka started elbowing me. She's been in love with him forever, and she always tried to get his attention. She started to say something to him, but he walked right past her... to me.

"Landry, are you going to be on *American Ingénue?*" he asked. I wanted to change the subject, so I said Mrs. Kharrazi wanted to enter one of my essays into a writing contest.

"Wow, good luck," he said and ran off to join the soccer game.

"I didn't know you were entering a writing contest," Tori said.

"Yeah, Mrs. Kharrazi said my story is one of the best she's seen in a long time," I said.

"Well, I'll have to ask you for help next time I have to write something for class since you're such an expert,"

Ericka said, rolling her eyes. The bell rang for us to go in, and Ericka linked her arm through Tori's as they hurried inside. I had to run to keep up.

I tried calling my dad at work when I got home to tell him about the writing contest. I had called him yesterday about the competition, and he said I got my good looks from his side of the family. He thought I had a good chance of getting chosen, but the only thing I've ever won was a pillowcase at a carnival and it always smelled like horse poo no matter how many times I washed it. I didn't get to see my dad a lot because he still lived in our old apartment in Chicago. Mom and I moved to Grand Rapids when she got a promotion last year. My dad was supposed to move, too, but the hospital he was planning on working at had some budget thing happen and they couldn't hire him after all, so he stayed to work at the medical clinic.

I kept hoping he'd move here to live with us, but my mom never talked about it when I asked. I tried talking to my dad about it, but he always said the same thing, "Go ask your mother." They're not separated or anything, but I was always worried one day they were going to tell me they were getting divorced. My dad wasn't at the clinic, so I left him a message saying I'd e-mail the story to him.

The next day Tori came out of Mrs. Kharrazi's room while I was waiting to go to my next class. I smiled at her, and she raised her eyebrows at me and said Mrs. Kharrazi had gone on and on talking about my short story. Ericka walked over and interrupted her.

"Oh look, it's the supermodel," Ericka said rolling her eyes. "Or are you a model *and* an author now?"

I couldn't respond because Mrs. Lacey started yelling at us "to move along," like we were cows or something. My stomach felt all twisted up as I sat down and somebody passed me a worksheet, but I couldn't concentrate. I just stared at it until the lunch bell rang. I tried to catch Tori's eye in the cafeteria so I could take cuts in line, but she never looked my way. I kept praying everything would be okay by the time I sat down to eat because I would die if they stopped talking to me.

By the time I got to the lunch counter they were out of pizza, and they only had oatmeal cookies left for dessert. What a choice: cream of broccoli soup or leftover steak sandwiches... yum. Tori and Ericka stopped talking as soon as I got to our table. I tried to ignore the sinking feeling in my stomach and acted like everything was fine, but I felt like puking. Ericka looked at my steak sandwich and said, "Ew," but other than her gagging, neither one spoke to me. The bread started sticking in my throat, and I realized I forgot to get a bottle of juice. They got up to leave and I wasn't finished eating, but I threw my tray out and followed them outside. Ericka ran over to Hana Ito and started talking about her "cute" jacket. Hana's had it for two years, but I knew it was just a slam on me and I tried to smile.

"Landry, your jacket is cute," Hana said.

"Thanks, it's Franciszka T," I said.

"Being a supermodel, I guess you know all the designers now," Ericka said.

A soccer ball came flying at us, and I ducked before it took my head off. Kyle ran after it and stuck his arm out like he couldn't stop. He pulled me back with him and then tried to lift me up even though I'm almost a foot taller than him. Ericka tried to get his attention, but he ignored her. Again. Ericka moved away and pulled out her wallet with some baby pictures of her little cousin, Isabella, to show Hana and Tori. Nobody passed me the pictures so I had to look over Hana's shoulder. I said Isabella was cute, but she looked like a fat raisin and she had Ericka's ugly hair color. Poor kid. Ericka didn't say anything to me, and I wondered if I had been bragging or something? I didn't mean to, but I thought Hana wanted to know about my jacket.

I felt like I was walking underwater the rest of the day. I had history with Tori and Ericka, and I sat at their table like always. Mrs. Hearst told us to get into groups of three to work on the questions at the end of the chapter. I thought everything was fine until Tori and Ericka got up to sit with somebody else and left me sitting by myself. I looked around the room, and the only group left with two people in it was India Allen and Peyton Urich's table. India and Peyton were best friends with Devon, the girl who was going to be in the *American Ingénue* competition with me. I took a deep breath and walked over to their table to ask if I could work with them.

"Sure. We're in luck. Loser here," Peyton said nodding towards India, "thought we were supposed to do the questions for homework last night, so ours are already done."

"I was at my grandparents' last night, and they don't have cable or Internet," India said, flipping her long honey blonde hair over her shoulder. "And they live in the middle of nowhere, so it's not like you can get Wi-Fi for your phone. It's like being in a cave or something."

Mrs. Hearst had us put our answers on the board, and I offered to go up and write the ones for our group. Mrs. Hearst asked if anyone had a different answer to each of the questions. No one had a problem until she got to our question, and Tori raised her hand. Tori probably thought I had come up with the answer since I wrote it on the board. Mrs. Hearst told her she only had it half right and moved on. Hah.

"Sorry it wasn't up to Tori's high standards," India said, rolling her eyes in Tori's direction.

The bell rang, and I started to walk to the next class when I heard Ericka telling Tori I had been talking bad about them to Peyton and India.

"How pathetic," Tori said.

I whirled around. "I didn't say anything about you guys."

"Oh yeah, right. Why don't you go flirt with your new boyfriend?" Ericka said. "It's sad how you throw yourself at Kyle."

"Maybe you could brag about your little story some more," Tori said. "Or your fabulous modeling career."

I went to French class and tried not to cry. I opened my book and pretended to read the next chapter on verbs. At least neither of them was in this class. Plus, it was Friday, and I'd have the weekend to get away from them. Of course, all this crap would start up again on Monday, but maybe they'd stop being mad at me by then. Otherwise, I'd have to pray for a freakishly early snowstorm on Sunday night.

At the end of the day, I waited until the last second to get on the school bus to go home so it would look like I was sitting in the front because there weren't any other seats. I didn't want anyone to know those jerks didn't want me around.

When I got home, Mom asked if I had any plans with my friends this weekend. I'd more or less have to have friends first. I shook my head, and she said we could order pizza and rent movies.

I headed over to the cartoon section at Movies 'R Us. I'd never admit this to anybody, but I love those girlie princess movies. They always cheered me up. Of course, my mother always had to remind me the whole "prince coming to rescue the girl thing" was dangerous for my "impressionable mind" and how women need to find their own solutions and not wait for some man to save them. Still, it was nice to escape to fantasyland for a little while. I was deciding between *Cinderella* and *Sleeping Beauty* when I saw Ericka's dad, Mr. Maines, at the cash register. I looked over at the new releases and saw Ericka and Tori, who were cracking up over a video game display. I ducked down and pretended to be interested in the bottom shelf.

"Landry, why are you sitting on the floor?" my mom asked.

I knew she'd wonder why I wasn't invited to hang out with Tori and Ericka if she saw them in the store, and I didn't want my mom to know what was going on. She bent down, and I asked her to help me decide between movies. She said I could get them both, and we went to pick up the pizza.

I tried to concentrate on watching the movie my mom had picked out, but all I could think about was what Ericka and Tori were doing. They were probably having a great time talking about how much they hated me. It was one thing for Ericka to be mad at me because she was always sorta mad about something, but Tori and I had never gotten in a fight before.

"Landry, stop twirling your hair. You're getting grease in it," my mother said.

My life was over, and she was concerned about greasy hair. She'd probably give my hair a nice rinse before calling 911 if I killed myself. Even if I did die, those two wouldn't come to my funeral. I bet the school would give the class a half-day to come to my funeral, and everybody would take the afternoon off to hang out.

"Why'd we get a half-day off?" someone would ask. "Didn't some girl toss herself off a bridge or something?"

"Yeah, the chick with the light blonde hair. What was her name? I think it's one of those names sort of like a last name... Smith or Harley or something..."

"I think it was Harley."

"Poor Harley. Oh well, off to the movies."

I spent the weekend watching movies and eating junk food. I know Sleeping Beauty falling into a deep sleep was supposed to be tragic, but right now I wouldn't mind a good coma. Then I wouldn't have to put up with those jerks giving me dirty looks and talking behind my back. It hurt to see Tori siding with Ericka because she always said I was her real best friend. I kept waiting for Tori to call and say we should make up, but the phone never rang, and I knew it was working because I checked it just in case. Sleeping Beauty had it made.

Then I realized Cinderella and I had a lot in common. Ericka was like the evil stepmother, and Tori could be both stepsisters because she was so two-faced. Of course, I didn't have a handsome prince to rescue me. We did have a rodent problem last year, but Mom called an exterminator. I don't think those mice would have been helpful in whipping up any designer clothing for me anyway. Maybe the modeling contest would make me a big star and I could leave this stupid town and never look back.

Three

I managed to avoid Tori and Ericka on Monday. I even ate one of my mom's protein bars in the bathroom so I wouldn't run into them at lunch. I was going to try to talk to them in the bus line, but then I heard Ericka and Tori talking about me. I didn't hear everything, but I did catch the "ugly jacket" part, the "so stuck up" part, and worst of all, the "I never thought she would have gotten picked in a zillion years" part. I stood in the back of the line and sat with Ashanti when I got on the bus. I didn't want to start crying in front of Ashanti, so I told her I liked her purse. We started talking about clothes, and we found out we like to shop at the same stores.

When we got to Ericka's bus stop, she made a big point of inviting Tori over to her house. The bus pulled up to my stop next, but Ashanti asked me if I wanted to come over so I waited and got off at her stop instead.

"I always record *As the Days Roll On*," she said as we walked into her bedroom. "I'm in love with Bradley McMillan."

"I love Troy," I said. "I'm so glad Savannah left the oxygen tank in the coffin when she buried him alive."

"I know, right? Remember the day the tank got messed up and Alfonso almost didn't dig him out fast enough?" she asked. "I was having an attack. Wanna watch today's show?"

"Yeah, I forgot to watch it on Friday," I said.

"Troy was in the pool on Friday. You have to see it," she said, cueing up the program.

We had a good time watching the show and later, when I got home, I saw Ashanti had added me as a friend on her social media page.

The next day, I waited inside for the bus so I wouldn't have to stand at the bus stop with Tori. Mom looked at my feet as she was leaving and freaked.

"Sandals? It's forty-five degrees out. Are you nuts?" she said. "And it's supposed to rain today, too."

Mom went to the front closet and pulled out these ugly little yellow rubber shoes she bought me to wear in bad weather. She jokingly called "rubber duckies," because they were the exact same color as a bathtub rubber duck. She thought they were cute, and I could keep my feet dry without anyone realizing I was wearing boots. Yeah, except for the fact I was wearing butt-ugly kindergarten booties. I tried to explain to her people were going to expect me to wear better stuff since everybody knew I was going to be a model. I was forced to wear the stupid Hillcrest uniform, but at least my feet could be cute.

"When you start making money like Talisa Milan then you can wear whatever you want on your feet," she said.

Mom made me change my shoes and told me we were going shopping after school for some "sensible shoes." There's nothing I hated more than shopping with my mother. She only bought me stuff *she* liked, even if it made me look four years old. I thought I heard the bus coming so I walked to the bus stop. Tori was there, but so was Devon Abrams, who was trying to pull her gorgeous curly dark hair into a ponytail.

"Why is the bus always late when it's cold? We should protest or something," Devon said.

Everybody liked Devon because she had a bubbly personality and was a lot of fun. She was also, like, TV pretty. She had huge brown eyes and long curly dark hair. Today she had on a button-down shirt, untucked, with khaki pants, and she looked gorgeous. I was wearing the exact same outfit, and I looked like a rumpled little boy standing next to her. I could understand why she'd be picked to model, but I couldn't figure out why they had chosen me.

Ericka's mom drove up, and Ericka rolled down the window. "Tori, wanna ride?"

Tori got in and they drove off, while the rest of us stood out in the cold.

"I wish Ericka had asked me if I wanted a ride so I could have said, 'No, thanks,'" Devon said.

With my luck, Ericka would come back tomorrow and give Devon a ride, too. The bus pulled up, but Ashanti was already sitting with someone. I started to ask a seventh grader to move his solar system project, but Devon told me to move to the back with her. She plopped down next to India, and Peyton moved her binder to make room for me. Peyton was trying to get her English homework done, so I let her borrow mine. She had just finished copying it when the bus pulled in front of the school.

"Thanks, I owe you," she said. I just shrugged as I shoved my notebook into my bag.

I hoped it would rain so I wouldn't have to go outside today. Plus, then my stupid rubber duckies wouldn't look so dumb. No such luck, but I managed to avoid going outside by offering to help Ms. Ashcroft put together the mid-month folders. We have to get our parents to sign the back of our folders to show they know how we're doing in our classes. Ericka and Tori always take out any assignment lower than a ninety-five percent before they show it to their parents.

It didn't rain until the end of the day, and I was soaked when I got to my bus. I sat behind the bus driver and scrunched down in the seat, hoping no one would see me. Ericka got on the bus and asked if my shoes were made of "designer" rubber. I stared out the window and pretended not to hear her.

Later, Mom and I went shopping, and she found a shoe which was fifty-percent rubber and perfect... if there was a flood.

"Mom, those look like boy shoes. How about these? They're cute and on sale," I held up a pair of pretty suede boots. She told me to try them on and asked the sales-clerk if they were waterproof. The salesclerk said they were better than bare feet, but they wouldn't keep my feet dry. Then the salesclerk showed me some ugly clunky things which made my feet look bigger than they already were. I found another pair of boots on sale, and Mom put her hand inside the boot to feel the sole.

"The sole is like paper. I could spit on it, and it'd soak right through," she said.

"Real classy. C'mon, please? I'll wear two pairs of socks, and I'll give you some money." I checked my pock-ets. "I only have seven dollars, but I've got twenty bucks at home."

"How much are they?" she asked. I said they were half off, so, "only" thirty-nine dollars and she shook her head.

"Maybe dad will send me the money for them. He's always asking if I need anything," I said, watching her out of the corner of my eye.

"Try these other ones on," she said. She handed me some boots with a thick rubber sole which could almost pass for normal boots. She said she'd buy the cute boots for me if I promised to clean my room. I swore I would, and she went to pay. I knew she'd cave in if I brought up Dad. Ever since we moved, she got weird about how much money she made and how much my dad made.

The next day I had gym class, which I dreaded, but at least Ericka and Tori weren't in this class. We had to sit on the bleachers and listen to Coach Daly talk before we could change into our gym clothes. I always tried to sit far away from the popular boys because they can be brutal when they get together. After all, they made Tad Johnston a complete outcast. Tad had never been popular or anything, but the other guys never had a problem with him before. He used to play kickball with the guys at lunch and everything... until Kyle moved here. Tad was always kissing up to the teachers and trying to act all grown up, but nobody was ever mean to him until Kyle showed up.

I didn't think Kyle was going to fit in when he first moved here from Boston because he was short and had a weird accent. New kids either became popular right away or they never fit in at all. When Arianna Seymour moved here earlier this year, I was the first person who asked her to eat lunch with us, but since then she has moved on to cooler pastures. Then there was Thalia Zimmer. Thalia seemed to fit in when she came to visit at the beginning of the school year, but no one noticed she was alive once she started going to Hillcrest. People only paid attention to her if she brought in chocolate from her dad's candy shop.

Thalia and I always sat on the bleachers during kickball and let people take cuts in front of us. She seemed to be the only person who lied and said they had their period as much as I did in gym. She told me it wasn't like Coach Daly was going to check. All you had to do was say the word, "cramps," and he'd let you sit the game out. In gym, we either had to play kickball in class or have a free day, which meant we could do anything we wanted as long as we were moving. However, if Coach Daly was in a bad mood, then he'd make us choose teams and play dodge ball. I was always picked second to last, and Thalia was always chosen last.

Any animal with half a brain knows it's best to get out of the way when an object comes flying at you, but I would stand there like a deer in the headlights hoping to get hit. Then I could sit down and wait for the next round of torture. There was this one time when the other team refused to hit me, and I was the last person left standing. I felt so stupid having to run after the balls by myself. I wondered if they did it to make a fool out of me. It was those days when I felt like the biggest loser on the planet. On those days I stayed away from Tad and Thalia so I wouldn't get lumped in with them.

❧

I got to class and found an envelope on my desk. I hoped it was a note from Tori, but it was an invitation to Thalia's birthday party. I guess she had mentioned it in gym class, but I didn't realize the party was this Saturday. She was having it at a roller skating rink near the mall, which was weird because who roller skated anymore? And do girls our age hand out invitations to birthday parties? I hadn't been roller skating since I was eight, but it wasn't like people were begging me to go to their parties either. I pretended to do my work while I watched Kyle walk over to the pencil sharpener. He goes up there every class period just so he can walk around the room and act cool. His pencils were all little chewed up stubs, but he kept on sharpening. He stopped by Thalia's desk and asked why he couldn't come to her party. He could be such a jerk sometimes, but there was still something kinda cute about him. Thalia ignored him and he said, "Oh, you're so cool, Thalia," and pushed her desk hard. I pretended not to notice.

When I got to history, Peyton asked me if I was invited to Thalia's party. I figured all the girls were invited, but I guess she had only invited a few people. Peyton said Thalia got the idea for the skating theme from reading about Melani Parkington's retro skating party in a fashion magazine. I was surprised Thalia even read *those magazines*, but even more surprised to hear Devon, Peyton, and India were all planning to go. I asked Thalia who else she invited to see if Tori and Ericka were going to be there. Thalia said she invited Ericka, but she wasn't sure if she was coming because she had a basketball game. Things were looking up. The basketball games always lasted forever, and I figured Ericka wouldn't bother going to the party because she thought Thalia was a "loser."

Later, I found out India's mom was driving Peyton and Devon to the party. I hoped India would ask me to ride with them, but nobody offered. I couldn't get too excited about the party because all I could think about was walking into the skating rink by myself. Everybody always went to those things in a group. Only losers walked in alone.

I decided to call India after school and pretend I forgot which questions to do for class. Then I brought up the party. India asked if I was going and I said I wanted to, but I wasn't sure if my mom could drive me. Unfortunately, she got a call on the other line. India switched back, and she said it was for her mom.

"We can pick you up on Saturday if you need a ride," she said.

Yes, yes, yes. I wouldn't have to walk in by myself like a loser.

I stayed up late on Friday worrying about what to wear to the party. I took a quick shower in the morning and got ready while my mother searched the house for wrapping paper and tape. She ended up putting the purse we bought for Thalia in a gift bag my grandma used for my present last Christmas.

"Mom, it has a bear wearing a Santa outfit on it," I said.

"It's the thought, and we spent a lot on the purse," Mom said.

India's mom pulled up, and Devon's face lit up when she saw me. She held up her present, which was covered with Hanukah wrapping paper.

"At least we'll be losers together," she said. "Maybe we can pretend we did it on purpose."

I hadn't been on roller skates in forever, but it sorta came back to me. India and Devon requested songs, while Peyton and I skated around the rink. I sat next to Thalia and Peyton when we ate lunch, and I was having a great time until I looked up and saw Ericka standing by the door.

"Thalia, I thought you said Ericka had a game today," I said.

"Yeah, but she was going to come afterward if there was time," Thalia said as she waved Ericka over. There was only one empty seat, and it was across from me so I couldn't pretend Ericka wasn't there. Devon and India got up to go to the bathroom just as Peyton got up to get more pizza. I went to talk to Thalia, but she had her back to me. I glanced across the table, but Ericka wouldn't even look at me.

"There was a huge line," Devon said as she sat back down. "Did we miss dessert?"

I shook my head, and Thalia's dad starting passing out cupcakes with blue frosting. I sat there focused on my cupcake while everyone talked around me. I couldn't wait to get away from Ericka.

Thalia's grandma gave us gift bags as we left, and we tore into them in the van. If parties were based on gift bags then this was the best party ever. Most of the time you get some cheap candy, a pencil, and a hair thing from the dollar store, but this bag had a music gift card, a lollipop, a tube of Little Rose lip gloss, some gum, and a glitter pencil.

"Devon, what color gloss did you get? I got 'Coral Ya Later'," Peyton said. Devon had "You Look Mauveulous," India had "Little Bo Pink," and I had "Jumpin' Jack Frost."

"This party was worth it for the gift bag alone," India said, turning up the radio. "I love this song."

It was the new Havana Carys single, and they all sang along. I felt dumb singing, so I just sat back and listened.

Later, I was spreading out all of the stuff I got at the party on my dresser when Mom came in to see if I had her favorite basketball team sweatshirt. I had gotten a huge grape jelly stain on it last week and had hidden it in the back of my closet where she'd never find it.

"How was the party?" she asked, peering under my bed.

"Good."

Did Thalia like the purse?" she asked.

"I guess."

The phone rang, and I answered it since mom was still underneath my bed.

"Hey, kiddo," Dad said. "How's school going?"

"I went to a party today," I said, thinking it wasn't a good idea to tell him I bombed the last two math quizzes.

"Did ya have a good time?" he asked.

"Yeah, I'll go get Mom."

Mom was in a bad mood when she got off the phone. I asked if we could order a pizza and she almost took my head off, so I settled for a chicken potpie I found in the freezer. I hoped my dad would call back so they'd make up, but the phone never rang. Why couldn't my stupid parents get along?

Four

~~~~~~

On Monday, I decided to walk to the bus stop after I saw Devon was already waiting there. She was finishing up a protein bar and offered me a bite from the other end. The apple kind makes me gag, but I took a bite just to annoy Tori, who was watching me. Devon wiped the crumbs off her mouth and looked in her backpack for her compact. Tori let her borrow a mirror, and Devon put on the gloss we got at Thalia's party. Devon handed me the mirror. I hadn't eaten my lip gloss off, but I made a big deal of reapplying it anyway. Tori snatched the mirror back as the bus drove up.

In homeroom, Ms. Ashcroft got called down to the office and told us to pair off and quiz each other. Thalia had the bag I gave her hanging on the back of her chair.

"I'm glad everybody ended up coming to the party. Well, everybody except Arianna. She had to watch her brothers," Thalia said as she drew a heart with her highlighter. "She said she was babysitting anyway."

Mrs. Hearst came in the room to make sure we weren't hanging from the ceiling while Ms. Ashcroft was on the phone. We pretended to be working as Mrs. Hearst watched us with pursed lips and narrowed eyes. I wondered what Thalia meant by her comment because I thought everybody liked Arianna. Arianna had this beautiful curly strawberry blonde hair. I wondered if she used the highlighting stuff you activate with a hairdryer to make it lighter. People were always trying to do stuff for her. Even Yasmin McCarty, who had been the most popular girl before Arianna moved here, wanted to hang out with Arianna. So Arianna had abandoned Ericka, Tori, and me for Yasmin's crowd the second they showed any interest in her.

"Do you mind if I sit with those guys at lunch?" she had asked us. "It's just for today."

And then she switched tables and never came back. She'd talk to me once in a while in class or give me one of her cutesy waves where she made bunny ears. At least she didn't ignore me when I sat at her table in science last month when my partner was sick. I wondered what she'd do if I asked if I could eat lunch with her? Even if she said I could, I'm sure Yasmin would stare me down until I left or Stuart would ask me if I got lost on my way to the losers' table.

After class, we went to the theater for a presentation, and Thalia and I sat together in the back row. I saw Ericka and Tori sitting together, and Ericka was whispering to her. Tori started laughing, and Ericka sat back with a smirk on her face. The presentation was some stupid science guy with fuzzy white hair sticking up all over. The science guy asked for a volunteer, and I shrank down in my seat as Arianna ran up on stage.

"She's so fake," Thalia said, rolling her eyes.

"Who?"

"Arianna. I mean, she's Yasmin's friend, but Kyle drools over her in math class and she encourages him."

"I dunno, she sits by Kyle and maybe Yasmin doesn't mind," I said.

"Please, I once borrowed a pen from Yasmin and she stood over me while I used it. Trust me, the girl doesn't share well." Thalia pulled out a cherry cough drop from her purse and offered me one. "I invited Arianna to my party because her mom works for my dad, but it bugs me how everybody thinks she's so great."

Crazy science guy sprayed Arianna with some water, and everyone started laughing. I noticed Ericka was hanging on Tori. After the show, I overheard Ericka say the science guy was my real dad.

"They have the same hair," she said, laughing. Tori found this hilarious. So I have pale hair. Big deal. I felt like pointing out that unlike Tori and Ericka's fathers, at least my dad had hair. Tori had seen my dad before and knew he had light brown hair, but did she speak up for me? Nope.

⋖⊹⋗

Later, I watched Arianna and Kyle in class, and he was flirting with her. He'd do something stupid, look over at Mrs. Lacey's desk, and then they'd laugh all silent-like. Ha ha, you're killing me. Then he shredded little pieces of paper and stuck them in the heating vent by the window. Arianna put her hands over her mouth like this was the funniest thing ever. Two minutes later, the heater made a weird noise and paper shot out of it. They almost wet themselves. Thalia looked over at me and rolled her eyes.

Mrs. Lacey walked over to the vent and looked at Kyle, who was now all innocent and doing his work. She sighed and said we were going to change seats. Fabulous. All I needed was to wind up sitting next to Ericka. Mrs. Lacey put Kyle right in front of her desk and moved Ericka across from him. Then she put me behind Kyle and next to Arianna. Kyle leaned back in between Arianna and me.

"I'm going to have to come over here a lot since I'm stuck at a loser table," he said.

I knew Ericka had heard him, and I wondered if he lumped me in with her even though she wasn't speaking to me. Kyle reached over, took my pencil, and went up to the sharpener.

"I don't know how you could write with it so dull," he
said, handing it back to me. Arianna said she only used
mechanical pencils.

"Yeah, but yours is boring," he said. "Landry's is
cool." Was he making fun of my glitter pencil? I had tak-
en the dangling kitten face off it, but maybe he knew it
was supposed to be on there. He showed me his hologram
pencil and said we should trade for the day. I still wasn't
sure if he was trying to make a fool out of me, but I
switched with him. I just hoped he didn't get glitter in
his eye, go blind, and then try to sue me.

I was walking to my next class when somebody
stepped on the back of my shoe and pulled it off my heel. I
squished my foot around my shoe until it slipped back on.
Then it happened again. I pretended not to notice, but I
heard Ericka's voice so I hurried into the science room. I sit
next to Hana, but she wasn't there yet, so I sat down and
opened my notebook. Stuart Graham walked over and sat
in the seat across from me. Okay, what's this?

"Hey Landry," he said, taking Kyle's pencil out of my
hand. "I heard you like somebody in here."

Tori was staring out the window, but Ericka was
watching us. My eyes burned. Okay, ignore me, but don't
humiliate me. I never should have told Tori I thought
Kyle was cute.

"Hey, gimme my pencil." I looked up, and Kyle
grabbed his pencil back from Stuart. "Landry, don't let a
loser like Stuart touch my stuff." Stuart punched him on
the arm, and Mrs. Tamar walked in with Devon and
Hana behind her.

"Everybody in your seats. Now." Mrs. Tamar
snapped the screen down over the board and flipped on
the overhead machine.

"I'm having the worst day," Devon said. "I had to
take Jay to the office 'cause he wasn't feeling well, and
then he puked in the hall." She squinted at the board.
"What's it say? Am-what?"

"Amphibian. What happened?" I asked, moving my chair further away from her. The stomach flu was my biggest fear in life. Well, tied with finding a centipede in my food.

"The secretary paged Mr. Ivanov to clean it up, and Jay went home."

All day long I freaked out every time my stomach hurt because I thought I was getting the flu. I was walking to the bus when Kyle asked me for the math homework. I pulled out my binder, and papers went flying everywhere. Smooth. He picked up the stuff next to his feet, while I chased after a book report.

"Um, it's in here somewhere," I said. I flipped through the pages, but it was hard to balance my binder on my knee.

"It's no big deal. I can get it from someone else," he said and ran toward his bus. At least he didn't laugh at me. When I got on the bus I heard Ericka say, "Nice job, Gracie." It took me a minute to figure it out. I slid down in my seat and pulled out my notebook. I started writing so no one would bug me. Mom always tells me to focus on positive things, so I wrote Kyle was nice to me and I liked my new seat in Mrs. Lacey's class. Maybe Arianna would even ask me to sit at her lunch table. It would show my old friends when popular people like Kyle and Arianna wanted to hang out with me.

The next day, Arianna told me Kyle called her last night for the homework. I wanted to tell her he had asked me first, but I didn't. She asked if I thought it would be weird if they started going together because he was so much shorter than her. I said height didn't matter, but I wondered why she was so sure he liked her. Kyle came into the room and ruffled my hair as he walked to his desk.

Later, Arianna ran up to me outside during lunch. "Guess what? Kyle just asked me to go out with him,"

she said. Her skin was glowing from the cold. "If you
hadn't talked me into it I never would have said yes, so
thanks," she said over her shoulder as she walked back
to her friends. Um, how did I talk her into going out with
the guy I liked? Could I be any more of a moron?

We got our reader response journals back in English,
and I got an A+. Mrs. Kharrazi wrote I should start
keeping a journal. Seemed like the thing to do since I only had two friends. Then I could end up like a crazy
woman in the attic rocking back and forth with piles of
journals around me. Good times, good times. I spent the
entire gym class holding my stomach on the bleachers
while everyone else got sweaty playing kickball. Once in
a while Thalia and I had to duck as balls flew at our
heads. The guys always have to show off how strong they
are by kicking the ball as hard as they can so it bounces
off the ceiling beams. Just once I'd like to go up to the
plate and kick the stupid ball so hard it went through
the wall and leave them all just staring. Of course, I
couldn't even get the ball to go up in the air. Once I got
the ball a foot off the ground and was so surprised I forgot to run to first base, and they got me out. I didn't
mind since when I was on base, I never knew when to
run and I'd have to ask someone on the other team to tell
me when to go.

After we changed our clothes, we had to line up and
wait for a teacher to walk us back because we're too stupid to find our classrooms by ourselves. It's so humiliating. In the public school they can do whatever they want,
but we're herded like sheep from one field to the next.
It's not like we could make a break for it since there's a
twenty-foot high chain link fence surrounding the school.
Plus, the grounds people patrol the area with walkie-
talkies in case one of us gets out of line. One time I ran
back to the gym because I forgot my gloves and this
woman almost bit my head off. She actually called me a
"smarty pants" when I said I didn't want to get frostbite.

When I got to lunch, Nikolas, this guy who rides my bus, said "hi" to me as I walked past him. He's sort of cute, and he sat with me on the bus one day. It was the first time a guy had sat with me because he wanted to instead of being forced to because there weren't any empty seats. I ate lunch with Ashanti and her friends, Maggie and Halle. Ashanti told me Nikolas had come up to them and asked her my name. I hadn't paid a lot of attention to him, but I knew his dad had been a professional soccer player, he was born in Toronto, moved here from Tampa, was into computer animation, only drank pineapple juice and hated beef jerky the first time he tried it.

In fifth hour, we had to go out in the parking lot because of an accident in the science lab. I was taking a test, and I had gotten as far as writing my name. I had been hoping for a fire drill, and when they told us to go outside, I thought I had become like the girl who could start fires with her mind. Mrs. Lacey said not to worry because we'd have plenty of time to finish our test.

I ran over to Ashanti in the parking lot, and we huddled together. I tried to pull my skirt down to cover my freezing legs and overheard Ericka ask what kind of moron wore a skirt in forty-degree weather. I pretended not to hear, and Ashanti rolled her eyes.

"Nikolas's looking over here," she said.

I tried to turn my head slowly like those shampoo commercials where the girl's hair fans out all sexy. Unfortunately, I had used too much hairspray this morning so when I moved my head it looked like I had a tick. Nikolas was leaning against the parking barrier and smiled at me. He even touched my elbow and said "hey" as we were going back into the building. Ashanti grabbed my arm and squealed.

"I love foreign men. They're so... worldly," she said. I pointed out Canada didn't count since it was attached.

Ashanti had her Franciszka T backpack on the seat when I got on the bus. She looked down and pretended to tie her shoe when I stood by her seat. At first, I thought she was mad at me, but then she whispered for me to sit behind her. I sat down and Nikolas moved up to the seat across from mine.

"Enjoy the sulfur spill?" he asked.

"Um, yeah. I enjoy anything disrupting the learning process."

"Huh? Can I get your e-mail address or something?" he asked. He didn't waste any time. I opened my backpack and searched for a pen. It was filled with three inches of tissues and gum wrappers, and I hated to stick my hand in there. Ashanti held up a lavender gel pen and a piece of notebook paper. I scribbled down my e-mail address and phone number. He went back to his seat, and I moved up to sit with Ashanti.

"Guys never ask girls for their numbers unless the girl is alone," she said. "So? Do ya like him?"

"I don't know. He's kind of cute and he's got an okay personality, but..."

"Is it the weird hair?" she asked. "Would it help to know his dad drives an expensive car?"

"No, but what kind is it?"

"I'm not sure. It looks like a clown car, but my dad said it was expensive."

"I dunno. Nikolas seems a little immature," I said.

"Well, he acts kinda young, but my mom says girls mature faster, and the hair... it's either trendy or his mom does it for him. Maybe it's a style they do where he's from and it just hasn't hit here yet."

I checked my messages fourteen times. I was still on Ericka and Tori's social media pages, and I forgot to switch my chat thing to "offline," so they were probably laughing at me for being on-line all night. They always used to check their messages around eight o'clock, and they never pop up in my "chat list" anymore. I had no idea how they kept themselves hidden. If I were smarter I'd know how to change mine, too. Ashanti instant messaged me while I was checking my mail for the millionth time.

> *TI22: Anything yet?*
> *Albright: No. You don't think he's some sort of master hacker and can read this?*
> *TI22: Doubt it. Besides he wouldn't know who "he" was anyway.*
> *Albright: Good point. Hold up, I just got mail. Not him :(*
> *TI22: Jay and I worked together in English today :0) Crap, my mom's home and I was supposed to clean my room, but I was too exhausted. See ya.*

I looked at my clock, and it was after nine. Okay, this was just stupid. Why ask for my e-mail address if you're just going to use it for a bookmark? What was wrong with him? I was going to check my mail one more time and if he—*yes-yes-yes*. I had got mail! Life was good.

> *To: Albright@alphamail.com*
> *From: NIK@romail.com*
> *Re: Hey*
> *Hey. What's up? I had a ton of homework tonight. Are you riding the bus tomorrow? –Nikolas*

My first e-mail from a guy, and this was the best he could do? I mean, you could send it to your grandfather or a nun or some homeless person you just saw on the street, although in retrospect, a homeless person wouldn't have a computer or e-mail access, but still.

Nikolas had lost his chance. I was not even going to respond. Let him sit up all night wondering if I'll be riding the bus.

I broke down fifteen minutes later and e-mailed him back. Maybe Ashanti can play hard to get with Jay, but some of us just didn't have those options.

To: NIK@romail.com
From: Albright@ alphamail.com
Hey, I had a ton of homework, too. I may or may not ride the bus in the morning. Same goes for the afternoon.
-Landry

And it took me ten minutes and five re-writes to come up with it. I used the same opener he used and didn't offer any more information than he did. It was simple, straight to the point, with a bit of mystery and a touch of, dare I say, intrigue?

I was at the bus stop early the next morning. I wanted to wear another skirt, but Ashanti hadn't said whether she was wearing one and I didn't want to be the only one wearing a skirt, like I was trying to show some leg. Tori didn't say anything to me, big shockerino. Nikolas tugged my hair as he got off the bus. I wasn't even sure if I liked Nikolas. He did annoy me when he got excited over video games or bragged about his soccer player dad, but it was nice to have somebody like me.

Five

I was making a sundae when the phone rang. Ashanti usually calls me around four o'clock so we can talk about *As the Days Roll On*. I licked the ice cream off my spoon and answered the phone, and it was a guy calling... for me. It wasn't too hard to narrow it down since no guys (other than my dad) ever call me. I swallowed too fast and tried to ignore the ice cream headache taking over my brain.

"Uh, hi. How are you?" I said. Ugh, so unoriginal.

Lucky for me, Nikolas likes to talk, and he took over the conversation telling me about his new computer game. I hit the mute button as I ate so he wouldn't hear. Then he did it—so fast I almost missed it. He asked me if I wanted to meet him and his friends at the mall on Saturday. I didn't know what to say. Did he mean I should come with my friends or did he mean it like a date? Did he like me, or did he just want to hang out at the mall? I said I'd check with my friends and told him I'd e-mail him.

I got off the phone and freaked out. Nikolas was the first guy who had ever asked me to do anything, and I might not be able to go because I had no one to go with me. My mom would never let me meet a group of guys by myself. I called Ashanti to see if she was free, but she wasn't home. I wanted Ashanti to go, but I was afraid she might already have plans. She was probably out with Halle and Maggie right now having a great time. I tried to focus on my math homework, and Mom brought home Chinese food for dinner. I cracked open my fortune cookie, but all I got was, "Patience is the greatest virtue." Not exactly fame and fortune there. The phone rang, and I almost knocked my mom over to answer it.

It was Ashanti. "Hey, my mom said you called. Are you eating dinner?" she asked.

My mouth was half full, but I managed to swallow and say I wasn't. Mom tried to get me off the phone so I could finish eating, and I hit mute so Ashanti wouldn't hear her. I tuned mom out and told Ashanti how Nikolas wanted to meet at the mall this weekend.

"Are you gonna go?" she asked.

I said I wanted to, but I didn't want to go by myself.

"I'll go with you if you want," she said. Happiness. I asked mom if she could drive us to the mall on Saturday, and she said she would if I got off the phone and finished my dinner. I got off the phone and dug into my food.

"I bet it's cold now," Mom said. It was, but I didn't want to admit it to her. "Put it in the microwave," she said, sighing.

Dad called after dinner, and I told him Nikolas asked me to meet him at the mall. He asked a million questions about Nikolas, his family, and his plans for the future.

"We're just going to meet up at the mall," I said. "It's not a date or anything."

"It better not be," he said. "So all's right in the world then? How's math class going?"

I didn't want him to know I was barely squeaking by in math, so I focused on the "A+" I got on my English lit journal.

⌐ ⋅ ⌐

I was at my locker on Friday when Ashanti yelled to me from across the hall that she had to stay after, but to call her about this weekend. Ericka and Tori were standing nearby at their lockers.

"Okay, I'll let you know if Nikolas wants to get together earlier."

I knew Nikolas wouldn't change the time, but I wanted Ericka and Tori to hear I was going to meet a guy at the mall. They just stared at me.

Saturday afternoon couldn't come fast enough. Ashanti and I decided what we were going to wear the night before, and we promised to call each other if either one of us changed our outfits. Ashanti had decided to wear the new jeans she had gotten for her birthday with a Franciszka T shirt. I was going to wear my jeans and a dark pink sweater.

I was having another bad hair day Saturday morning and ended up sticking it back in a bun. We picked Ashanti up ten minutes late and Mom lectured me about the importance of being on time up until Ashanti got in the car, and then Mom became all sweet and friendly.

Mom dropped us off, and we met Nikolas and his friend in front of the arcade. I thought we were just meeting there, but he wanted to go inside. The guys went to play a game which involved shooting the living dead. They thought it was tons of fun. The worst part was you couldn't just shoot a zombie and be done with it, you'd just shoot part of its face off or knock half a limb off and it was disgusting. Ashanti and I had a good time playing air hockey, even though Nikolas never paid any attention to us.

Ashanti and I told Nikolas we were going to the food court and he nodded, but kept his eyes on the screen. We bought tacos and tried to find a place to sit, but the food court was nearly full. We found an empty booth over near the Corn Dog Hut. Ashanti didn't talk much at lunch, and I was worried I was boring her. I asked her if everything was okay, and she said she was just tired. After we ate, we went back to the arcade, but Nikolas and his friend were still playing games, so we decided to ditch the guys and go shopping. We walked around until she said she was exhausted and called her mom to pick us up.

Six

Ashanti didn't ride the bus on Monday, but Nikolas sat with me. I hoped he didn't expect me to talk to him or anything because I have a hard enough time remembering to breathe at seven in the morning. In the mornings I just sit like a blob on the bus. Ashanti wasn't in class, so I went to the library and checked to see if she e-mailed me.

To: Albright
From: TI22
I tried to call you this morning, but you had already left. I'm sick and my dad's taking me to the doctor. Call me when you get home... if I'm still alive :(
Ashanti

To: TI22
From: Albright
Sorry you're not feeling well. I'll get your homework for you. Hope you feel better.
Landry

I asked Jay if he would call her with the English assignment since she likes him. Then I walked to the cafeteria by myself and went to sit at Ashanti's table with Maggie and Halle.

"Ashanti's sick today," Maggie said, flipping her dishwater blonde ponytail. I didn't know if she was trying to say, "So you don't need to sit with us," but I sat down anyway. Halle was busy reading an article in *Seventeen* on how to make your eye color stand out.

"It says lavender shadow makes brown eyes pop, but I think my azure liner works better," she said. "It also recommends slate and pewter." She moved the magazine closer to Maggie, making it impossible for me to see, so I got up to get a cookie. I asked if either of them wanted anything and they both looked up like, "You're still here?" Devon got in line behind me and reached over for a brownie.

"What's up?" she asked.

"Not much. I just listened to a fascinating conversation on eye shadow."

"Learn anything?" she asked.

Yeah, to skip lunch when your friend was out sick. The bell rang, and she stuffed the brownie in her mouth as she paid the cashier. I walked back to class with my cookie in my pocket.

When I got to science, Mrs. Tamar said she was going to change our seats. I said a prayer I wouldn't be moved near Tori or Ericka. My understanding teacher decided to make a game out of it and had us draw numbers out of a hat to assign our seats. I had number twenty-four, and the first table had four spots. Even if both of them wound up at a table there would still be a chance I'd have one person there who didn't hate my guts. Ericka ended up with Arianna, Anthony, and Tad. One down. The next set of seats had three desks in a row. Okay it would suck, especially if I was stuck in the middle with Tori on one side. I prayed as Mrs. Tamar's hand went into the hat.

"Twenty..." Please Lord, I won't spend all my money on celebrity tabloids, I won't think about boys, I'll devote my life to homework, and—"two. Who has number twenty-two?" she asked. There were still a couple of other people I didn't want to sit by, like Stuart or Yasmin.

Seat after seat was taken until we got to the last table. I had been so busy going over whom I didn't want to sit next to, and I hadn't paid attention to whose name hadn't been called. We were down to the last table of four desks. This was it... the moment of truth.

"Twenty-four and fifteen. Okay, you may pick up your things and move in an orderly fashion to your desks. Quietly people," Mrs. Tamar said.

No one else had raised their hand when she called the last two numbers so all I knew was there were only two of us at the table. It would either be amazing if it was someone I liked or awful if it was somebody stupid who couldn't help me with the lab work. I took the desk facing the windows, but no one was moving in my direction. Oh no, what if they saw me sitting here and were trying to plea bargain with Mrs. Tamar to sit somewhere else. I'd have to spend the whole quarter without a lab partner.

"Cool, we'll be partners." I looked up as Devon slid into the seat across from me. "I was worried I'd end up sitting with Stuart," she said. "I gotta warn you, science is not my thing."

I went over to Ashanti's house after school to drop off her homework.

"Hi, Landry. How are you doing?" Mr. Russell asked. "I'd invite you in, but the doctor said she's got mono. She slept all afternoon, and she's going to be out of school for a while," he said.

"Tell her I hope she feels better. I picked up all of her assignments for her. Oh, and tell her Jay Crane might call her about the English assignment," I said.

His eyebrows flew up. "You mean *the* Jay might call my house? I better prepare my answering voice. 'Ashanti, a gentleman caller for you,'" he said in a British accent. He thanked me for getting her assignments and said he'd have her call me when she woke up.

I went home and looked up the symptoms of mono and how you caught it. Since Ashanti and I hadn't shared a drink and she hadn't spit on me, I figured I was safe and I went to hang out on the couch. Might as well get comfy since I had no place else to go as long as Ashanti was sick. Yup, Mr. Couch and I were going to become real close pals for the next couple of weeks. I sat there watching *Simpsons* reruns until Ashanti called a few hours later.

"Jay called me. You are the greatest person since the inventor of Super Yummy Scrummy snack cakes, and you know how much I love those things," Ashanti said. "And the homework thing — it gave him a reason to call without looking like, you know, a boy calling a girl thing."

"So what happened?" I asked.

"He told me you were worried about me getting the directions for our paper—"

"Your grades are my first concern," I said.

"Of course, so then he asked how I was feeling, and I told him I'd be out for a while so he offered to get my English assignments. Now my dad talked to all my teachers this afternoon who said they'd e-mail the work to me, but Jay doesn't have to know about it."

"Great," I said.

"Yeah, except my dad said the words 'gentleman caller' with an English accent. I died."

"Maybe he'll think you have a butler," I said.

"Well, my dad is going to be working from home part time while I'm sick, but I don't think he'll pretend to be the butler. Anyway, will you miss me?" she asked.

She had no idea. Ashanti had made it easier to get up in the morning. I had found a friend who liked the same things I did, and we had a lot of fun together the last couple of weeks. In fact, getting to know her was the one good thing which came out of the fight. If Ericka and

Tori hadn't stopped speaking to me, then Ashanti and I wouldn't have gotten to know each another so well. I could tell she was getting tired, so we got off the phone and I decided to start my history homework. I was completely friendless with Ashanti out sick, but maybe my grades would go up with all the extra homework time. However, I forgot to write down the assignments, so I called India for the homework, and we talked until her mom called her for dinner. She was nice to me, but she wasn't in my lunch hour so I was stuck sitting at Maggie and Halle's table or hiding out in the library. Still, I wondered if I'd ever be able to break into India's group of friends.

Seven

The next day, I stood in the cafeteria doorway trying to find someplace to sit. I decided to try Maggie and Halle's table again. They said "hi" to me when I put my tray down and then went back to their conversation on some reality show. I pretended to be interested in my food and escaped to the library when I finished my sandwich. I picked *Jane Eyre* off the shelf and sat down to read. It was nice and long so I would have something to do during lunch for a while.

Devon wasn't in science class because she hadn't finished her math test in her last class. I kept watching the door hoping she'd come in since we were doing a lab, but Mrs. Tamar told me to work with Yasmin's group. I pulled my chair up to Yasmin's table and basically sat there while the rest of the table did the lab. No one said a single word to me. After class, as I was walking to social studies, Mrs. Kharrazi called me over.

"I got the contest results today, and you got second place in the short story contest. Congratulations," she said.

It was like the light at the end of a crappy, crappy day. Suddenly I didn't care about Tori or Ericka. I had just gotten second place in a writing contest, and even they couldn't take it away from me. Then I got called down to the main office. Everybody made an, "Ooh," sound, but I knew I wasn't in trouble. How sad. I was too boring to even get suspended.

"Landry, your mother is on the phone," the secretary said, giving me the evil eye for getting a personal call at school. I should have told her at least I didn't sneak a cell phone into the bathroom to make calls like Yasmin and Arianna do.

"Hi, sweets. I hate to bother you at school, but Mrs. Myeski called, and they want you to have your picture taken for the paper today. The *Ingénue* people are paying for it, but you'll have to get out of school early to do it," Mom said.

"Cool!" I said. "Do I—"

"Wait! Don't say anything. I had to say you have a dentist appointment so I could get you out early. Make sure you're in the office at two o'clock and remember — don't act excited because they think you're going to the dentist," she said.

"Right. See ya, Mom."

I was psyched I was going to be in the newspaper. Tori had her picture in the paper once, but it was for playing soccer and she looked constipated as she kicked the ball. Those losers were going to be so sorry they got mad at me when they saw I was on my way to being a celebrity. And, if I did become famous, then I was never going to talk to either of them again. Let them see how it felt to be ignored. I ran into Devon on my way back to class. She had already gotten a call from her mom, but her excuse was "going to the doctor." We stood in the hall talking about what we were going to wear until the door to the office opened, and we scattered like cockroaches.

I got out of class at two and had just enough time to stick a few of Mom's hot rollers in my hair. I washed my face and put on some makeup and went to change. Mrs. Myeski said it was just a headshot, but I wanted to wear something nice since a little of my shirt would be showing. I put on my red sweater, but Mom thought it looked ratty. It was pathetic, but I didn't have a lot of clothes which weren't school clothes. Mom told me to wear my navy sweater to the shoot, which sucked because I didn't want my first publicity photo ever to be in a Hillcrest sweater. I ended up wearing it, but I guess it didn't matter too much because when we got to the photography studio, they said the photos were going to be black and white. Devon and I sat together. The other girls in the waiting room seemed super stuck up. One girl stepped on Devon's foot and didn't even apologize. They only took three shots of each of us. Afterward, they put them on a screen for us to see, and Mrs. Myeski came over to inspect them.

"Your eyes are sort of shut in this one," she said. "And you're trying too hard to keep them open wide in this one."

She was right. I looked like a crazed lunatic with my eyes almost popping out of my head.

"But this one is nice and natural. You just need to work on relaxing your face," she said.

Two of Devon's pictures were perfect. Her mom wanted them to use the one where she was smiling, but Mrs. Myeski said the serious pose was more flattering.

Devon's mom said we should go out to celebrate. I knew my mom wanted to go back to the office, but she agreed to stop for some ice cream at Ignatowski's Ice Cream Palace. I got a caramel marshmallow sundae with extra strawberry whipped cream. Devon ordered the brownie n' fudge extravaganza. Our moms sat at a separate table from us. There weren't a lot of people there in the middle of the day, so we took the good table, which was a round booth which looked like you were sitting in a hot air balloon. There was also a booth like a gazebo, but it was where the older high school girls and their boyfriends sat. I was halfway done with my sundae when Devon said we should switch sundaes.

"My friends and I always switch so we can taste what everybody got," she said.

I tried to ignore what I had read about salvia and mono online. It was kinda cool she would want to share with me. After all, Arianna and Yasmin always shared food at lunch, but my ex-friends never wanted to share anything with me — not even popcorn at the movies. I slid my dish over to her and tried not to gag as she told me about the time she, India, and Peyton had all gotten the flu after they shared a triple chocolate explosion. I guess Devon hadn't learned anything from our chapter on germs and bacteria in our science book.

The next day I missed the bus and I expected Ms. Ashcroft to glare at me when I walked in late, but instead she congratulated me on getting second place with my story in the Michigan Young Pens Contest. However, I overheard Ericka talking about me in science class.

"It's not like it was first place, you know," she said and Tori agreed. So I didn't win the contest. What had they won lately? Then Ericka made a remark about my hair.

"Looks like a dye job," Ericka said.

"A *bad* dye job," Tori said.

"She only got picked because models have to be super scrawny. Who knows, maybe washed-out hair colors will become trendy," Ericka said laughing.

I walked over to my seat and slammed my books on my desk. Tad congratulated me on the writing contest, but all I could focus on were my ex-friends whispering on the other side of the room. Devon was absent, but we were doing a worksheet so I didn't mind sitting alone. We watched *Anne Frank* in history, and India and Peyton congratulated me on the contest.

"So what are you wearing for your audition?" Peyton asked.

"I got an outfit from Franciszka T. It has a black and grey striped long sleeved sweater, and then it's like a strapless grey dress which goes under it with a wide black belt."

"It sounds cute. Devon's super excited about the whole thing," she said. "Her mom kept her home because she's had a sore throat last night."

Great, the girl I shared ice cream with was home with a sore throat. Fabulous.

"Her mom's so overprotective," India said peering at the TV. "Hey, is it the guy from *Schindler's List*? I can barely see from here."

"Put your glasses on, dork. Yeah, it's him. Landry, what chapter are you guys on in French?" Peyton asked.

"Oh crap. I forgot to do the homework for chapter nine," I said. I couldn't even do the work now because I had left the handout in my locker.

"Chapter nine? She handed those back in my class." Peyton went through her binder and pulled them out. "Here, just copy them on notebook paper and tell her you spilled something on your sheet." I started to thank her, but she cut me off. "No, you helped me out before."

I spent the rest of the movie copying her work. It was a good thing I had my homework done because Mrs. Aniston freaked out when Thalia forgot hers, and she wouldn't give her a pass to get it out of her locker. Mrs. Aniston said we had to be mature enough to bring our homework to class.

Devon was back the next day. "Congratulations," she said. I asked if she was feeling better.

"Yeah, but now I have all this extra work. I had to take a math quiz during lunch, and now I've got the stupid lab from the other day to do," she said as Mrs. Tamar came over to see if Devon was going to stay after to make up the lab assignment.

"I don't have a ride home today," she said. "Could I do it during lunch on Monday since the field trip is tomorrow?"

"Well, I have an appointment, so I won't be here then..."

"I could come in during lunch to help," I said. It's not like I had anything better to do.

At the end of the day, Ms. Ashcroft announced what cars we'd be in for our field trip to the art museum. It took about a half hour to get there, and it would suck if I got stuck in a car with one of my ex-friends. Ms. Ashcroft read off my name, along with three boys, and Ashanti and Tori. Great, with Ashanti out sick and Tori acting like Ericka's new best friend, the trip would be a blast. I thought about pretending to be sick tomorrow, but Mom would never let me miss school unless I was throwing up. I called Ashanti when I got home to see if she was feeling any better. I was hoping she'd say the doctor realized she didn't have mono after all, but then she told me she had a blood test and she was definitely going to be out of school longer.

"We never go on a decent field trip, and I'm on my deathbed the one time we do. Too bad you got stuck in a car with Tori — she follows Ericka around like a puppy," she said.

I checked my e-mail before bed. I was hoping Tori would want to make up, but I didn't have any mail. I couldn't believe they were still mad at me. I went into the living room where my mom was watching TV.

"I don't feel good," I said, remembering Ashanti had said she had a lot of high fevers. "Check my temperature. I think I've got mono." She slid her hand onto my forehead.

"Hate to disappoint you, kiddo, but you feel cool as a cucumber," she said.

"I feel sick. I don't think I can go tomorrow," my voice broke, and I moved away so she wouldn't see me cry.

"What's the matter?" she asked. "Are you crying?"

"I just feel so bad." She told me to go to bed and see how I felt in the morning. I did feel sick. My stomach was cramping, and my head hurt. I lay in bed wishing I would wake up with mono and be out of school for weeks. I didn't want to fall asleep because the sooner I went to sleep, the sooner it would be time to get up for school.

Eight

~~~~~~~~~~~~~~~~~~~~~~~~~~~~~~~~~~~~~~

Mom made me go to school, but I didn't eat breakfast because I didn't want to puke in Mrs. Carangi's van on the way to the museum. Mom gave me a ride to school, and I prayed this would be the world's shortest school day. Ms. Ashcroft and the other teachers were in the parking lot, and I checked in and went to Mrs. Carangi's van. Jared, Tad, and Hakeem were already sitting in the back so I could either sit in the front seat with Jared's mom or sit next to Tori, who would ignore me the entire trip. I got into the front seat, and Ms. Ashcroft came over and asked if we had room for one more. *Not Ericka,* I prayed, *not Ericka.*

Mrs. Carangi nodded, and Peyton got into the van. However, it's not easy to talk to someone in the seat behind you, so I spent the trip down listing to the radio. When we got to the museum, the teachers told us to pair up with someone from our car, and Peyton grabbed my arm and said "partner," which was great since Tori got stuck with Tad. Our guide, Antonio, walked us to the Egyptian room, and I told Peyton I've had a fear of mummies ever since I saw *The Mummy* on TV. She told me to look at the floor as we walked through the room. Peyton had to go to the bathroom, but we couldn't find the restrooms on our map. She felt dumb asking Antonio,

who was super hot, but she was about to wet her pants
so I asked for her. Tori sighed loudly, like I was bothering her, and Peyton gave her a dirty look as he told us
the quickest route to the bathroom.

"Go back through the Pharaoh's room—"

"Um, is there another way? I have a thing about
mummies," Peyton said. I shot her a grateful look.

"You can go through the contemporary art section, but
it'll take longer. Meet us in Impressionists, okay?" he said.

We got lost on the way back and ended up in the
lobby, and a security guard radioed Antonio and led us
back to our group. We found our group, and Mrs. Carangi said we were going to break for lunch. There was a big
sign for bathrooms as soon as we walked into the museum cafeteria, and we started laughing. Everyone else
had already begun eating, and we sat with India and
Devon as we helped ourselves to pizza and soda. India
soaked up the orange oil on the top of her slice with her
napkin while she told us about a painting which freaked
her out in one of the galleries our group hadn't been in
yet. She wouldn't tell us what it was, but Devon put her
hands over India's ears and said it was of some dead guy.

"Peyton, what time do you want us to come over tonight?" India asked.

"Six," Peyton said through a mouthful of cheese.

Antonio asked us to get back into our groups to finish the tour. I was glad since I felt uncomfortable when
they started talking about their plans for the weekend. I
knew they didn't mean to leave me out. I just wasn't part
of their group. It wasn't their fault my own group didn't
want me anymore.

We went into the room with the dead guy picture,
and Peyton grabbed my arm. She said if a decomposing
mummy freaked me out, then I'd never sleep again if I
saw the painting. She led me past it, and Antonio said
we might want to skip the next room with the sculpture
of another dead person.

"You guys can meet us at the gift shop. I'll mark the map for you so you won't get lost again," he said. I was starting to like him until I realized the gift shop was practically around the corner. How stupid did he think we were?

Devon's tour group came into the gift shop next, and we started looking at the jewelry. Devon decided to buy this cool woven bangle bracelet, and India and Peyton decided to get one, too. I wanted a bracelet too, but there were only three. Instead, I bought a postcard of a Monet painting to send to my dad.

When we got back to the car, Peyton asked Tori if she'd mind sitting in the front seat. Tori looked annoyed, but she got in the front and Peyton and I had fun on the ride back, which seemed a lot shorter than the ride down. I started to head to the bus line when we got to school, but Devon offered me a ride home.

"Landry, do you want to come over to my house tonight?" Peyton asked. "We're going to watch movies."

I wondered if she was just asking me because India had mentioned it in front of me, but I said I'd love to and then felt stupid for looking so excited. Devon's mom said she could take me to Peyton's tonight, and I said my mom could probably bring us home. Devon said she was going to wear her new black sweater with her new jeans tonight. I went through my closet trying to find something cute and fairly clean. Mom was happy to see I'd be off the couch for the evening, and she let me borrow her sweater.

"Who am I taking home? Tori?" she asked as she rifled through the mail.

"No, Devon," I said.

"Is Tori going? Because I could take her home since she's right on the way."

"She's not friends with these girls," I said.

Mom asked how Tori and Ericka were, and I didn't want her to know they weren't talking to me. I said Tori had a bunch of soccer stuff going on and Ericka had a new babysitting job.

"We've been e-mailing each other," I said.

"Uh-huh," Mom said, reading a bill. "What time should I pick you up? Eleven-thirty?" I nodded and went to get ready.

Peyton led us into her family room, which had two long navy couches facing one another, a square coffee table, and cream colored bookcases covering the whole wall.

"I went out with my dad, and we got a couple of movies. We got the new Evan Reynolds one for India, the new Blake Alderson one for Devon—"

"Thank you," Devon said as she helped herself to some potato chips.

"—and *The Mummy* for Landry," she said. "Just kidding."

I took a snack cake and two slices of pizza and settled down on the sofa next to Peyton to watch *Take Back the Skies II*. Devon was sitting on the couch across from me with her legs tucked up underneath her.

"Blake is so amazing," Devon sighed.

"Isn't he, like, way older than your dad?" Peyton asked.

"It doesn't matter, although I hate his tattoo," she said through a mouthful of pizza.

I said Blake looked a little bit like Peyton's dad, and they all cracked up.

"Watch her if she leaves the room because my dad's not safe," Peyton said.

"Ew, what's wrong with you people?" Devon said, laughing.

"What's wrong with us? Um, we're not the ones with crushes on our friend's dad," said India.

After the movie, Mom came to pick us up, and India joked Devon might want to stay over. Devon blushed.

"You'll have to excuse her, she wants to be my step-mother," Peyton said as Devon shrieked. We walked to the car, and Devon said she didn't think she'd ever be able to look Mr. Urich in the face again.

"I wonder what the *Ingénue* audition will be like next weekend," Devon said when she calmed down. "My mom's already freaking out about the whole thing. She's called, like, fifty times to check on things."

I had been trying not to think about next weekend. Every time I thought about getting in front of the judges my stomach would flip over and I'd end up running to the bathroom. I had been trying to get through one day at a time. Now I could worry Mrs. Abrams would decide not to let her go and it would just be me by myself. I could just imagine me tagging along behind my mom because no one else would talk to me. Well, at least having my mom there would be better than nothing.

The next morning, my mom came into my room. She said her manager had been taken in for emergency surgery, and they needed mom to cover for her in some important meeting. Then mom dropped the bad news.

"The meeting is on Friday afternoon."

"So I can't go to the audition? Mo-om, this could be my big—"

Mom put up her hands to stop me. "I called Mrs. Abrams, and she said you can ride with her and Devon to Lansing. I don't see any other way of getting you there."

I shrugged. I guess it was better than missing the competition, but I wanted my mom to be there with me. Mom said since she already paid for our room, Devon and I could share it, and Devon's mom would stay in the other room. I was glad Mrs. Abrams would be there because I wanted somebody's mother to be there... even if it wasn't my own.

Nine

~~~~~~

On Tuesday, I went to sit in the lunchroom because I thought I could sit with Devon. I was halfway through the line when I remembered she was eating lunch in Mrs. Kharrazi's room because she had to make up a quiz. Maggie and Halle had their matching pink purses on the chairs next to them, and I didn't feel like having to ask them to move their stuff. I didn't want to have to beg to sit at their table. I could sit with Tad and his friend, but none of the girls had ever sat by themselves with a bunch of guys. Besides, then everybody would think I was his girlfriend or something. I had been standing there way too long, and I started to walk toward Maggie and Halle's table when Hana walked past me to get a napkin.

"Hi, Landry. What's up?" she asked. I almost kissed her on the mouth.

"Hey, can I sit with you?" I asked.

"Sure," she said. "What did you think of the math quiz?" she asked as we sat down. "The story problem was crazy."

Oh crap, I thought it had been pretty easy which should have been a huge sign since math is never easy for me. Hana was a brain, and if she found it tough, then I was sunk. My mouth was full, so I shrugged.

"I read your story. It was cute," she said.

"Thanks."

Tori walked by, and Hana asked if we were still fighting. I rolled my eyes.

"I know you guys were friends and all, but doesn't it bug you how she has to be the best all the time? I've seen her ask for extra homework to challenge her," she rolled her eyes. "Why are they mad at you anyway?"

I told her it was because of the audition, and she wasn't surprised since Ericka and Tori were always so competitive. I didn't mention Ericka was also mad about Kyle paying attention to me because I didn't need to hear the fact Kyle would never be interested in me. Hana and her friends had finished eating, and I started to gather up my tray to go, but they told me to finish my lunch.

The rest of the week flew by as I worried about the trip. We were leaving Friday afternoon, and we even got to leave school early. I wanted to bring my favorite stuffed mouse with me as a good luck charm, but I'd die if Devon saw him, so I shoved him into the bottom of my suitcase next to my makeup bag so I'd know he was there even if I couldn't take him out. Devon's mom was in the driveway packing up their SUV when my mom and I walked over.

"This is so exciting," Devon said.

"I'm kinda nervous," I said, but I don't think she heard me.

I said goodbye to my mom and got in the Abrams' SUV. Devon had flipped down the two middle seats so we could sit in the backseat and put our feet up.

"Are you hungry?" Devon asked when we sat down. "My mom packed a ton of snacks. I have animal crackers, pretzels, juice boxes, and candy bars." We pulled down the middle seat tray and made a little buffet. "You know, I'm glad we're only auditioning for the young teen group," she said. "I hear the older girls get asked if they'll pose naked, and they have to wear swimsuits."

I almost choked on an animal cracker. "I would have passed out," I said.

"Yeah, they can't make girls under eighteen wear swimsuits because people would, like, protest or something," she said rolling her eyes. "Whatever."

When we arrived, Mrs. Abrams checked us into our room at the hotel and told us where her room was. She said we were supposed to meet in the banquet room for orientation at five o'clock, and we'd eat at six. We had plenty of time, and Devon said she'd do my hair. She took out a curling iron with a bunch of different attachments. She used a waving iron on my hair, and it looked gorgeous. Since her hair was already curly, we used the straightening iron on it and then the big curling iron to put a little wave in it. Her hair looked just as gorgeous straight as it did curly.

We went downstairs to get our information packets, and I got a funny feeling when I saw our nametags. My nametag was yellow, but Devon's was blue. Oh no, they were going to split us up into groups. We sat down and the group leaders made us go around the room and say our names and what school we were from. I was glad Devon was there because the other people didn't look friendly.

Then we were divided up by the color of our nametags and had to sit in a circle and do this stupid getting-to-know-you game where we had to ask each other dumb questions. The first girl I was paired with never even looked at me. She kept leaning across the aisle to talk to her friend. I was getting sick of her saying, "Bella, oh wow!" every five minutes. I asked her if she had any pets, and she rolled her eyes. I reminded her I didn't make up the questions.

"A Bichon Frise," she said. I figured it was one of those little frou-frou dogs who wore a bow in its hair and could fit inside of a purse.

The next girl I was paired with looked like she thought she was too intellectual to sit with the rest of us or play such a stupid game. She called it "infantile."

"Hm, my favorite book... I like Paula Danziger's books, the *Harry Potter* series, and *Jane Eyre*," I said. I hadn't actually finished *Jane Eyre*, but I thought it might impress her. She stared at me.

"I'm currently reading Joyce and I love Faulkner," she said. Okay, what was I supposed to say now? She spent the rest of the time staring at the clock above my head and snapping her gum. I don't know why they even bothered with the book question anyway. It wasn't like reading was important for being a model anyway. The servers began bringing out our dinners, which was some kind of chicken and vegetable thing smothered in a slimy gray sauce. I ate two bites, and Devon and I hit the vending machines before we went back to the "fun" activities.

"Is it just me or are the people here stuck up?" I asked.

"People suck. Aw crap, my chips are stuck." She hit the machine, and a tall guy came up behind her and expertly tipped the machine making her chips fall down.

"Thanks," she said staring up at him.

He winked and walked away. "Whoa. He looked just like the singer — what's his name... um, Mason Fraser," she said. She narrowed her eyes at me. "You're not going to tell me your dad looks like him are you?"

"Nope, although I just downloaded Mason's latest song," I said. "I wonder if the Mason lookalike works here."

"I think he had a hotel shirt on. We should clog up our toilet and maybe they'd send him up to fix it," she said. "Of course, it would be kinda embarrassing, but we have to see him again."

Later, we went back up to the room and changed into sweats. Devon flipped through the TV stations, and we sat on her bed and ate our snacks from the train.

"You know what I'm craving?" she asked. "Cupcakes." We decided to go to the vending machine down the hall, but neither one of us felt like changing into our regular clothes.

"How bad do I look?" she asked.

She had on a gray sweatshirt and navy sweatpants. They were baggy, but she looked fine, and she said I looked okay in my sweats.

"Should we risk it?" she asked.

We peered around the corner, and the hall was empty. We made sure we had the room key and tore down the hall to the machines. We bought cupcakes and bottled water and checked the hall to make sure it was still clear. I dropped my cupcake package, and I heard her gasp.

"Another junk food run?" The Mason Fraser lookalike was standing in front of her.

"Um, yeah," she said.

"Cupcakes, huh?" he said. She offered him one, and he took a bite and thanked her as he walked down the hall.

"I'm dying," she said. She narrowed her eyes. "Aren't you the one who said, 'Who will see us?'"

"Oops."

"My hair's a complete mess from lying on the pillow, too. Oh well. He's probably too old for me anyway," she said.

"At least this guy isn't as old as your dad," I said.

"I wish I hadn't given him a cupcake though," she said.

We went back to the room, and she asked if I wanted to watch a movie. I knew we should go to bed, but there was no way I was going to fall asleep. I was too nervous about tomorrow to sleep. Devon found a movie on one of the local channels, and I said one of the actors looked like Nikolas.

"You mean the guy on our bus?" she asked. I nodded. "Did you know he skipped a grade or two?"

"He did?"

"Yeah, he's pretty smart, and he's like only eleven or something," she said.

Oh no. Total humiliation. He probably saw the nesting doll keychain on my backpack and thought, "Ooh toys." Ericka and Tori would have a field day when they found out. Why did I have to go bragging in front of them about meeting him at the mall? Could I be any dumber?

"I have to tell you something, but you have to swear you won't tell anybody," she said.

"Promise."

"Okay, you know how India is in love with Stuart? Well, I asked him if he liked her, and he told me he likes Arianna," she said. "India said he's been acting weird around her lately, but I don't think she knows I talked to him."

"So you lied when you said you thought he stunk like moldy burritos?" I asked. She nodded.

"Promise you'll never talk to a guy for me," I said.

"Too late, the hotel guy already knows you're after him," she said through a mouthful of cupcake.

"He's all yours," I said.

"But don't you think it's better to just go for it? If I like someone then I just go up and tell them," she said.

It helps if you have curly dark hair and happen to be gorgeous. Kyle would fall over laughing if I went up to him and told him I liked him. Then he'd tell all of his friends so they could laugh at me, too.

"Yeah, like how you were so brave in the hall just now," I said.

"Hey, he's not an ordinary guy. He's like actor hot or something," she said. "But don't you think it's better to know? What's the worst thing he could say? If they don't like you back... then you just move on."

Easy to say when guys fall all over themselves to talk to you. I bet she had never been rejected by anyone she liked. Devon's mom knocked on our door to say goodnight and reminded us we needed to get up early for the audition.

"Do you like anybody right now?" Devon asked after her mom left.

Like I was going to tell her about Kyle after she had gone behind her best friend's back. "Nah. Besides, guys never seem to go for me. They all want girls who look like Yasmin or Arianna or you. I wish I had dark hair and big brown eyes like yours."

"Funny," she said as she snuggled down into her pillow. "I've always wanted blonde hair and blue eyes like yours."

Ten

My stomach felt like I had psychotic butterflies clog dancing in there the next morning. Devon and I spent a half hour doing our hair and makeup. We weren't supposed to wear makeup, but there was no way I was going to the audition with puffy eyes, a blotchy broken-out face, and without any brow color. I put on sheer foundation to cover my spots, powder because I get greasy, Little Rose mascara and brow pencil, lip stain, and I borrowed some of Devon's cream blush. Devon had a black wrap dress on and I put on my outfit.

Mrs. Myeski gave us our numbers, and we had to wait in a huge line to do a quick interview. A man named Noah interviewed me and asked me about my modeling background. Somehow I didn't think he'd be impressed with the fact I pretended my hallway was a runway, so I said I had a big interest in fashion and photography. I had to admit my cell phone pics always came out excellent. He stared at me for a minute and then nodded. He gave me a packet to fill out and called the next number. Devon was already filling out her forms in the lobby.

"Some of the girls are doing their auditions," she said. "Wanna sneak in and watch?"

I nodded. We sat in the back as one girl practiced walking for the judges. She had thick dark hair down to her waist, and you could tell she knew she was hot.

"Monique, your nose is a little flat from the front. I don't think print work will be right for you," one of the judges said.

They thought *her* nose was flat? She could win a beauty pageant compared to me. Devon and I looked at each other.

"She's amazing," she said.

The next girl was almost six feet tall with long spiral curled dark hair. She didn't even walk in front of the judges. She, like, sashayed or something. The judges asked about her hair, and she said it was natural. She claimed she never even used a curling iron or rollers either. I thought I was going to puke. There was no way I could compete against her. No way. Devon and I sat through the first hour of auditions. Out of all the girls there were maybe three who weren't sophisticated, and even they looked better than me. I felt bad for Devon since the judges had already told four other girls how curly hair was the most difficult to deal with. I bet they still picked the tall girl with the spiral curls though. Devon grabbed my hand, and we went into the hallway.

"I feel sick right now," she said. "I should have straightened my hair again. Why did I bother washing it this morning?"

"You could still run up to the room and change it," I said. "But it looks gorgeous natural."

"Sometimes it gets frizzy when I use a flatiron, and I wouldn't have time to fix it right. I only washed it and wore it curly today because the stupid sheet they handed out said to look as natural as possible. Crap, I'm sweating so bad," she said. "I'm going to start frizzing for sure now."

We were in the next group to audition. I watched one African-American girl curling her eyelashes in the practice area. She looked like she was thirty, but somebody said she was only sixteen. There was no way I could go in there. I didn't belong there, and I wasn't even sure I wanted to. A couple of the girls were talking about their hair extensions, and it was obvious some of them had had plastic surgery already. I looked like a little kid. Devon tried to make me feel better and reminded me that the judges said they were looking for a "fresh faced girl next door." Yeah, tell it to the girl in the super tiny dress over there. Plus, there was the fact we'd have to do "modeling challenges" on the TV show if we made it to the third level. In the past the show had made girls pose with snakes and have pictures taken underwater.

I would die if they made me touch a snake or pose with a tiger like Talisa had to on the show last season. I knew it was just to get people to watch the show, but it made me want to throw up just thinking about it. As I glanced around I wondered what kind of look they were hoping to find in this competition. A bunch of gorgeous girls had already been cut from the morning group, and some odd, scrawny girls had already moved on to the next level. I looked around the room to see if there were any regular, normal looking girls there. I saw one plain girl who was going in for her audition. I stood in the doorway to watch. As she walked the runway, I noticed she had slouched the whole way. I thought she'd get cut for sure, but the judges applauded when she was done. Devon and I just stared at each other.

"They liked *her*?" Devon asked.

"Don't get mad, but I'm not doing it. I can't go up there. I'll make a fool of myself, and to be honest, I don't want to hear what they're going to say about me," I said.

"Come on, we made it this far."

I shook my head.

"Would you at least pretend you're going to so you can go in with me and be there to give me moral support? Then you can back out right before it's your turn. If you don't want them to focus on any flaws then just trip on purpose so they'll focus on the falling instead," she said. "Besides, you got this far, and aren't you a little curious about what they'd say?"

Part of me was dying to know what the judges would say. One time Ericka and I played "Truth or Dare" and she asked me what I thought her best and worst features were. I went first and said her eyes were her best feature, and I didn't want to hurt her feelings, so I said her only bad feature was how her hair got a little frizzy in the rain sometimes. However, she told me my worst features were my "super pale" hair which just "lay there," and how I was "too tall." She said my best feature was my hands. Hands. Who even looks at those? I couldn't sleep all night. I just kept picturing myself looking like a used mop.

"Please go in with me?" Devon asked. "You can even get out of line right before you're called, but I'd feel a lot better if I knew you were there with me."

I had gotten this far and maybe the judges would say I wasn't as gross as I thought I was or maybe they'd point out something I could do with my hair. Besides, my mom had spent a lot on the hotel room — not to mention all the stuff she had bought me for the competition. I decided to try out, and we went to line up. Devon's number was called. The rest of us had to stand backstage to wait, so I couldn't hear what the judges were saying to her. She looked so beautiful under the lights and walked in like she owned the place, but there were girls here who already looked like professionals. She came backstage, and her eyes were watery.

"Are you okay?" I asked.

She nodded. "They said I was probably too short even for petite modeling and how curly hair is hard to work with. I know I won't make the cut, but at least I tried. Let's just go to the lounge and watch TV or something. I don't want to see my mom yet," she said. "I feel kind of stupid for dragging her here in the first place."

A woman with a headset came over to us. "Number forty-seven is next."

I held up my number.

"Oh, you're still going to try out?" Devon asked.

I shrugged. "Might as well. Wait for me outside?" I walked onto the stage, and the judges had me walk and turn for them.

"Is this your real hair color? Or do you lighten it?" one of the judges asked.

Great, it was so freakishly light they thought I bleached it.

"It's my natural color."

"Can you pull your hair up away from your face?" the woman asked me. I pulled my hair back in a pony-tail, and they had me look side to side to check out my profile. "Thank you. Please get your information packet from Janette. We'll see you in Detroit."

"What?" I asked.

The male judge smiled. "You're moving on to the next round. Congratulations."

I was stunned as I walked away. Janette, the woman with the headset, handed me an envelope with release forms and told me the next segment would be televised. I almost knocked over a potted plant as I headed for the door. Devon was outside waiting for me.

"I made it," I said. "They put me through to the next round.

"For real?" she asked. I nodded and she gave me a half-hug, but then her arms went sorta limp. "This is gonna be so embarrassing. Everyone back home is expecting me to be a model. I feel so guilty for making my mom come here," she said as her eyes filled up. "What a waste."

"Yeah, but nobody has to know what happened," I said. "We can tell people you thought it over and decided not to do it because you'd have to miss too much school."

"Nobody would believe I quit because of school. This sucks. I wanted to be on the show," she said.

We sat in the lounge trying to come up with a believable story before we went to see her mom. We decided to tell people she didn't even try out because we found out there was a lot more to doing the show than she thought. We went to tell her mom she changed her mind, and I thought Mrs. Abrams looked relieved. Her mom took us out to lunch, and Devon wanted to split a hot fudge cake, but I was worried the chocolate might break me out.

"So? Just use some skin cream. This cake looks so good," she said.

I wanted to say, "But what if my skin doesn't clear up in time for the next round?" but I didn't want her to be jealous and get mad at me. She ordered the cake and I tried a little, but said I was full from lunch. We packed up and got in her mom's SUV. I thought we'd talk about the auditions, but she took out her headphones, put on some music, and curled up with her pillow. I couldn't tell if she was sleeping or not, so I just stared out the window. Mrs. Abrams dropped me off, and Devon gave me a hug as she helped me unload my stuff. When I got inside, I told my mom all about the competition. She was happy for me, but she was in a weird mood. Normally, the weekend was our lazy time, but as soon as I finished telling her about the audition, she was telling me it was time to redo my bedroom. Where was this coming from? I liked the wood paneled walls because it made my room feel, I dunno, warm and cozy, and I didn't want to change it.

I wanted to call my dad to tell him about the competition, but mom said we could call him later since the free long distance minutes on her cell phone didn't kick in until the evening. Instead, we went to the home improvement store and looked through the wallpaper books while I finished telling her about my trip.

"I'm excited for you, but I'm a little... apprehensive," she said.

"Huh?"

"Are you sure you want to go through with this? There's going to be even more competition in the next round, and I don't want to see you get hurt," she said.

Great, my own mother didn't think I stood a chance. I told her I was just doing it for the experience, which was what Devon had told her parents to convince them to let her try out in the first place. Apparently, as long as Mom thought I wasn't in it to be a supermodel, she was okay with it. I changed the subject by showing her a wallpaper sample. Mom scrunched up her nose and said she wanted something classic, which meant boring. We tried the kid's wallpaper books next since the designs were more fun. The smell of the glue and turning page after page and finding the same design in different colors was driving me crazy.

"How about painting the room?" she asked. "It might be harder since the wood is dark, but we could check into it."

Mom got up and asked a worker about painting the wood in my room. He said we'd need to clean and prime the walls, but it wouldn't be a problem. I wanted a bright shade of royal blue, which was the color of my favorite fleece blanket. I looked at every paint chip of blue in the store, but I couldn't find one I liked. Mom suggested a pale blue, but I wanted something darker.

"You don't want too dark and gloomy. The room is small, and a lighter color would make it look bigger," she said. "And we can put up a border, too."

I was tired, thirsty, and about to give up on life when she pushed a peach colored paint chip in front of me.

"Whaddya think?" she asked. I lifted my head off my arms and shrugged. It didn't make me sick.

"Grapefruit. Not too light, not too dark and one of the flowers in your blanket is this color," she said.

We stood in line with drop cloths, rollers, and other painting supplies. Mom asked if I was sure about the color, but I was too tired to argue and it wasn't like I had to worry about how it would look in front of my friends. No one would see it but my mom and me. We got home and Mom and I moved my furniture out of my room and cleaned the walls. I didn't do a great job, but I figured I could always put up posters if the walls looked bad. I thought using a roller to put on the primer would be easy, but my arms and legs hurt like crazy. We finished putting the primer on and then collapsed on the couch.

"Where are you going to sleep tonight?" she asked.

"In my bed — oh crap, my bed is in pieces. Do you think we'll be finished by tomorrow?" I asked.

"Doubt it and even if we were I wouldn't want you breathing in paint fumes at night. You're crazy enough already," she said yawning. "We can pull out the loveseat in the den."

The den was so small the foot of the bed touched the bookcase across from it. I put on my sweats, grabbed my stuffed mouse and blanket, and slid under the covers. I still hadn't called my dad, but I was tired so I went to bed anyway. I ended up sleeping in until one o'clock the next day. Mom and I were too tired to put on a second coat of primer, even though the walls looked kind of splotchy.

"Do you think it matters it looks… stonewashed?" she asked. "Should we call and ask the guy at the store?"

"It looks stone-*what*? I don't care what it looks like. I can't do it again," I said.

Mom pried open a can of paint, and we both stopped when we saw the color.

"Was it this orange in the store?" she asked.

We decided to put on the first coat and hope for the best. Painting was easier than putting on primer, but the paint went on darker in some parts because of my crappy job as a cleaner/primer applier. Oh well. I slopped paint on the ceiling and on the floor a couple times, but the spots on the floor could be covered up with furniture, and who looks at the ceiling anyway? I went to see how mom was doing and saw her staring at the wall she had just finished.

"Maybe it'll look better when it's done," she said. She sighed and her breath blew her white-blonde bangs up.

It wasn't until I moved to paint my closet that I noticed the room had become ultra bright. The soft peachy-pink shade on the paint chip was now a bright orange sherbet color.

"Well, it's certainly lighter in here," Mom said. "But it *is* dark outside, so we can't judge the color until tomorrow."

We were nearly blinded when we checked my room the next day. It was so bright and so *not* what I wanted.

"Did they give us the wrong color?" Mom asked as we stared at the walls. I pointed out the can said "grapefruit," but maybe the company had put the wrong label on it.

"Or we're stupid," I said.

"Do you like it?" she asked.

"Well, it's not what I wanted…"

"I'm not repainting it. I can't go through it all again."

After we took a break, I called my dad to tell him about the contest.

"Guess what? I got picked to go on to the next round," I said.

"Great news! So what do you have to do next?" he asked.

I told him I would be going to Detroit to compete and I would be on TV, too, but only in Michigan, not in Illinois.

"You have to promise to record it for me if I can't be there. I have some good news of my own," he said. "I have some time off from the clinic, and I'm coming to see you guys early this week. Can you put your mom on?"

He used to visit us every weekend when mom and I first moved here. Dad would come over and everything would be fine, but then he and mom would start fighting over who was going to pay for dinner or something equally dumb. Once Dad bought me a CD Mom had said I couldn't have, and she freaked out. I knew they tried going to a marriage counselor because I overheard my mom telling her friend about it on the phone. I guess my dad didn't like the last one they had so they stopped going.

Then Dad hadn't been able to get away from work for a while. I got off the phone with him and tried calling Ashanti to tell her about the competition, but her mom said she was sleeping.

"Landry, I need your help," Mom said after she got off the phone. I went into the hall where she was pulling out the vacuum. "Do you want to vacuum the living room or dust it?"

"Um, neither," I said. "Can't I do your room instead? It's smaller."

"I'm not bothering with my room. Just the living room and bathroom," she said. "Besides, your dad will be staying at a hotel anyway."

I assumed Dad would stay at our place like he always does, but Mom said it would be "less of a hassle" for her without all of his stuff around. I asked why he wasn't going to stay here and why she was suddenly so worried about his stuff being in the way since our house is never super clean, but she just handed me a dust wipe and told me to get started.

I called Ashanti after dinner. Her dad answered and told me she had been waiting all day to talk to me.

"She has shocking news for you. You might want to put all the sharp objects away," he said as Ashanti snatched the phone from him.

"I was reading *Soap Opera Hotties* and they asked a bunch of actors how they start their day, and your man said he starts each day with a back massage from his 'darling Mirabella,'" she said.

"Is Mirabella a back specialist who makes morning house calls?" I asked.

"Well, maybe she's his great-aunt who lives with him because she's a hundred years old and doesn't get around too well," she said.

"And he's such a sweet guy he takes care of her, and in return, she helps his aching back," I said. "Or he's a jerk with a live-in girlfriend."

"*He* can be a jerk because you love his character, Colin, and Colin would never let some chick move into his place and then brag about getting massages to prove his manhood," she said. "So how was your trip?"

"I almost backed out since the other girls all looked like they were thirty, but then I changed my mind and they picked me! Well, me and a bunch of other girls."

"So cool. How did Devon do?" she asked.

I told her Devon had changed her mind about trying out at the last minute. "It was scary though. I mean, I know I'm not pretty enough to be a model, but it's nice to know someone out there didn't think I was a hideous freak."

"Landry, you are beautiful, but looks aren't the most important thing in the world," she said. "Did I ever show you a picture of the actress who plays Savannah without her makeup on? She looks just like Mrs. Tamar. Looks aren't everything."

Eleven

~~~~~~~~~~~~~~~~~~~~~~~~~~~~~~~~~~~~~

On Monday I had one of those days where nothing went my way. My hair was extra static-y, I broke out above my lip, which looked like a cold sore, and everybody at school seemed surprised I was going to be on the *Ingénue* show. Not just surprised, but shocked. I overheard Yasmin say it was probably because "I was so tall and painfully tiny." Jerk. Plus, I failed a math quiz and had to play dodge ball in gym, but at least my dad was coming to visit.

After school, I got off the bus deep in thought about Colin and *As the Days Roll On*.

"Hey Kiddo!"

I looked up and saw my dad standing in the driveway. As he hugged me, I breathed in his cologne, and it was like we were never apart. Dad was surprised my bedroom was so bright, but he said he liked it. He asked why I chose this color when I always bugged him about having a blue room in my old bedroom back in Chicago. I shrugged and said Mom and I painted it, but I wasn't crazy about it.

"You did a nice job," he said. "But let me know if you want to change it to blue. I'll help."

He looked at the school pictures I had on my dresser of Tori and Ericka. I had put them in little heart-shaped frames last year. He asked me about "the soccer player," and I said Tori was fine. He hadn't met Ericka before. Lucky man. I showed him the second place certificate I got from the Michigan Young Pens contest, and he was excited to hear about my trip.

"A ton of girls didn't make it. My friend Devon got cut, and she's beautiful. I almost backed out at the last minute, but then I got chosen," I said.

"The judges had excellent taste," he said. "I'm excited for you, kiddo."

Dad said he wanted to read some of the stuff I had written lately. I ended up letting him read a story I had started in math class. He was still reading when Mom came home from work. Dad gave her a kiss on the cheek, and she said we were going to have an early dinner. Dad offered to help with dinner, but Mom said she had everything under control.

"Dad said he'd help me with my room," I said.

"We haven't picked a border out yet, and it's a unique color so it may take some time," she said. "Anyway, we can do it ourselves."

"Just trying to help," he said as he picked up my stuffed mouse, who was sitting on my dresser.

While we were eating, I casually mentioned I was thinking about repainting. I glanced at my mother out of the corner of my eye. She had a mouthful of potato salad and couldn't respond. I thought about how to word it. I didn't want to upset my mom by saying it was butt ugly. Instead, I went with saying, "It gives me a headache."

"I thought you liked how cheerful it is," she said, tearing into a roll.

Dad wasn't sure which side to take so he kept eating and staring at his plate as if nothing was going on. I started to point out it didn't match any of my stuff, but then my mom gave me her famous "not now" look, which included a raised left eyebrow, pursed lips, and a stare which could turn me to ice. I could live in a neon grapefruit, but I couldn't live on my mother's bad side.

"This potato salad is delicious," Dad said, finally breaking into the conversation.

"I got it at the deli, so you can thank Leon for it," Mom said.

Dad went back to studying his plate. I shoved a spoonful of potato salad in my mouth as I matched my mother stare for stare. However, I began choking and started sputtering potato and radish all over the table. Dad leapt up and whacked me on the back, and Mom pushed a plastic cup of apple juice at me.

"You gonna make it?" Dad asked as he removed a piece of spit-up radish from his shirt. I nodded as I forced the juice down my burning throat. Mom asked if we were ready for dessert, and I almost choked for the second time. Dessert? I mean, for us dessert meant passing a bag of fun-sized candy bars back and forth during a TV show, and "preparing dessert" meant pulling the foil off the pudding cup. Mom brought out little bowls of pudding with whipped cream and chocolate sprinkles on top. I knew she had spooned the pudding out of the prepackaged cups, but my dad didn't.

"Hey, butterscotch, my favorite," he said, digging in. It had to be a lie because butterscotch was nobody's favorite. Dad wasn't aware we were having butterscotch because we only eat the chocolate pudding out of the variety pack so we had a fridge full of butterscotch, and the chocolate sprinkles were from a package of cookies we never got around to making.

After dinner, Mom asked me to clear the table, and without thinking, I almost threw my plate in the trash. Then I remembered we had used real dishes and silverware. I wasn't even sure what to do with a real dish since I was used to eating off paper plates. Did she want me to wash them, put them in the dishwasher, or hide them in the oven? We always hid the dirty dishes in there, and last summer Grandma Albright came for a visit and we freaked out every time Grandma suggested baking some of her famous brownies.

I put the dishes on the counter and figured if mom insisted I wash them I could say, "What? These aren't paper?" and that would be the end of it.

We went into the living room, and I noticed a gift bag hidden behind the recliner. When was Dad planning on bringing it out? I looked over at Mom, who was sitting so far away from us she was almost in the dining room. Dad handed the bag to me and gave my mom a box of candy.

"I remembered how much you loved chocolate covered cherries from Maxie's," he said. Maxie's was a store where it cost twenty-five dollars for a big caramel apple.

"Landry, open yours."

He didn't have to ask me twice. I tore into the first present, which was a big book about young adult authors. There was a smaller aqua box in the bag. I slid the white ribbon off. Inside was a silver link bracelet with a dangling heart. Mom said it looked expensive and helped me put it on.

Dad asked my mother about work, and I had to give him credit for managing to look interested. He must have been listening because he said, "mm-hmm" and "uh-huh" in all the right spots. Mom let me stay up until eleven o'clock, and then I listened through my bedroom door. They seemed to be getting along. I peeked around the corner and saw Mom had opened the chocolate covered cherries. My parents were still where I had left them. Mom on the chair and Dad was still on the couch, but at least they weren't arguing.

Later, she poked her head in my room. "I just wanted to say goodnight." She shut the door and then came back into the room. "If you want to repaint the room... it's okay with me."

"For real? It's like a tangerine exploded in here. Can I get the paint roller thing they show on TV? They promise you can paint any room in an hour or your money back," I said.

"No, I hate the actor in the commercial. I don't have any free time for a while, but I suppose we could hire someone," she said.

"Ashanti's mom hired a guy after her dad did a crappy job on the living room. Mrs. Russell thinks he did a bad job on purpose so she'd never ask him to paint again," I said. "I'll call Ashanti tomorrow." Mom left and I went to bed dreaming of a room which wouldn't hurt my eyes.

Twelve

~~~~~~

My mom had a business dinner the next day, so Dad
went out to get groceries so he could make dinner for me.

"I thought I'd make spaghetti with lots of ant poison," he said.

I used to put tons of Parmesan cheese on my spaghetti when I was little, and Dad used to tease me the
cheese looked like ant poison.

He asked me about school as I helped him with dinner. I avoided the fact my best friends hated me and told
him about Colin's betrayal with the evil Mirabella.

"I bet she is a back specialist. Is he the guy you have
hanging on the back of your door?" he asked. I nodded.

"He's kind of... pretty, and he's wearing more
makeup than your mom does," he said.

"It's not makeup," I said, even though I suspected he
used tinted lip balm, bronzer, and possibly mascara. "Oh
guess what? Mom said I could repaint my room. I forgot
to ask Ashanti who painted their living room."

"I'll help you. Do you have a color picked out?" he
asked.

He said he'd pick me up from school tomorrow and
we could get all the stuff. Dad picked out the movie after
dinner. We watched *Field of Dreams*, but then he saw

my old *The Truly Mean Queen* movie in the pile and said
I was terrified of the Queen in it when I was a little kid.

"We took you to the amusement park and you wanted to go on this ride, and we didn't know it was basically
a queen like her chasing you throughout the whole thing.
You screamed your head off, and we ended up buying
half the gift shop to calm you down," he said.

"I still have the mouse."

"I noticed."

The next day, Devon had to skip lunch for tutoring
and Hana was absent. I went to the bathroom and wolfed
down a peanut butter sandwich in the last stall before
going to the library. The school library never carried any
books we might actually want to read. I couldn't find my
usual copy of *Jane Eyre*, so I read an ancient looking
Nancy Drew, which smelled like our attic.

We had a pop quiz in history because we were being
"highly disruptive." I had to correct Tori's quiz, and I
made big red check marks next to all of her wrong answers. I knew I had gotten them all wrong too, but it
made me feel better knowing Ms. Brainiac failed the
quiz. When she got her quiz back, her hand shot up in
the air, and she asked Mrs. Hearst if she would also ac-
cept Churchill for number five. Mrs. Hearst shook her
head, and Tori tried again for half-credit. I heard somebody whisper, "Loser" at the next table.

After school, Dad was over at the house waiting for
me.

"How was your day, kiddo?" he asked. "Ready for op-
eration re-paint?"

We went to the home improvement store and I
picked out royal blue paint. Dad told me to call Mom on
his cell phone and find out what she wanted us to pick
up for dinner. Mom said she had another business dinner
with Ronald and Alfred from the office. I had met Ronald

when he had offered us his daughter's old bedroom furniture when we first moved to Grand Rapids. At the time, he thought my mom was single and he kept flirting with her — big time. It was disgusting, and I've hated him ever since.

"Maybe you guys could order pizza," she said.

I couldn't believe she'd go out with Ronald while my dad was in town. *So* not right.

"Can't you cancel?" I asked.

Mom said Alfred was leaving on a trip tomorrow, so I told Dad she had plans.

"Another meeting? Well, let's get a pizza," he said.

Dad felt bad she had to work late, and I let it slip I thought Ronald liked Mom. Dad's slice stopped halfway to his mouth.

"Does she work with this Ronald person a lot?" he asked.

I shrugged and reached for a napkin. "I dunno. He's kind of weird."

"You've met him? What's he like?"

"Kinda boring. And he sweats a lot."

I told him Ronald dyed his hair a weird shade of blond, was a lot older than Mom, and he was kind of pudgy. Dad nodded and chased a piece of pepperoni around his plate.

After we ate, I spread out the drop cloths while dad stirred and poured the paint. It wasn't hard to cover the grapefruit color, and we decided to finish up instead of wasting a good Saturday afternoon. I was all sweaty when we finished and went to take a shower. I heard my parents arguing when I got out of the shower. I slipped into the den and crawled under the sheets without bothering to dry my hair. I heard the door slam. My mom came into the den, but I pretended to be asleep.

Thirteen

Dad called the next day and asked if I wanted to go to the park. Mom was all on me wanting to know if my homework was done. Like my homework had ever been finished on a Saturday before. I was lucky to have it done by Sunday night. She sighed and told me I could go.

"Great. I saw this park by the expressway, and it looked nice. There's a zoo there, too," he said.

"I've never been to the zoo, but Ericka and I played tennis there."

"Do you want to play?" he asked.

I asked Mom if he could borrow her racket, and she sighed again. I went to look for a clean pair of sweatpants, but all I found were ones stained with tomato sauce, chocolate, and blueberry... blueberry? When did I have fruit?

"Don't let your father put the case on the filthy court, and my racket is not to touch the ground," she said. "I'm not sure which one of you I trust less with it."

Dad pulled in the driveway and honked the horn. We went to the zoo first and walked through the birdhouse. However, the sign for the birdhouse didn't tell you you're going to be attacked by butterflies or the fact you end up in the amphibian house, which led into Snake County. I about puked when I almost walked into a glass case with a four-foot snake wrapped around a branch.

"Um, Dad? Remember, I'm not a huge snake fan. Can we go back through the birdhouse?" I asked.

"Didn't you just call the butterflies 'objects from the devil'?" he asked.

I pointed out that normal butterflies wouldn't fly in your face, and he said he'd form a human shield from them. However, we couldn't get back in because some lady had passed out in front of the door. A zoo worker rushed to help her, but I couldn't get through unless I walked over her... which I was more than willing to do to avoid the snakes, but there just wasn't room.

"Okay, Snake County it is then. Just close your eyes and I'll lead you to the exit," Dad said. "It's not far."

"I could handle it if there's just one or two snakes around the corner," I said and he went to check.

"A couple of boas and a cobra that freaked me out." He put his arm around my shoulders and led me through, while I kept my eyes shut.

"Almost there. All right, small dip in the floor, watch your step, now we're five feet away," he said. "Okay, cobra — keep 'em closed. And we're out. You made it."

I was nearly knocked over by a kid yelling, "It was so cool when the zookeeper fed it the mouse. You could see the shape slide down."

I looked at my dad with horror.

"Why do you think I told you to keep your eyes closed? It wasn't pretty," he crossed his eyes.

We headed over to the tennis courts, but there were two older high school boys playing on the first court, and I didn't want to play in front of them. We went to the last court, and I hit the ball right into the net. Dad had me running all over the court even though he was hitting the ball right to me. I was starting to get the hang of it when a little kid and his dad started playing next to us. The kid was about seven, and he returned every ball even though his dad wasn't hitting them directly to him. Of course, I hit, like, fifty balls on their side. My parents

both played on tennis teams in college and there I was
tripping over my own feet. I was panting, and Dad suggested we stop and head back. Mom was in a better mood
when we got home.

"Did you guys get your flu shots yet?" Dad asked.

Mom said she had been busy at work, but we were
going this week. A complete lie since she's even more
afraid of needles than me. We watched a movie, and I
snuggled up in the recliner, while Dad put his arm
around Mom. Things were looking up. I went to the den
to read and woke up at one in the morning with the light
still on. I guess Mom never came in to say goodnight.

Dad was there when I got up in the morning, and he
took us out to breakfast. I ordered scrambled eggs and
hot chocolate with whipped cream and candy cane pieces
in it. After we ate, he packed up and gave me a goodbye
hug. I felt the peppermint taste burn in my throat as my
eyes filled with tears. His coat started to smell like a wet
dog from my crying.

"Sweetie, it won't be long until we can see each other
at Thanksgiving," he said squeezing me. "And then
there's your birthday and Christmas."

I didn't trust myself to say anything, and I moved
my head when I let go so he wouldn't see me cry. I dug in
my coat for a tissue, but I had to use a gross old one to
blow my nose. He kissed us both, and we watched him
leave. Mom's eyes were red as we walked back to the car.

"We could still make it to church," she said. "We'll be
a little late, but earlier than we usually are. You could
say it'll be the earliest we've been late."

After church, I went to see my room as soon as we
walked in the door. The room smelled, but the walls were
a nice cool blue. It was freezing since we had left the
window open all night, but my room was finally the perfect color. Mom came in behind me.

"Nice, although the grapefruit had a certain charm,"
she said. I reminded her we had plenty left over to paint

her room. "Don't you have some homework to do?" she asked.

Fourteen

~~~~~~

I woke up late and missed the bus. I looked semi-okay in the bathroom mirror, but I almost puked when I flipped down the visor mirror in the car. My eyes looked squinty, my skin was blotchy, and my forehead was breaking out. I put some of Mom's powder over the red mountain on my forehead. I had read in a magazine Talisa Milan used lipstick instead of blush, so I dabbed some on my cheeks. I think Talisa lied because I didn't see her running around with bright red clown cheeks. I rubbed my face with a tissue, but it just made my face redder. Maybe the *American Ingénue* makeup people would have some tips on how to cover up huge forehead volcanoes.

"I can't go to class like this," I said.

"It's school, not a beauty pageant. Just put more powder on."

I slunk in late, and Ms. Ashcroft greeted me with a tight-lipped grimace. So I was five minutes late, it wasn't like I ran over her dog. I went to the bathroom during second hour and washed my face with a rough paper towel. Ericka walked in and I pretended not to see her, even though we were the only people in the bathroom.

I went over to Devon's house after school. She had pictures all around her dresser mirror, and there were

photos of her with India and Peyton as well as magazines cutouts of Blake Alderson and Mason Fraser.

"This is from a picnic two summers ago. India made
me climb to the top of this enormous playscape," she said
pointing to a photo. "I couldn't figure out how to get back
down, and I was stuck up there until Peyton's dad said
he'd catch me if I jumped."

There were also pictures of her and Peyton on a roller
coaster. I knew they were a tight-knit group, and India was
her best friend. It seemed like everyone was already in a
group, and I was just moving around trying to find my spot.
I was so sick of being on the outside looking in. I just wanted to belong somewhere, and I wanted a best friend again. I
wanted somebody who I could be myself around and talk to
after school. Someone who I could just look at and she'd
know exactly what I was thinking. Most of all, I wanted
somebody who liked me more than anybody else — even if I
acted like a total dork. Tori and I used to be able to exchange glances and talk about everything. I wondered if
we'd ever start talking again. I missed her, but I also knew
I'd never be able to trust her again.

When I got home there was a message on the answering machine from Tori asking me to call her. She
and Ericka must want to make up. Finally. I called her
back and she answered on the first ring.

"Hi Tori, it's Landry. I just got your message."

"Oh, Mrs. Dennis wanted me to call everyone to tell
them tryouts for the play are on Tuesday," she said.

How humiliating. Well, there went my hopes of making up and being friends again. I felt so stupid because I
had gotten on the phone all cheerful and hopeful. She
hung up, and I sat on the floor and started to cry. The
phone rang again and I thought it was Tori calling back,
but it was Grandma Albright.

"Hi, sweetheart. How's school?" she asked.

"Fine." I hit mute so I could blow my nose into a paper towel.

"How's your mother?" she asked. I knew she was calling to find out about my dad's visit because she thought it was horrible we weren't all living together.

"She's okay. She's still at work," I said.

"Have you cleaned up the house after your dad's visit?" I started to answer when I got another call. It was Mom, and I told her Grandma was on the other line.

"Oh, great. What does she want?" she asked.

"She was wondering if our house was a mess for some reason."

"The house? Oh my — did you tell her your father stayed in a hotel?" she asked.

"No, why?"

"It might upset her. Listen, I'm going to bring fish and chips home for dinner, so don't fill up on junk," she said.

I clicked back to Grandma, and she tried to find out what was going on with my mom and dad. Why didn't she just call my dad, who lived two blocks away from her? Finally, she realized she wasn't going to get anything interesting out of me so she let me go.

Since the next phase of the competition was coming up next week, I started worrying about what to wear. Mom suggested we go to the mall and look for a new outfit for me. I swear we had, like, fifty fights before we even left the first store. She wanted me to wear a dress which made me look about five years old. Then she found a dress Anne of Green Gables would have worn. I tried to explain to her I needed to look older, and I showed her a short leather skirt with a white off-the-shoulder sweater.

"Over my dead body," was my mother's understanding response.

"Moth-*er*, I can't look like a kid. I'm supposed to be a model, not a baby," I said. "You would not believe the outfits some of the girls wore to the auditions."

Mom let up a little and let me try on a short skirt, but she would only let me get it if I wore it with a preppy sweater so I "wouldn't look like trash." I agreed, but I switched the sweater with a smaller one when she left the dressing room. The smaller sweater was a little tighter, and it showed off a bit of my stomach, too.

I also got my hair cut for the competition. The *Ingénue* people had already told us not to do anything drastic with our looks, but the form said a trim was okay. The hairstylist wanted to cut layers in my hair, but I wasn't allowed to do anything other than "shaping" according to the forms I had signed. My hair looked a lot fuller after the woman styled it with rollers and sprayed it. It looked so good my mom even bought me some rollers from the drugstore and, shock of shocks, she even sprung for the volume spray and conditioner they used at the salon, which she never did. She always lectured me on how it was "a waste of money."

On the day of the competition, I got out of school three hours early to get ready. Nobody wished me luck, other than the teachers, but at least I hadn't woken up with a huge pimple or something. I washed my hair when I got home and put in the new rollers. However, I yanked out a ton of hair when I tried to get the rollers out. I guess they held a little too well. Mom had packed my outfit so it wouldn't get wrinkled on the car ride. I barely spoke during the drive to Detroit. I was just so nervous. They were only choosing ten girls tonight to go on in the competition. But at least if I didn't get picked, only people in the state would see it since it wasn't being broadcast anywhere other than Michigan. We were recording the show at home, but I had made Mom promise not to show it to anyone if I didn't get picked.

Dad called on the cell phone to wish me luck, and Grandma was at his apartment telling me I'd get chosen for sure. I hoped she was still taking her heart pills because I didn't want to cause her a heart attack if I didn't win. At least Grandma thought I had a chance, unlike any of my so-called "friends." The phone rang again, and it was Ashanti calling to wish me luck.

"I'm recording it," she said. "My dad said you should do something memorable on stage so you'll stand out to the judges." I could hear her dad yelling, "Good luck, Landry," in the background. I felt better knowing at least two people, other than my family, cared.

We finally got to the hotel. Mom took a zillion pictures while I got ready so she could send them to all the relatives in Chicago. I felt nervous — like my skeleton was going to leap out of my body and run around the room. The *American Ingénue* people had put a little gift basket in our room with candy and sodas. Yeah, I'm sure real models ate candy all the time. I went to the bathroom five times and ended up throwing up ten minutes before I had to check in at the *Ingénue* table.

"Maybe a soda would settle your stomach," Mom suggested as I curled up in a ball on the bed. "Or how about some of this banana taffy. You love banana—"

"Why would you offer banana flavored anything to a sick person? What's wrong with you?" I said groaning.

Mom gave me a cough drop to cover the barf smell because I couldn't handle the thought of putting minty toothpaste in my mouth. She walked me down to the check-in spot, although I noticed none of the other girls had their mommies with them.

"You were right," she said looking around. "These girls look like they're my age."

To make matters worse, one of the competition organizers tried to give her a number as she was leaving. Everybody stared at me while she explained she was actually my mother. Fabulous. Not only did I look pathetic for bringing my mommy with me, it looked like my mom had me when she was thirteen or something. We lined up, and the organizers said we'd all take turns walking down the runway and then give our names and where we were from. Then the judges would narrow the group to ten girls. Those girls would go on to model different clothes the organizers picked from the racks backstage. I noticed Franciszka T had provided outfits for the girls who were chosen. They were gorgeous clothes, but I knew I'd probably puke again if I had to do a quick change. The organizers scrutinized all of us and gave us accessories to wear. I tried not to take it personally when they put a sailor hat on my head. I mean, the lady did say I had a "nautical" looking outfit on, but all I heard was "your hair sucks." The volunteer, Georgia, also gave me a heavy gold chain belt to wear over my skirt. It looked like a belt Ashanti's mom had.

We got back in line, and I stood behind a girl with dark blonde hair and amazing blue eyes. I asked her if she was nervous, and she told me she was used to doing pageants.

"It's no big deal after a while," she said as she told me all the different titles she had won. She pointed out a couple of other girls who had been in the pageants with her. Some of the girls weren't what you'd call "pretty," but there was something interesting looking about them. Others... well, maybe their mothers bribed the judges or something. Or maybe I had no idea what the judges were looking for in a model. I started to ask the pageant girl if my hair looked okay, but then Talisa Milan walked in the room.

All the girls crowded around her until the organizers made them back off. Everybody was going crazy over her outfit, but it looked like somebody wound a purple rag around her. An expensive rag. She had sleek, glossy dark hair which seemed to swing when she moved. She seemed laid back, and she told us to relax and have fun. One of the girls asked her if she was still dating Lorenzo from the band Puking Baby Dolls.

"Yeah, he's a sweetheart," she said, tilting her head and doing an annoying half smile you always see popular girls doing. "And he's writing a song for my album. It should be coming out this summer so look for it, okay?"

"I heard she can't sing," the girl next to me whispered. "And she's super phony."

Talisa was acting like we were all best friends when this was the first time she had ever seen any of us. But she was sorta nice, and at least I could tell people I met someone famous.

"You guys all look so cute. I wish I could stay, but I have to go right after I do the intro," Talisa said, pouting. "I have to do a TV appearance tomorrow at five, so I gotta fly to Chicago."

Like we were supposed to believe she'd rather stay here with a bunch of people she didn't know instead of being on TV?

"Ladies, line up. We go on in ten minutes."

"Good luck you guys," Talisa said. "I'm so excited for you."

I didn't think she meant it, but she looked over at me for a second and winked. Before she went on stage, she brushed lint off one of the girls and tilted my hat to the side. She smelled like gardenias when she leaned in to smooth my hair.

"Good luck," she said. I never realized how pretty her mouth was. She had small Cupid 's bow lips which looked like my Cadia doll. One of the other finalists from the show, Rae Ellen, was there, but I didn't remember her as well. I think she was the one who got sent home for refusing to do the photo shoot with the cougar.

"Hi y'all," she said. "I bet y'all thought I was going to wear red lipstick again. There's a fan website keeping track of how often I wear it, but it's my signature look. You were thinking I'd have it on, weren't you? Y'all are funny."

The rest of the girls seemed to be going along with it, but I wondered who in their right mind cared whether or not this weirdo wore red lipstick? And she just walked in the room, so how did she know what we were thinking or that we were funny? We were all strangers. People were acting so fake it made me feel sick... well the stress-induced diarrhea and vomiting wasn't helping much either.

The stage manager came over and made sure we were lined up in the right order. From backstage we could hear the opening music playing. The girl behind me said she felt like throwing up.

"I already did before I came," I said. "So at least I don't have to worry about it anymore."

"Unless you get the dry heaves," she said.

Crap. What if I got the dry heaves on stage? And what if it got so bad one of my eyes bulged out or something? I should just go back up to the room... double crap. Mom had the room key. At least there was a bathroom for when I had to worry about... the other end.

While I was deciding whether or not to chicken out, the stage manager, Georgia, started having the girls go out on stage. I overheard somebody say one girl fell out of her shoe as she stepped on the runway.

"Is she okay?"

"Yeah, she's fine. She just pretended to have two heels on and walked on her tip toes," Georgia said.

I would have burst into tears and run off the stage — kind of like I did when I was four years old and in a dance recital. We were supposed to be little ballerinas and have scarves attached to our tutus, but my mom was still in school at the time and she came home late and forgot to give me my scarves. So all the other little girls pulled out their scarves, and there's a video of me looking on either side of my tutu for my scarves and then bursting into tears crying "Mommy!" as I ran off the stage. My grandmother said I was adorable, but I don't think it was any coincidence my grandfather died two weeks later.

At least I didn't have to worry about missing scarves tonight. All I had to do was focus on not tripping. If I could just make it down the runway and back, I'd be fine. Unless, of course, I suddenly came down with Tourette's Syndrome and started swearing live on the air... but I'd know if I had Tourette's, right? It doesn't just come on out of nowhere, does it?

"Okay, girls. Your group is next," Georgia said.

I took a deep breath. All I had to do is say, "My name is Landry, and I'm from Grand Rapids." Easy—as long as I didn't get the dry heaves or puke into the microphone and electrocute myself...or get diarrhea on live TV. Why did I ever go to the audition in the first place? Everything was fine when I was just boring old Landry fading into the background. The girls at school were a lot nicer to me when I was nobody special. I mean, before this stupid competition I had friends, but now it seemed like there was no one I could trust. Maybe if I lost this stupid thing I could go home and everything would be back to normal.

"Okay, girls. You guys are next." Georgia pushed me in the back. "Don't forget to smile," she said in my ear.

Then the girl in front of me morphed into a different person. She straightened her spine and walked with a little skip in her step. "I'm Desiree, and I'm from Sterling Heights," she said in a low sexy voice. Great, I had to follow her.

"I'm Landry, and I'm from Chicago, Illinois," I said. I moved away from the microphone and realized I said "Chicago" instead of "Grand Rapids," so I went back to the microphone to correct myself and slammed into the next girl. She acted like she didn't notice, but I had hit the microphone and it made a shrieking noise. I heard laughter. People were laughing at me. On television. I wanted to die.

I saw Georgia gesturing at me to get off the stage, and I walked off. I had been practicing my stupid runway walk for weeks and for what? A chance to humiliate myself on live TV? I've always been sorta accident prone. If anybody was going to do something stupid and embarrassing it was probably me, but I thought I could control myself for two seconds on live television. I'm such an idiot.

"Don't worry about it, kid," Georgia said.

"Um, excuse me," a blond girl pushed her way in front of me. "Don't you have to be from Michigan to participate in this? I thought we didn't get to other states until the regionals?"

"She's from Michigan, honey. She just got a little confused," Georgia said.

The blonde girl looked at me like I was a complete moron. "Did you just move here or something?" she asked rolling her eyes.

"Yeah," I said. So what if I've lived here for a while. It wasn't any of her business. My face got hot, and I went to the bathroom to cry. I was blowing my nose when I heard a group of girls come in.

"Did you hear one girl forgot where she lived? What a loser," somebody said.

"I know. Did you see the girl in the short red dress? Ew."

I heard the girls walk out and was about to leave the stall when I heard the bathroom open.

"Landry? Honey, are you in here?"

Oh crap, it was my mom. I held my breath, but then she knocked on the stall door. "Sweets, I can see your shoes," she said.

"Go away."

"I just thought you might want to go out and get some ice cream," she said.

I opened the door. "It's not over, is it?" I asked.

She shook her head and said they were about to have everybody line up again while they narrowed the group down to ten.

"No, I'm staying and finishing this," I said and went over to the sink to fix my makeup. I was not going back on TV with raccoon eyes. I couldn't get all the mascara from under my eyes with the crappy bathroom soap, so I borrowed Mom's concealer to cover it up. A couple girls came in to do last minute touchups on their makeup, and Georgia poked her head in the bathroom and told us to line up.

"Good luck," my mom whispered as I went to line up. Like I had a chance. I got back in line behind Desiree.

The room was silent. Everybody was wondering who'd get chosen and who would cry on stage. I didn't have to worry either way — I wouldn't get chosen, and I was all cried out. All I had to do is stand there and pretend to be excited for everybody else who was picked. I figured the camera wouldn't be on me at all, but Desiree was the second name they called. She shrieked, and I gave her a hug just like all the pageant contestants always do. Nobody else hugged anyone, so I probably just made myself look even stupider. They called the rest of the names and then had the audience clap for us losers who were still standing on the platforms. We walked off stage, and Georgia put her hand on my shoulder.

"Nice job, kid," she said. I thought she meant because I hadn't crashed into anybody this time, but she said I showed a lot of "class" hugging Desiree when her name was called. She said there were free "promotional items" in the lobby. Mom and I walked to the lobby, and they gave me a big plastic bag filled with stuff. They assumed Mom was a contestant, so they gave her a bag, too.

We went back up to the room so we could check out all the free stuff. This time there were actual Little Rose makeup samples. Little tubes and jars with French words on them. And a makeup palette with shimmer powders, eye shadows, lipsticks, and blushes. There was even a tiny eyeliner and lip liner pencil with a teensy sharpener. Not worth making a fool out of myself on live television, but still cool. The lipsticks were too dark on me and so were the eye shadows, but I could wear the rest of the stuff. I tried using the lip liner, but it looked like I had a chocolate ice cream ring around my mouth.

"Your dad wanted you to call him when it was over," Mom said as she cracked open a free soda. I wondered what to tell him. Did I tell him everything went okay and then destroy the tape of me crashing into the other girl on stage? I didn't get a chance to get my lie straight because my dad called on the cell phone.

"How'd it go?" he asked.

"It went okay, but I didn't get picked," I said.

He said the judges must have been blind and said he was proud of me for going up there. He might not have been so proud had he seen me body slam another contestant and forget where I was from. Grandma got on the phone next and said modeling wasn't a good career for young girls anyway. Then she went on about how she used to model for a department store when she was a teenager. Just what I needed to hear — how my grandmother could cut it as a model, but I couldn't.

"I was proud of you for going back up on stage," Mom said after I got off the phone.

I asked what she meant, and she said I could have just stayed backstage or left after I messed up my line. I hadn't realized it was an option. I just thought it would have been worse not to go back out with the other girls. Everybody who watched would have assumed I didn't come back because I was crying backstage.

I sat on the bed watching TV and ate a couple of free candy bars and drank some free sodas. Candy and pop were the only things sounding good to me after I had thrown up before. Besides, food tasted better when it was free. Someone knocked on the door, and I was afraid they were going to make us leave the hotel early... or maybe they realized we took an extra free bag and they wanted it back. I hid the extra bag in my suitcase while my mom answered the door. It was Mrs. Myeski.

"Landry, I just finished reading your comment sheets," she said. I nodded as I wondered what comment sheets were. "You got a lot of positive remarks on how you handled yourself up there. There are five agencies interested in you."

Even after I made a fool of myself? We sat on the bed, and Mrs. Myeski told my mom we should look into each agency to see if there was one which might work for me.

"And just because they're expressing an interest today doesn't mean they will necessarily take you on," she said. She said my mom could call to set up an appointment, and I would need to bring a picture with me.

"This is an exciting opportunity for you, but only if you can handle it. A lot of girls get caught up in the glamour aspects of it, but it is a job and you have to look at it as a professional," she said. She left us a sheet with the agency names on it and suggested we start researching them soon.

"Is this something you want to pursue?" Mom asked as I stared at the names. Three of them were located in Lansing, which was an hour away. One was in Detroit, which was too far, but there was one in Grand Rapids owned by two women named Delilah Rice and Anita Carter. Mom chewed the side of her mouth as she stared at the sheet.

"Let's deal with this later. It's too much to think about right now. Why don't we do something fun? I heard there's a great mall nearby. Wanna check it out?" she asked.

I must have looked pathetic onstage if Mom was offering to take me shopping. Still, I can't say no to a mall. I changed into jeans and a hoodie, and we got directions to Somerset mall. I picked out a few things to try on, but everything looked like crap on me. I was too tall for Capri pants (they looked like I was expecting a Noah's ark type flood), but too short for the new jeans they were showing. I found a couple of halter tops on the sale rack, and even though I wouldn't be able to wear them for months, I wanted to see how I would look in one of those tops. I mean, the judges didn't find me too hideous if I got through two rounds of the competition, right? However the halter tops made me look extra skinny and flat. Models were supposed to be able to make anything look good, and so far, everything looked blah on me. The only thing which looked halfway decent on me was a sweatshirt, and everyone looks good in a sweatshirt.

Mom could tell I was getting depressed clothes shopping so we went to the music store next. I hardly ever get CDs. I found a couple I wanted, and I was surprised mom was willing to buy them for me. Maybe I should humiliate myself in public more often. We went to dinner, and I had a hamburger and fries — my first real food all day. I was starting to have fun when I looked across the street and saw a sign advertising something on Friday. Just seeing the word "Friday," reminded me of the word "Monday," which reminded me I'd have to go back to school and face everyone who had seen me make a fool of myself on TV. My stomach rolled over. There was absolutely no way I was going back to school. Not on Monday. Not EVER.

"Do you want to head back after dinner?" Mom asked. I shook my head. "Well, I guess we don't have to leave tonight. I could get the room for another night, and we could go see a movie or go back to the hotel and watch TV."

I started to say I never wanted to watch TV again when I got a brilliant idea. Tomorrow when we were supposed to leave, I could pretend to be too sick to go in the car. Then there would be no way I could get back in time to go to school on Monday.

"Okay, can we stop at the bookstore on the corner?" I asked. "It's huge. I didn't realize Detroit had such great shopping."

"Sure. Wanna order a sundae before we leave?" she asked. I must have made a real fool of myself on TV if she was letting us stay another night and offering me dessert.

While we were in the bookstore, I picked up a copy of *Young and Fun* magazine with Talisa on the cover. The article talked about how busy she was, and there was a breakdown of her day: yoga at four in the morning, then hair and makeup, publicity appearances, meet with the songwriters for her album, meet with her vocal coach, meet with the music video show's producers, tape the show, more publicity stuff, and then work on the album some more. There's no way Talisa and I were even the same species. I mean, I come home from school, flop on the coach, and try to cram in as much TV watching as possible, which was a full day for me. Maybe the whole celebrity thing wasn't for me. I always thought Talisa's career was just standing around looking pretty except for the one hour a day she introduced music videos.

Sunday morning, I heard Mom in the shower. I took out my new makeup case and dabbed a little of the deep plum lipstick on my eyelids. Last year when I got the flu my eyelids looked all red and weird, so I figured this would do the trick. However my mother just looked at me and said, "You've got something funky on your eyes."

I pretended I couldn't lift my head off the pillow. "I don't feel so good," I said fake coughing.

"I'm going to run down to get coffee," she said. "I'll bring you some tea, but you better be up and in the shower by the time I get back. Checkout time is at noon, and I'm not paying for another night."

So much for sympathy. "My throat feels weird. Maybe I caught something from one of the other girls. Somebody at the competition said they thought they had a sinus infection," I said.

She put her hand on my forehead. "You look fine to me other than the eye shadow you've got on. Didn't you wash your makeup off last night? Seriously, we've got to be out by twelve. I'm not paying for another night."

She gave me her "I-mean-business-move-your-butt-now" look. No wonder Dad wasn't exactly killing himself to move in with us. Who'd want to live with her? I could have Ebola or the plague or something, and she was worried about having to pay for another night. It would serve her right if I got sick and died right on the elevator — no, wait, if I died in the room so she'd have to pay for another night and replace the sheets I died on. I dragged myself to the shower and Miss Speedy was back with the tea and coffee in, like, ten seconds.

"I brought you a blueberry muffin, but eat it while you pack," she said, checking under my bed. "Landry, you're not any neater on the road than you are at home. Your socks are everywhere."

As she went on about "how many feet did I have to need five pairs of socks anyway on a short trip?" I threw my clothes in an overnight bag. I didn't care if my stuff got wrinkled because I never got invited anywhere to wear my good clothes anyway.

We made it to the checkout counter with three minutes to spare so I don't know why she was all freaking out. Of course, she ditched me in the elevator with all the bags and ran down the hallway to make it to the lobby in time. I had to drag all our stuff out front. A bellhop grabbed one of the bags to help me, and later my mom lectured me for letting him help because she had to tip him a dollar. All her sympathy for me had run out sometime last night after dessert. We got in the car, and she said I could put one of my new CDs in if I wanted. I said I didn't feel like listening to music because I still felt sick.

"Do you want to stop for some soup or something on the way home?" she asked. I shrugged and asked if we could get some cough drops before we got on the expressway. I felt bad for lying, but I had to admit I didn't feel good. Sure my throat didn't hurt, but I did have a headache and I was kinda nauseous thinking about school tomorrow, so in a way, I did qualify as being sick.

"Here's some money for cough drops and get some aspirin, too," she said, smoothing back my bangs. "You're probably just rundown from the excitement yesterday."

Let's not forget the extreme humiliation I faced where all of the state watched me not only make a fool of myself but fail. I had been rejected on live television.

How much worse could it get? It's one thing to feel like you're not pretty, but it's another to be told you're not good enough with everyone watching.

When we got home, I had two messages on the answering machine from Ashanti and Devon. I called Devon back first because I figured she would understand what it's like to get rejected by the *American Ingénue* people.

"You're back," she said. "How was it?"

"Well, at first it was cool. I was nervous, but I'm sure you saw how I made a fool of myself on stage. I blanked, and I almost died when I said the wrong city and then I ran into someone."

"It wasn't too noticeable," she said.

Devon acted like it was nothing, so I started to feel better. She asked me what it was like backstage, and I told her about meeting Talisa and about how a lot of the girls had done pageants and stuff before.

"Probably why a lot of them got picked. They already knew what to do and what the judges wanted," she said. "Did you get any free stuff?"

"I did get some candy and makeup and stuff. Oh, there are a couple of agents interested in me, too."

"Even after you messed up on stage and all? Listen, I've gotta go. India and Peyton are coming over so I'll see you tomorrow."

She hung up so I called Ashanti, who said she had been waiting by the phone to hear from me. Her phone is right next to her bed anyway, but it was nice knowing somebody cared.

"You looked so cute," she said. "I loved your hat. My mom said you looked 'darling.'"

"Even though I messed up?"

"Please, you were great. Just a sec, Dad! Hold up. Landry, my dad's bugging me. He wants to say something," she said.

"Hi Landry. We enjoyed watching you last night. You did a great job," Mr. Russell said.

"Thanks, I just wished I hadn't screwed up."

"You handled yourself well up there. You showed a lot of poise, and you should be proud of yourself. I'll put Ashanti back on before she pulls my arm off."

"Okay, so give me backstage dirt," she said.

I told her about how nice Talisa was and how all the girls looked so much older than me. I told her the *American Ingénue* people thought my mom was the contestant instead of me. She wasn't surprised because even her parents thought the girls looked way older than the age limit. I told her I got free makeup, and she could have some of my samples.

"And I have enough free soda to last me forever, so I'll save some for you," I said.

"Cool. Have you seen yourself on TV yet?" she asked.

I was dreading it, so I told her I'd watch later. Much later. I got off the phone with Ashanti so I could work on my sick act. I sat next to my mom on the couch and started adding symptoms to my fake illness.

"Mom, I feel like I could just fall asleep and, like, go into a coma. Wait, do you think I have mono?"

"No, I don't. You'd be a lot sicker if you had mono. I had it once in college, and trust me, I'd know if you had it. What's going on?" she asked.

"I told you. I don't feel good," I said, laying my head on the armrest.

Mom made me some tea and had me get into bed, which meant I couldn't watch TV. I read until it was time for bed. My biggest fear is getting the stomach flu, but if I ever had to get it then I wished I could get it now.

Unfortunately I woke up healthy. Even my skin was glowing for the first time. It was going to take an Oscar winning performance to get my mother to let me stay home today.

"Mom, I think I'm going to throw up—"

"Landry, I know what you're doing. You've been paving the way so you can stay home, but it isn't going to happen," she said.

She was smarter than she looked. "No, I'm sick."

"Do you honestly think it's going to be any easier going to school tomorrow? Or the next day? It's always going to be there, honey, so you're better off just going and getting it over with," she said. "Trust me. Once you get there, it'll be fine. The worst part is the anticipation."

I said everyone was going to laugh at me, and she gave me the speech adults always give, but nobody ever believes about how, "Your true friends wouldn't laugh at you." Well, I obviously didn't have any true friends besides Ashanti. Even Devon got all weird on me when I told her about the agents. After arguing for ten minutes, Mom promised to drive me to school all week and get me a subscription to *Young and Fun* magazine as long as I went to class. Little did my mother realize it was a weekly magazine so she would be paying more. Hah. But I still had to go to school.

I put on a navy sweater and pants and wished I could just fade into the background. I knew I couldn't hide, so I put on more makeup than usual hoping everybody would focus on how good I looked instead of on the fact I didn't make the cut. Mom didn't say anything when she saw me, so I figured I looked okay. Then she told me to blot some of the lipstick.

"It's a little dark," she said.

Even my mother's a critic. When we got to school I made my mom drive around the parking lot so I wouldn't have to stand outside with everyone and talk about the show.

"Landry, I have to go to work. Just tell them it was fun and it'll be the end of it," said my mother, who I'm guessing had been homeschooled in a cabin outside of the limits of civilization.

"The first bell is going to ring in a minute, and I'll go in then."

The bell rang, but I didn't budge. Mom sighed. "Am I going to have to push you out of this car? You're going to be late, and then you'll call attention to yourself."

Crap. She was right. I got out of the car and walked in behind a group of seventh graders. I thought I was so smart, until they went around the corner leaving me exposed. Peyton waved to me and didn't yell, "Hey loser," so I figured it was safe to walk over to her.

"How was it?" she asked.

I shrugged as Hana walked over. "You should have gotten picked, Landry," she said. "Did you get to meet any celebrities?"

I told her about Talisa and how none of the celebrity judges were celebrities you ever heard of before. The panel was mostly modeling people, but they threw in some local people who were semi-famous. One lady hosted a talk show in Detroit, one was a baseball player I had never heard of before, and there was some news anchor guy. I saw the talk show host for one second backstage when she wished us luck, but the news anchor guy and the basketball player never bothered to come back to see us.

I expected to get laughed at or to hear mean comments in the hall, but nobody brought it up. It was kind of weird. As far as I knew, nobody at our school had been on TV or won anything major. So how come when I got the chance to be on a popular show nobody even mentioned it? Maybe nobody cared or they were trying to spare my feelings since I made a fool of myself. No, no one at my school was nice, so they probably just didn't care. Unless the principal had made some big announcement about how anyone making fun of the "poor reject from TV" would get suspended. Devon didn't even bring it up, but we had talked about it on the phone. However, Tori waved to me in the hall, so I started to feel a little better. Then came lunch.

I got in the lunch line with Hana, and Tori came up behind me. I was telling Hana about how nervous I was before going onstage when Tori interrupted to ask if I got to keep the clothes I wore.

"No, it was my outfit, but I borrowed the hat and belt," I said. She acted like it was normal for us to be hanging out, and I kinda felt like I wasn't supposed to make a big deal out of it. I went on with my story and then said I had a couple of agents interested in me.

"Wow, so cool," Hana said, but Tori didn't say anything. Not, "Oh great," or even a, "You suck." Nothing at all. I asked her about her weekend, but she just shrugged. I started to say it would have been cool if we could have done the show together, but then she ignored me and ran off to talk to somebody in the back of the line. I grabbed a dish of macaroni and cheese and followed Hana to her usual table. Devon was already there, and I asked her if she was doing anything on Friday night.

"I think I have plans with Peyton and India," she said. I was hurt she didn't say, "Do you want to join us?"

When I got home, there was a message from Grandma telling me how pretty I looked on TV. I was surprised she had seen it.

"How did Grandma see it?" I asked. "Did you send her a link?"

"I don't know, maybe Uncle Martin found a link," Mom said. I gave her a look. "Okay, you know your grandmother. She has to be the first one to call and pretend to be in the know—"

"So she just said I looked pretty on TV without ever seeing me?" I asked. How depressing. Even my grandmother had to lie to me. I bet she'd freak if she saw the actual footage. Of course if I had anything to say about it, she never would. Grandma just figured out how to send an e-mail, so I was guessing finding a video online was a little beyond her abilities.

"How was school? Was it as bad as you thought?" she asked. I could tell she was getting ready to put on her smug "I told you so" face. I almost wanted to tell her I had gotten beaten up for being a reject. It was almost as bad to admit almost no one had even brought it up. Instead, I said Hana seemed interested.

"Have you decided about calling the agencies?"

I said I wanted to think about it a little more. I knew Mom didn't want me to start modeling, but I kept thinking if the *American Ingénue* judges saw something in me then maybe I wasn't as hideous as I thought. Or maybe I was picked just because I was tall and skinny. I decided not to think about it, but then I saw Talisa while I was watching a music video countdown show. She was wearing a white tank top with a short hot pink mini skirt. For some reason Talisa always looked weird when she dressed trendy. Like she was a doll somebody had dressed up. She was introducing the next video, and she mentioned one of her *Ingénue* costars was in it.

"You guys remember Bianca Laurel from the show?" she asked the studio audience. "Cause she's in Lars Anderson's new video, and she gets to play his girlfriend." The girls in the audience started making *"whoo"* noises. Lars Anderson was only the hottest singer ever. I knew Bianca was only, like, seventeen, so it wasn't like she was much older than me, and if Lars was interested in her then maybe I could meet a famous guy by modeling, too. Sure, Bianca had made it to the major *American Ingénue* competition, but it wouldn't hurt to try modeling and see if I could get a part in a video or something. I told my mom after dinner I wanted to try modeling.

"Okay, I'll check out the agencies tomorrow," she said.

The next day I couldn't wait to find out what the agencies said, but Mom came home in a bad mood.

"Landry, do you think I could get in the front door before you come charging at me?" she asked. I backed off, and she dumped her stuff on the kitchen table. I guess I was crowding her or something because she sighed and asked, "Don't you have some homework or something to do?"

I went to my room and stayed out of her way until dinner. She made chicken pot pies, which I hate, but I ate the whole stupid thing (except for the soggy crust because it made me gag). She still hadn't brought up the agents, so I asked.

"I went online and they all seem legit, but if you're going to do this then it has to be the local one. I talked to one of the owners of the Grand Rapids agency, and I can set up an appointment for you to meet with them if you still want to," she said.

Okay, so my chances of Lars Anderson (or any rock star) calling a Grand Rapids modeling agent weren't good, but maybe I'd be so popular as a model I'd get to move to New York or something.

"I just want to make sure you have realistic expectations for this," Mom said.

Like any one famous ever got anywhere from having realistic expectations. All I knew was I wanted to make enough money so I could leave school, get a private tutor, move to New York (or someplace cool), and do magazine covers and music videos. I didn't even have to have a modeling career. I could just model until I got some sort of acting job. I'd rather be an actress than a model anyway. I just wanted to be famous, and I didn't even care how it happened. I wanted to be like Talisa who was always in *SuperTeen* magazine and a Little Rose model. Plus, she was dating the lead singer of the Puking Baby Dolls. I just wanted to get out of this place and have everybody who was mean to me see I was special and they were all too stupid to notice me when they had the chance.

The next day, Mom called the Rice-Carter agency and made an appointment with me to meet Delilah Rice. I had no clue what to wear, and Mom told me to put my plaid kilt on.

"But I wore it to my first audition. What if she was there? Then it'll look like I have one outfit."

"Do you have another option?" Mom asked. "It's your cutest outfit."

I sighed. I needed to get some better clothes. Mom said I was supposed to come looking natural with no makeup on. I just used a little concealer on the pimple forming on my chin, put on a touch of mascara and brow pencil, and some tinted lip balm. We had to wait for Ms. Rice for twenty minutes, but when we went into her office she was nice and asked me if I wanted some tea.

"I have chamomile, jasmine, and Earl Grey," she said.

Chamomile tasted like dandelions in dirty bath water to me, so I said jasmine would be fine. The jasmine tea was okay, and it kinda tasted like flowers. She asked if I had a portfolio, but all I had were the pictures the *Ingénue* people had taken of me. She set up a test shoot with a photographer for me on Wednesday and told me to bring two outfits.

"Bring some sort of accessory, a prop, an outfit for a close-up, and something for a full length shot — nothing baggy. We need to see your shape," she said. I had to fill out some forms, which were confusing. I had no idea what my bust measurements were, but she told me to leave those blank and someone would measure me later. She had me stand up, and she walked around me the same way my dad walked around the last car he bought. I felt stupid standing there, but then Delilah nodded and said I could sit down.

"Your weight is perfect, but you could use some toning," she said.

"Sure," I said. And as soon as I figured out what she meant, I'd get right on it.

"Nothing over five pounds," she said as I stared. "You know, for the free weights," she said as she mimed lifting a dumbbell. Oh, muscle toning. Duh. I thought she meant, like, using astringent or something on my face.

I got home, and Devon texted me about going to the apple orchard for cider and donuts with Peyton and India after school on Wednesday. She said they've gone there every year since they were eight. I wanted to go, but I had my test shoot then. At first, I felt bad about missing out because it had been a long time since anyone had invited me anywhere. Then I started thinking about how Talisa had told *Young and Fun* magazine she had to "miss out on a lot of fun things with friends." But I bet she thought it was all worth it since now she was famous.

I laid out my outfits for the test shoot. I was going to wear a black turtleneck for my close-up. I was also bringing a scarf, my black hat, and a huge white teddy bear (actually an old bear of my mom's which I stripped of his little scarf and ski hat) for my props, and I was going to wear a peach and black sweatshirt and matching skirt I had gotten a year ago for Christmas. The skirt was too short for me on its own, so I was going to put black pants underneath.

⋙⋘

Ms. Rice loved the stuff I brought when I showed up at the agency. They put the scarf in my hair for the close-up pictures. The photographer took shots of me standing, sitting on the floor with the bear, and posing with the hat. A week later Ms. Rice called and asked us to come to the agency.

We went to her office after school, and I was so nervous I could actually feel sweat drip under my arms. I thought she was going to say, "Sorry, I changed my mind," but Mom said they would have just said it on the phone. Ms. Rice (she told me to call her Delilah) called us into her office just as I was getting up to go to the bathroom for, like, the hundredth time. I needed to pee, but I went in and hoped I didn't have an accident in her office because those pink chairs looked expensive.

"I'd like to sign Landry to a six month contract," Delilah said. I almost leapt across the table to kiss her. She
pulled out my proofs to show me which pictures I should
get for my portfolio. I was surprised to see how great
they ended up. I didn't look like Talisa Milan, but for me,
they were great. Although you could kinda see my forehead breaking out in one. Delilah gave my mom some
papers to sign, but my mother, being Miss Overprotective, asked to take them home to read. I bet Talisa's mom
didn't take her contracts home to read back in the day.

"Are you sure you want to do this?" Mom asked me
for the millionth time in the car.

"Yeah, I can start making some money for college," I
said, thinking I would impress her with my responsible
planning.

She laughed. "Right, you just wanted this to save up
for college. Good one."

I called my dad when I got home. While my mom was
all weird about me doing this, my dad thought it was great.

"Of course they'd want to sign you honey, you're gorgeous," he said. "After all, you get your looks from my
side of the family."

In reality, I looked almost exactly like my mom except I have my dad's eyes and chin. My mom is like a
softer, prettier version of me. I was just glad to hear my
dad say I was pretty enough to model. I knew it was my
dad so of course he was going to say I was cute, but it
was still nice to hear. I wondered if Mom kept asking me
if I was sure I wanted to do this because she didn't think
I was pretty enough to model.

"Landry, come in here. I want to go over the contract
with you," she said.

We sat at the kitchen table as she read these boring
forms. I put my head on the table while she was going
over them.

"This is going to be expensive," she said, poking me
with her pen.

"Why? I thought Ms. Myeski said you should never have to pay to model."

"But the pictures for your portfolio cost a lot. And you need something called a comp card," she sighed. "They're supposed to take it out of what you make, but... I dunno. Are you sure—"

"Yes. Why do you keep asking me? You know, Dad thinks I'm pretty enough to be a model, so how come you don't?"

"It has nothing to do with — I know you're pretty, but I just don't want to see you get hurt—" I started to interrupt, but she put her hand up and gave me "the look." "Of course your dad thinks you're beautiful, but remember guys think it's what a girl wants to hear. There are a lot more important things than just being pretty. Sometimes people put too much focus on a girl's looks to distract her from other things."

Mom went on a big thing about how people focus on the appearance of a woman running for President, while they focus on the guy candidate's career. I made the mistake of yawning, which just made her mad and extended the stupid lecture. Mom went and got one of my teen magazines and started showing me how the articles on the guy singers focused on their songs, but the female singers' articles focused on her clothes and makeup.

"But guys don't wear makeup," I said.

"Look at this cover. Tell me Drew Bernard doesn't have eyeliner on," she said holding *Seventeen* up.

Ew. Drew did have eyeliner on, and it looked like he had gloss on his lips — not like the super shiny kind or anything, but his lips were definitely glossier than most guys. Okay, so she had a point.

"And look at this," she said turning to another page." Salma Dagwood writes her own songs and plays the guitar, but the article focuses on how to get glowing skin like her, while this boy here doesn't even know how to play the guitar he's holding. And did you know Talisa

Milan was an honor roll student? They don't tell you the important stuff."

It did seem unfair, but what did she want me to do about it? I asked her if I could still try modeling, and I promised I wouldn't get all caught up in my looks and stuff.

"You have to promise to keep your grades up — even in math," she said. "And absolutely no dieting. If I even suspect you're eating less I will come down to your school and watch you eat your lunch."

I rolled my eyes. Like I could give up food. Please. I promised I wouldn't diet or do anything drastic to my looks without asking her first. It meant I couldn't pluck my eyebrows or dye my hair, which was fine. I tried plucking my eyebrows once after seeing an article in a magazine, and it hurt so bad. And I had a huge fear of hair color after Grandma told me about some girl who went blind when hair dye dripped in her eye. She was probably just trying to freak me out so I wouldn't dye my hair, but you know what? It worked.

"This is a big commitment to make, and you're going to miss out on a lot with your friends," she said. "I'm not going to let you take off from school, so you can only work on weekends, which will cut into your social life."

Like I even had a social life. Ashanti was still sick and other than inviting me to the apple orchard, Devon hadn't exactly been dying to hang out with me. People talked to me at school, but no one asked me to do anything outside of school. I hadn't had a comment or a "like" on my social media page in weeks. I even considered setting up a phony account just so I could post fake comments on my real page and not look so pathetic. I could work every weekend from now until I was eighty and I wouldn't miss a thing. Actually, working would give me a good excuse for not having any plans on the weekends.

Mom told me according to the contract, I wouldn't be allowed to work much because of my age. I couldn't do any of the perfume promotions where models stand in a department store and ask to spray you with perfume because I was too young. I would be limited to fashion shows, ads, and maybe commercials. I guessed music videos were out of the question, but it was still better than nothing. Plus, it was only for six months so I could quit if I hated it.

When I got to school it was pretty obvious nobody seemed to care I had an agent. Ashanti thought it was cool when I called her about it on the phone, but no one else said much. When I told my dad people at school didn't seem to care, he said the other girls could be jealous. Maybe, but it was hard when the girls I went to school with were more impressed with winning basketball games, and I'm just not good at sports. Plus, during lunch, I overheard Arianna in the bathroom saying she was surprised I was chosen to model at all.

"She doesn't look like a model," she said. "But I guess they do have to be super skinny."

I couldn't see whom she was talking to through the crack in the stall, and the other girl didn't say anything. I waited until she and the other girl left before I flushed the toilet. However, when I came out of the bathroom I saw Arianna walking back to the lunchroom with Ericka. I went back to my table and told Hana and Devon I wasn't feeling well.

"Do you want us to walk you to the office?" Devon asked.

I was just going to sit in the library for a while, but I guess Devon wanted me gone. I shook my head and Hana told me to "feel better soon," and then they went back to their food. I went to the office and said I didn't feel well. The secretary asked if I felt like I was going to throw up, and I nodded. Then she stuck this gross looking barf-colored bowl in front of me. I'm surprised nobody puked just from looking at it.

"I'll call your mother to pick you up," Mrs. Beckham said. Just then a kid with a real stomachache came in.

Now there was a guy who looked like he was going to puke. He needed the bowl way more than me. I decided I had enough of fake-sick land, so I told the nurse I felt better. She was busy with the sick guy, so she waved me off. I thought it was the end of it until I got called down to the office in math class.

"Landry, I tried calling your mom to pick you up, but she was out of the office all day," Mrs. Beckham said. "So I called someone from your emergency contact card and Mrs. Robins said she could come pick you up if you still needed to go home."

I forgot my mother had put Tori's mom on my emergency contact card. There was no way I was having Mrs. Robins come pick me up. I told Mrs. Beckham I felt better, and I didn't need to go home.

The next day Ericka made gagging and puking noises as I walked past her in the hall. I guess Tori's mom had told them about my little illness yesterday. Way to keep it to yourself, Mrs. Robins. Meanwhile, my own mother never got the message. The secretary at her office didn't think it was important enough to write down my mother's only child was sick and dying. I loved the world. On the plus side, I did get a commercial lined up for Saturday. My first job was for a stain removal product.

Delilah had sent over a handbook which said models had to be prepared for anything. Most of the time there wouldn't be hair and makeup people at the shoots, so you were expected to do your own. I also had to put together a "model bag" with hair rollers, makeup, pantyhose, a strapless bra, extra shoes, and anything else I might need while on a job. Plus, I needed to buy a thong, which I thought was super gross. I knew Yasmin wore them because I had seen one sticking out of the back of her pants before in gym.

I didn't want to tell my mom I needed to buy a thong, so I just told her about the strapless bra. She was going to help me find one, but I told her I wanted to go in and try it on by myself. We went to the mall, and I grabbed a bunch of bras to try on. I must have tried fifty bras on and only two fit without sliding down. Mom was sitting outside the dressing room waiting, so I asked her if she could pick out some pantyhose for me.

"Can't you just get those at the drugstore?" she asked.

"Mo-om, I'm supposed to be a professional."

She sighed and went to pick some out. Meanwhile I went over to the underwear display and picked out a thong. It was in a box, so I hoped mom wouldn't notice what it was. I went over to the counter and paid for the thong while mom was over in the pantyhose section. I couldn't believe how much a tiny little string cost, but it was worth it if it kept my mom from freaking out. I tried the thong on when I got home and it was the most uncomfortable thing I had ever experienced. There was no way I was ever wearing it. I was also out fifteen bucks since underwear was non-refundable.

I showed up at the Averline agency for the shoot on Saturday morning. They had several pairs of white Capri pants waiting for me to wear — a clean pair for each take of the commercial. I sat down, and the hair stylist went to work on my hair. She yanked the comb through my hair and almost took my head off.

"How do you deal with this tangled mess every morning?" she sighed. She began spraying something all over my hair and then combed through it easier.

"What is this stuff?" I asked.

"Leave-in conditioner. You might want to pick up a bottle to use on your days off," she said. "Your hair is fine, so I'm using the one for babies. It'll get the tangles out without weighing your hair down like a lot of conditioners do."

Once my hair looked shiny and smooth, I had to sit at this picnic table and smile until some loser ran up to me and dumped spaghetti sauce on me. I knew they were going to get the pants dirty, but I didn't think the guy would dump half a bucket of sauce on me. Who would ever eat so much spaghetti sauce? The director loved the grossed out look on my face, so I only had to do a couple takes of it. He was thrilled, but I was covered in cold sauce — not even real spaghetti sauce. They had put some junk in it to make it thicker and so it would cling better to the material. It was all gooey, too. Gross. I'd never buy their crappy product. They gave me the tiniest little spray bottle of the stain removal spray. I'd be lucky if I got two squirts out of the container. Still, I made some money... which all went to the agency to pay for the photographs in my portfolio. Oh yay.

Hana asked me at lunch one day how modeling was going. I noticed Devon got weird whenever modeling was brought up. I just shrugged and said it was okay.

"Yeah, but she can never do anything because she's always busy working," Devon said. "You must hate it."

I had only done one job, so I wasn't exactly working my butt off.

"I can still do stuff," I said, but she just shrugged.

Fifteen

On Friday, Devon asked me to go ice skating with her and India and Peyton. I was nervous because I had never figure skated before, but I thought it couldn't be too much harder than roller skating.

"Are you any good?" I asked.

"Don't laugh, but one time I slid across the ice and knocked an old couple over," she said. "They were super nice about it, but I felt so stupid."

I told Mom I was going to the ice rink, and she freaked out.

"Are you crazy? You've never even been on ice skates," she said.

"Devon said she's not good, and I'm sure I'll be okay," I said.

"I could barely stand up my first time. Both my ankles caved in, and I fell three times and once *while* I was holding onto a tree," she said.

"Dad used to play hockey in high school. Maybe I inherited his talent."

"Your dad started skating when he was five. Five-year-olds aren't afraid of falling on their rears. Call her and tell her you can't go. You'll break something," she said. "Or you'll get bruised or something and you won't be able to model."

I decided to tell Devon I couldn't go when I got to the bus stop, but she got a ride from her mom. Then I tried telling her at lunch, but she swore I'd be fine. In social studies, I told Peyton and India I had never skated before and was worried about making a fool of myself.

"We can teach you how. It'll be fun," Peyton said.

"Can you skate?" I asked India.

"I'm so bad. I spend most of the time on my butt," India said. So I said I'd go.

India's mom picked me up at four o'clock, and I got a bad feeling when I got into the van and saw both Peyton and India had brought their own ice skates. People who never skate don't own their own ice skates. Devon told me not to worry because she was going to rent skates, too.

We got to the rink and I realized I had only brought one pair of socks and the other girls had two pairs on. My rental skates had some weird metal thingies on them. I didn't know what to do with them so Peyton laced them up for me. I went to stand up and my right ankle caved in. I could walk on the carpet, but I slid when I hit a wet area. Being on blades and having the loss of control over my balance was the most horrible feeling in the world... and I hadn't even made it to the ice yet. I got on the ice and my feet went in different directions. I grabbed the rail with both hands.

Devon skated out to the middle of the ice while I was desperately trying to get my feet under control. Devon said I could hold onto her arm, and she'd take me around the rink. India skated in front of us, and Miss I'll-be-on-my-butt-the-whole-time skated backward and did little spins on the ice. I felt myself tipping backward, and Devon told me to lean forward and I almost pulled her arm off. Then my feet shot out from under me, and I landed on my butt. My legs were twisted under me, and I couldn't get to my feet. Peyton and Devon tried to help me up, but I had to crawl to the side of the rink to pull myself up. How embarrassing.

"Are you okay?" Peyton asked. My ankles were aching, but I said I was fine. She helped me off the ice and bought me a hot chocolate. I told her she could go back on the ice, but she waited until India came off the ice. I thought India was going to sit with me, but she went to buy a snack and left me alone.

After a while, Peyton convinced me to try skating again. She swore she wouldn't let me fall. Devon had said the same thing and I had landed on my butt, but I went out anyway. I didn't think Peyton would be able to support me because she was shorter than me, but she put her arm behind my back so I didn't have to worry about falling backward. My feet glided along, and she showed me how to push off on the ice. Devon said I should try it on my own, but I threatened Peyton not to let go. India came back out, and for someone who was "so bad" at skating, she seemed to be doing pretty well. She hadn't fallen once. I couldn't completely let go and skate the way she could. I was too afraid of falling again and having to crawl off the ice.

When I got home I limped over to the computer and hoped my mom wouldn't ask too many questions. I was on my social media page, and I decided to look up Tori's page. I was shocked when I saw Ericka's picture in her "friends" section. Her parents finally let her have one. Tori hadn't unfriended me, but she listed Ericka as "her sister," in the family members section. I read three of Tori's blog posts, and they were all about soccer or doing stuff with Ericka. It was like I never existed. Devon didn't have a page because her mom said, "Social media is the devil," but I knew Peyton did, so I looked up her page. I decided to send her a friend request.

The next morning my right leg felt like it had been wound up. I walked like a doll who had her leg popped in wrong. My mom, with her cat-like alertness, had to make a big deal out of it.

"I told you you'd hurt yourself," she said as I limped over to get the cereal.

"I'll be fine. It just has to... pop back into its socket," I said.

Devon called and asked if I wanted to go to the mall this afternoon. Walking around a big mall wasn't the smartest thing I could do, but I wanted to go.

"We'll pick you up at one. What are you going to wear?" she asked.

"Probably my new jeans and yellow sweater."

"Why don't you wear your green shirt and the jean skirt you wore on 'jeans day,'" she said. "It's kind of like mine."

We only have one day a year when everybody is allowed to wear jeans, but this year my only clean pair had a hole in the butt so I wore a jean skirt instead. Thalia told me Ericka said I was trying to get Kyle to notice me by wearing a skirt. I tried to ignore it, but why couldn't Ericka leave me alone?

I told Devon I'd put on a skirt, but I felt weird wearing one just to go to the mall. Ashanti wore skirts a lot, but she was shorter and super pretty so she looked good in them. I felt like a toothpick wearing a rubber band when I wore one. Devon had on a short denim skirt with a black fuzzy sweater under her coat. She looked great while I looked like her freakishly tall friend.

Devon said we should get a locker for our coats. I thought we could just carry them, but I went along with it and dug some quarters out of my purse. She pulled me into a toy store and whispered there were two boys watching us. I started to turn, but she grabbed my arm.

"Don't look," she said. "I wonder if they're going to come in here."

She finally let me turn around, and I saw the guys standing outside of the toy store. They were both short, but it wasn't like they were interested in me anyway. The two guys walked away, and Devon wondered where they were going. I figured they either went to play video games or eat, but I didn't want to find them and have to sit there while they flirted with her. We went to a jewelry store, and she went up to the case to look at the more expensive stuff. She pulled back her hair to try on a gold necklace. A piece of her hair got caught in the clasp. I was surprised at how different her curly hair felt from mine when I pulled her hair out.

"Look, best friend bracelets. My cousin has one of these," she said.

I had always wanted to get best friend necklaces, but Tori thought they were stupid and a waste of money, so we bought matching school supplies instead. Yasmin and Arianna had best friend necklaces, but all I had was a stupid binder with fish on it.

"Do you want to get them? The bracelets are twenty-five dollars, but if we split the price of the charm..." She looked at me. Devon Abrams with the perfect hair, who all the boys liked, and was way more popular than I could ever dream of being, wanted to get best friend bracelets with me? I had enough money to buy the charm, but not enough to get the bracelet. The lady behind the counter said the silver charms and bracelets were cheaper, so Devon picked up a silver one.

"The silver matches your other bracelet," the woman said, pointing to the bracelet my dad had given me. We paid for them, and she put the little silver heart charms on the bracelets. Devon took the "best" half and I got the "friend" side. We walked around the mall, and I kept looking at my wrist in every mirror we passed. I couldn't wait to wear it in front of Ericka, but I wondered what Tori would think when she saw it.

"Let's go to the drugstore and look at the makeup," Devon said.

We went to the cosmetics aisle, and she started to look at the nail polish. I hadn't worn nail polish since I was little and my grandma had given me peel-off nail polish. Devon picked up a bottle of bright red polish.

"I bought this last week. You should get this color," she said. I took the bottle from her, and she led me over to a display. "I love their gloss. This one's my favorite," she said handing me a purple tube.

We went to the music department and decided to split the cost of a Crazytones CD. I didn't know much about the band, but I gave her some money. I wanted to get a slice of pizza for lunch, but I only had enough money left for a hamburger and then I had to ask for a cup of water because I couldn't afford a drink. Devon got extra ketchup so we could share her fries. I started to head toward a booth in the back when she said she wanted to sit in the middle of the food court. She sat down near three guys who had been checking her out in line. One of them tossed a straw wrapper on our table, and she rolled her eyes. Then one of the guys leaned over and started talking to her.

A lump formed in my throat and I could barely swallow the piece of fry in my mouth, but she was relaxed and joked around with them. The red-haired guy said his name was Doug, and the other two were Jeremy and Cristian. Cristian was the cutest. He had big brown eyes and seemed sweet. I wanted to take a drink of water to push the fry down my throat, but I was afraid I'd start choking and spit water all over him.

"What school do you go to?" Cristian asked.

"Hillcrest Academy," she said.

"Pretty good school," he said.

"Yeah, but your football team sucks," Doug said. "All private schools have crappy teams."

Devon laughed like this was the funniest thing she had ever heard. We found out the guys went to Gregory Baker High School and were in the tenth grade.

"Hey, do you talk at all?" Jeremy asked looking at me. My face got warm, and Devon told him not to be a jerk.

Cristian elbowed him and said he wasn't interesting enough for me to talk to, so Doug changed the subject.

"Do you guys ever go to the basketball games at the public high school?" Doug asked. His brother was on the varsity team, and he said we should meet up at a game. Devon and Doug exchanged phone numbers before the guys left.

"We've gotta go to a game," she said.

"When are they?" I asked.

"I have no idea, but I bet it's listed in the stupid community schools calendar," she said.

Oh yes, the dreaded school calendar which came in the middle of August to remind you the summer was ending and school was about to begin. It always ruined the rest of August for me

I showed my mom the bracelet when I got home. I put my new gloss on, but it was kind of dark on me since my skin was lighter than Devon's. I thought it looked okay, but Mom said the color wasn't quite right for me so I put a little lip balm over it. I started to worry about what Tori would say when she saw my bracelet, but I figured she wouldn't notice it if I wore it under my sleeve. I painted my nails with the red polish, but the color made my hands look pale. Red looked a lot better on Devon than it did on me. Before I went to bed I checked my social media page to see if Peyton had added me to her page, but there were no new messages or adds.

Sixteen

~~~~~~

I was running late on Monday morning and forgot to put on my bracelet. Of course, Devon noticed at the bus stop.

"Where's your bracelet?" she asked. She said she had slept with hers on, and I told her I woke up late and barely made it to the bus stop. Tori looked surprised when Devon mentioned it. I didn't want to make a big deal out of it because I was still hoping Tori and I could be friends again.

"Landry, I like your headband," Peyton said as I got on the bus.

"At least you remembered to put it on," Devon said.

"I'm sorry. I'll wear it tomorrow — promise. I wore the lip gloss and polish though," I said. India didn't look up from her book.

I was at my locker after first hour when Ericka called my name from across the hall. I thought it was a trick and I ignored her, but after the third time, I had to look up.

"Did you read the stuff for English class?" she asked. I nodded. "Kharrazi was mad nobody in our class read, and she gave us a pop quiz."

"Oh, okay. Thanks," I said. What was going on? Was she trying to be nice to me now? She even walked out with me when class ended. Um, what's going on? Suddenly everything's all happy between us? She never stayed mad at Tori for as long as she had been mad at me. Of course, no one ever got mad at Ericka. Well, Tori and I had been, but we never did anything about it. I walked to my locker, and Tori came over and asked me to sit with her at lunch.

"We haven't talked in a long time," she said. "I don't even remember why we stopped talking in the first place."

Funny, I sure remembered. Tori asked me about the bracelet, and I tried to act like it wasn't a big deal. She asked if Devon was my "new best friend." I said they were both my friends. I had gone from having no friends to having two best friends. I felt like asking Tori what kind of "friend" turns on her best friend, but I didn't. In science class, I told Devon that Ericka and Tori had started talking to me again. She got quiet and then asked if I was friends with them again. I shrugged.

"I figured you'd go running back to them," she said. "So I guess you'll be eating lunch with them from now on."

"I was planning on eating lunch with you and Hana—"

"Wouldn't want to keep you from your best friend," she said slamming her science book on the desk. Mrs. Tamar came in and passed out our homework. I tried to get Devon's attention by poking her book with my pen. I flipped her page, and she put it back. Then I shut her book, and she snapped it back open.

"Devon, why are you—"

"Landry? Are you having too much fun back there?" Mrs. Tamar asked.

I pretended to take notes off the board, and Devon didn't look at me for the rest of the hour. I thought she would be happy for me since she knew how upset I had been when Ericka and Tori were mad at me. We had "B" lunch today and I got up slowly to see what she would do when the bell rang, but she headed for the lunchroom

and never looked back. I decided to skip lunch and started to walk to the library when Tori yelled to me she'd
save me a seat in the cafeteria.

"Okay, I just have to get my coat," I said.

I went over to our old table where Ericka was sitting
with her lunch spread out. Ericka always brought the
same lunch: a bologna and mustard sandwich with the
crusts cut off, a baggie full of carrot sticks, and cookies
wrapped in tinfoil.

"Hi Landry. I love your jacket," Ericka said.

"Thanks." I held back the urge to say, "What? This
ugly rag?" I dropped my coat off, and Tori let me cut in
front of her in line. I hadn't taken cuts in forever. I got
the last piece of pizza, and Tori got stuck with the cream
of broccoli soup. I waved to Maggie and Halle just to
show them I had people to eat lunch with now.

"Ew, you got the soup," Ericka said wrinkling up her
ski jump nose at Tori's lunch.

"Landry, wanna trade?" Tori asked.

Normally, I would have offered to switch, but I hated
the grease on top of the cream.

"There might be some peanut butter sandwiches left
in the cold lunch line," I said.

"It looks like someone threw up milk and broccoli,"
Ericka said. She made a wall with her lunch bag so she
wouldn't have to look at Tori's bowl. Ericka's mom always made her lunch. Ericka started talking about
Thanksgiving plans and precious little Isabella while I
zoned out. Then she got up to throw her lunch away. Tori
was still eating, but she dumped her soup when Ericka
started making gagging noises. I was done eating, but I
sat there and drank all my juice and picked at my pizza
crust. We went out to the courtyard to sit when I was
ready. Devon was sitting outside on the parking barrier
with Hana and some other girls. I said I'd be right back
and walked over to Devon.

"Hey," I said. She looked up at me.

"What'd they say to you?" she asked.

I shrugged and she rolled her eyes.

"All I heard was how mean they were to you and then you ran right back. They treated you like crap and now they're sick of each other—"

"It's not like I'm over it, but it's not easy to ignore somebody in such a small school," I said. I couldn't believe she was getting mad at me for making up with my old friends.

"They had no problem doing it to you," she said getting up. "I think your friends are waiting for you." I walked back over to Ericka and Tori and it seemed like the courtyard was bigger than ever.

In social studies, Peyton started to tell me about the pop quiz in French when Ericka called me over. Peyton's eyebrows shot up.

"You guys made up?" she asked.

"I guess," I said.

"Landry, come sit over here," Ericka waved me over. I told her I had to talk to Peyton about something. Mrs. Hearst had us work on the chapter questions and Ericka tried to get me to work in their group, but I pretended I was too lazy to get up and move. India and Peyton didn't say anything, and I asked if they wanted to do something this weekend. I almost asked if they wanted to come over, but I figured I'd just make Ericka and Tori mad again if I had people over and didn't invite them.

"Maybe we could do movie marathon at my house," Peyton said.

"Can't. I have to help clean the house for my grandparents this weekend," India said.

"Who invited you?" I said. I smiled to show I was kidding, but she didn't say anything. Peyton walked me to class and told me about the extra credit question on the pop quiz.

"We had to write a recipe in French, and I put eggs in the fruit salad. I shoulda gotten half credit for even remembering how to spell the word for 'eggs.' Tori would have argued—" She stopped. "I better shut up since you guys are friends again. Oh, by the way, I got your friend request and added you this morning. I'm never on there much. ."

I relaxed. After class, Ashanti was waiting by my locker.

"Welcome back," I said, giving her a hug. "Why didn't you tell me you were coming back today?"

"I wasn't sure last night, but I felt a lot better this morning. Listen, I have to stay after to talk to Mrs. Tamar, but do you want a ride home?" she asked.

I went to the library after my last class to wait for her and Ericka was on the computer. I sat with her, and we looked up websites on *As the Days Roll On*. I was going to print out a picture of Brad McMillan for Ashanti, but the stupid librarian came over, so we had to pretend we were looking at research stuff. Later, Ashanti's dad took us through the drive-thru for ice cream to celebrate her first day back.

"So what's up with you?" she asked, licking caramel off her spoon. "You guys are talking again, huh? I saw you and Ericka sitting together, but you never said anything about it on the phone."

"We just started talking today," I said.

"Are you still mad at them?" she asked. "It's kind of weird for them to assume they could just come up to you and everything would be okay."

I hadn't thought about it. Why did they think I wouldn't still be angry?

"Oh, guess what?" she said. "My dad's addicted to *As the Days Roll On* now."

"I hate the new girl who is always flirting with Colin," I said.

Ashanti nodded and said Carrington's dresses were too low-cut, but her dad didn't say anything until she kicked the back of his seat.

"Oh yeah, what is she thinking with those outfits?" he said.

"Carrington better not go after my Bradley," she said.

She asked if I wanted to come over, but I had to get home. I wanted to talk to Devon before my mom got home in case things didn't go well. I didn't want to have to explain what was going on to my mother. Devon's mom answered, and I could hear them talking and then I heard the sound of the phone scraping against the counter.

"Yeah?"

"Hi." She didn't say anything so I kept talking. "I know you're mad at me because I made up—"

"No, you *don't* understand. I don't care if you're friends with them. I care they treated you like crap and now you're going back to them like everything is fine," she said. "Just a second, I've got another call." She clicked over and came back saying it was for her mom.

All I wanted to do was to make up with my old friends, and now it seemed like my new friend was dumping me. I could never be myself around Ericka, but I didn't have to worry about Peyton and Devon talking behind my back when I left the room. When I told Devon I wished I had dark curly hair like hers, she said she loved my hair color. Ericka had called it "albino blonde" and made me feel ugly. Now I had messed everything up.

I called Tori, but she was still at soccer practice, and Ericka was too busy helping her mom to talk on the phone. I had never called Peyton before, and I always got nervous when I call someone for the first time. Just because you can talk in person doesn't mean you'll have good phone conversations. I took a deep breath and called her.

"Hey, are you okay?" Peyton asked. "You sound upset."

"Devon's mad at me. I tried talking to her, but she said her mom got another call and... I think she just didn't want to talk to me," I said.

"Devon hangs up on the people she doesn't want to talk to — just ask India," she said. "I don't think she's mad, but her feelings are hurt. She said she feels used. I guess we're all kind of wondering what's going on now since you're friends with those guys again," she said.

"They just started talking to me and I ate lunch with them, but I have more fun with you guys," I said.

"Are you going to start sitting with them in class?" she asked.

"No. I mean I'm glad to be talking to them again because it sucked when they were mad at me, but I want to hang out with you guys."

"Are they going to get mad at you if you do?" she asked.

I wasn't sure. I didn't owe Ericka or Tori anything after the way they had treated me. I was relieved Tori and I were friends again, but I felt weird around her because she had changed on me so fast after the competition.

"I wasn't supposed to say anything, but you know how India's been acting weird lately?" she asked. "Well, she and Devon got into a fight right after you guys got those bracelets. She felt you were taking Devon away from her."

I felt sick. I thought everything was okay, and all this time there was stuff going on behind my back.

"India and Devon have been getting on each other's nerves," she said. "But they've been close for a long time, and I think India got jealous when you came along."

"Is India mad at me?" I asked.

"No, it sorta worked itself out," she said.

I had noticed India had been quieter around me lately, but I didn't have as much in common with her. I felt weird knowing she had been resenting me all this time.

"I'm glad you told me. I don't want you guys to think I'm going to run from one group to another when things get bad," I said.

"I know. I mean, you stayed with us when Ericka kept trying to get you to move over to her table," she said. "Anyway, I think Devon's jealous of Tori since you guys were best friends for so long. Don't tell Devon I told you though. I gotta go. We'll chat later, okay?"

Whenever Tori, Ericka, and I got into a fight it was always me calling them back over and over again until we worked things out. This last fight had been different, but now I guess I was back to doing the same old thing, but with a different person. I was going to call Devon, but the phone rang before I could even dial her number.

"Sorry," Devon said. "My mom was on forever. Listen, I'm sorry I got mad at you for talking to them, but it makes me so mad they treated you bad," she said. "And then you didn't wear the bracelet, and I got tons of crap from India about it."

"I meant to put it on. Tori wasn't thrilled about it either. Maybe we shouldn't wear them to school. I don't want India to be mad—"

"What?" she shrieked into the phone. "Are you kidding? Because you better be kidding."

"Okay, I'll wear it every single day. I'll even get a tattoo," I said.

"Well, I'd get one, but between the 'Blake Forever' on my arm and the 'I Love Doug' on my butt, there's no room," she said. "Sorry I acted like a jerk today."

I told her I was sorry, too, and asked her what was going on with India since Peyton wasn't supposed to tell me about it. This was the first time anyone had called me during a fight and the first time anyone had apologized to me. I guess this was what normal friends did.

Seventeen

Devon grabbed my arm as soon as I got to the bus stop. She pushed my coat sleeve up to make sure I was wearing the bracelet. Ashanti had gotten a ride to school, and she was waiting for me when I got off the bus. She handed me a copy of *Soap Opera Hotties*.

"Page twenty-four," Ashanti said. I went to the page, and there was an interview of Colin.

"You can tear it out if you want," she said. "I was bored last week so I made a collage of Brad on the back of my door. You've got to see it. Can you come over after school?"

I nodded as Ericka ran over to us. Ericka stayed glued to my side until I went to class, and Thalia made a comment about me being "Miss Popular" all of a sudden.

At lunch, Devon and I split up to go to our lockers. Ericka linked arms with me and started to lead me to the cafeteria, but I said I had to wait for Devon. Devon looked surprised to see her hanging on me, and Ericka said she'd save me a seat.

"Are you sitting with them today?" Devon asked.

"Do you want to sit with them?" I asked, hoping she'd agree so I wouldn't have to deal with it.

Devon made a face. After we went through the lunch line, Devon started to head to our usual table when Ashanti called me over.

"Um, would you mind sitting with Ashanti?" I asked.

"I guess not. I can't stand Halle, but if it's just for one day..."

I realized I had to say something to Ericka or else she'd get mad again. Ericka started to move her coat off the chair, but I told her I forgot I had promised to sit with Ashanti.

"My stuff's already there," I said. Before I had to beg someone to let me sit at their table, and now I was trying to keep people from getting mad at me for not sitting with them.

Ericka and Tori came over to our table and started talking about what we should do for Tori's birthday. Devon kept poking me, but what could I do? Say, "Oh excuse me, we're going to go sit over there now" and walk away? Devon said she was going to play basketball with Hana in the courtyard. I started to follow her, but Ericka grabbed my arm.

I waited in the hall before class so Ericka couldn't ask me to sit with her and Tori. Jay asked me why I was waiting in the hall, and I said I had to ask Mrs. Hearst something. Unfortunately, Mrs. Hearst was right behind me and she asked me what I needed.

"I was wondering..." I saw the TV in the classroom, so I asked what we were watching.

"*Gandhi*. Have you seen it?" she asked. I shook my head and followed her into the room. I sat with India and Peyton, but Tori pulled out a chair for me when Mrs. Hearst started the movie. Peyton moved her chair to Tori and Ericka's table so India and I followed.

Kyle leaned over. "Am I crazy, or am I seeing Anne Frank's dad?" he asked.

"What? It *is* Mr. Frank. How many movies is he in?" I asked.

Tori tore off a piece of notebook paper and wrote, "Do you still like him?"

"That actor?" I whispered.

She rolled her eyes and pointed to Kyle. I shrugged and she passed me her pen. I wrote he was cute, but he was going out with Arianna. She wrote back Arianna liked Stuart. Arianna had called Kyle a "loser" in math so maybe she did like Stuart now. I made a mental note to do my hair tomorrow. Kyle moved my chair back when the movie was over. He didn't have to move it too far, but it was still nice.

"My chair's heavy, and I have to move it all the way over there," India said, pretending to be annoyed. I picked up her chair and dragged it back for her.

"Thank you, dah-ling," she said.

In French class, I wondered if Devon would get weird on me when she found out I was going over to Ashanti's house. I was going to tell Ashanti I had to stop home first and then I'd walk over to her house. However, Ashanti came over to my locker when I was talking to Devon to say her dad would pick us up. Devon raised her eyebrows. I told Ashanti I'd meet her outside.

"Are you going to Ashanti's for math tutoring?"

"Where's my notebook?" I said pretending not to hear.

"You already put it in your backpack," Devon said. "So why are—"

"Devon, hurry up," India said as she walked by. "We're gonna miss the bus."

"Call me tonight," Devon said as she followed India to the bus line.

Ashanti couldn't wait for me to see her room. "I saved a bunch of Colin pictures so we can do your door if you want," she said.

Devon called me the second I came home from Ashanti's. It was like she had seen me walk in the front door or something. She wanted me to come over tomorrow after school, but I had already invited Ashanti to come over. I said she could come over, too, and hoped it would be okay with my mom.

The next day, we decided to order a pizza after school. Ashanti wanted sausage, which Devon didn't eat, so we ended up with a plain cheese pizza. We watched *As the Days Roll On* while we ate, but Devon talked through it. She was only quiet during the commercials. Ashanti and I went to work putting up the Colin pictures on my door after we ate, but Devon flopped on my bed and asked if she could look at my books. It was obvious she was bored.

Devon started talking about Doug, and I told Ashanti about meeting the guys at the mall. Devon said Doug was super hot, which I didn't see, but I nodded anyway. Ashanti asked me about Cristian after Devon left. I said he was cute, but he'd never be interested in me.

"Sure he would," she said. "So who do you think is cute in our class?"

I had to say Jay because they were going together, but she freaked out when I said Kyle.

"You like Kyle?"

"No, I just think he's funny," I said. "Besides, he likes Arianna."

"Arianna likes Stuart now," she said. "I know for sure because Halle liked Stuart and he stopped e-mailing her because of Arianna."

Even if Arianna broke up with Kyle, he'd never consider me. We didn't have the same friends, and it would be uncomfortable even if he did ask me to eat lunch with him. I would never fit in with his friends, so why couldn't I stop thinking about him?

Delilah called me about doing a photo shoot on Saturday morning. She wanted me to work with a new photographer named Eddee Lane. I wouldn't make any money or anything, but I'd get free photos for my portfolio. It wasn't like getting to do a photo shoot for *Teen Vogue*. I was starting to realize all models start out at the bottom. Talisa and the girls who made it to the *Ingé-nue* finals were just rare exceptions.

"Eddee needs pictures for his portfolio, too, so you'll be helping each other out," she said. She gave me directions to his studio and told me to have my mom call her if there was a problem. Mom was okay with it, so I started organizing my outfits for the shoot. I was almost finished when Devon called and asked me to go with her to meet Cristian and Doug at the mall on Saturday.

"I have to work on Saturday," I said.

"Please? Cris was asking about you," she said.

"Cristian asked about me? I'd love to go, but I'm working with this new photographer and—"

Devon interrupted to ask if I could meet them after work. I had no idea how long the shoot would run, so I had to tell her I couldn't go. I knew India was staying with her grandparents over the weekend, and I felt a little better knowing she wouldn't be able to go either. Devon said she'd ask Peyton or Hana since I couldn't go. There were so many weekends when Tori and Ericka were mad at me and I had nothing to do. I would sit home all weekend before and finally I had a life, and now I had to work. Part of me wanted to be a big star, but part of me just wanted to have a best friend. Oh well. It would all be worth it when I got my big break.

Eighteen

I got to Eddee Lane's studio, and Mom insisted on coming in with me. Like Talisa Milan's mother sat in on every photo shoot she did. Whatever. Eddee didn't seem to mind she was there, but he did ask her to sit in the lobby while we went into the studio. Not like there would have been room in the studio for her. It was super tiny with cloth backdrops hanging from the ceiling and a dirty drop cloth on the floor. There was barely enough room for Eddee and me. He adjusted his camera on the tripod and told me to pick out some music. I picked out a country one because it was the only name I had ever heard of on his playlist. He said it was a good choice because she had a soothing voice.

"Okay, do you want to do your close-ups first?" he asked.

I nodded because my skin tends to get greasy quick and my hair falls pretty fast, so we might as well do the close-ups while I still looked fresh. He had me sit on this stool which was shorter on one side. I had to keep balancing myself so I wouldn't tip over. Plus, I had to act like I was having fun even though his studio smelled like pee and mildew. How glamorous. I'm sure Talisa always worked in places with the smell of dirty litter boxes in the air.

"Can we open a window? It's kind of hot in here," I asked.

"Can't. Window's stuck," he said. "Can you just tilt your head like — yeah. Perfect."

I couldn't breathe. I felt like I was going to pass out, but I didn't want to land on the filthy drop cloth on the floor.

"Okay, let's have you lay on the floor now, so I can shoot you from above," he said.

Crap on a cracker. Lay on a filthy rag? In my good jeans? Was he insane? I stood there for a second deciding how to tell him "No way," when I realized it would get back to Delilah I was "uncooperative." Bianca Laurel had been kicked off *American Ingénue* for doing the same thing. The photographer on the show wanted her to pose while hanging suspended from the air, and she refused. I didn't blame her for not wanting to hang from the ceiling, but the judges had used it as an excuse to vote her off the show. So I got down on his filthy floor.

The afternoon went by slowly. Eddee had me pose outside in the freezing cold for a little bit, but he let me wear my coat for the shot, so it wasn't too bad. Still, I felt sick from the smell in his studio, and he was kinda weird. He made strange noises and talked to himself while he was shooting, and it was starting to freak me out. He took a million shots of me and then said we were done. I couldn't leave fast enough.

"It reeked so bad," I said to my mother when we got in the car.

"Either he has fifty cats hidden away or he doesn't have a working toilet," Mom said. "I kept going outside for fresh air while you were in there with him."

I asked if I could call Devon, but Mom said it was almost dinnertime and I needed to study anyway.

"But I never do my homework on Saturday," I said.

She went into this whole thing about how I had promised to be responsible if she let me model and blah, blah,

blah. I said, "Forget it," just to end the lecture. It wasn't fair I couldn't see my friends just because I was modeling. The world wasn't going to end if I failed a quiz. I thought about bringing up the fact I only had three days of school next week because of Thanksgiving, but she was in one of her "don't-mess-with-me" moods. So I stayed in all stupid weekend long. You always see pictures of supermodels dancing in clubs and hanging out with pop stars, but I couldn't go to the mall for, like, fifteen minutes.

On Wednesday, Mom started freaking about cleaning the house for Thanksgiving.

"This place is a dump. I want you to dust everything in the den. You know how sensitive your grandmother is to dust," she said.

We didn't have to worry about cooking a meal because we were buying a pre-made turkey dinner with potatoes, stuffing (which only my grandma eats), and a pumpkin pie. The only thing we were making was sugar free gelatin for Grandma. Mom dusted and put new sheets on the pullout bed and I made the dessert, which took forever to stir. Mom usually does it because I always make it too gritty, but she was too exhausted from vacuuming.

Thanksgiving morning should be about watching parades in your pajamas and smelling pies baking. It should not involve your mother screaming at you to get ready and yelling, "You better not mess up your room, young lady," and not even allowing you a simple glass of juice because you might mess up her precious kitchen. I'm sure Dad would love to know she was starving me for the sake of a clean kitchen.

We got to the grocery store a good ten minutes before they closed so I don't know what she was so worried about. Even if we didn't get the meal, we could have gone to a Chinese buffet down the street where they have the best fried rice in the world. We loaded the food in the car, and the stuffing stunk. We had to drive home with the windows open even though it was freezing out. Dad and Grandma didn't arrive until after twelve o'clock, and Grandma sneezed as soon as she sat down.

"Oh my... dusty," she said. I thought Mom would kill her.

Dad put Grandma's suitcase in the den, but she took one look at the pullout couch and said it would bother her back. They all looked at me. Terrific. Grandma would probably die from a wheezing attack because I haven't cleaned under my bed since we moved in here. Dad helped Mom get dinner set up, and I sat with Grandma, who basically blew her nose and told me about my wonderful cousins.

"Lucy — oh so smart," she said tapping my knee. "She's an honor student and captain of the swim team. Oh, and Bryan's going away to college next year. He wants to be a doctor, but a specialist — not like your dad." She said the last part in a whisper.

I tried to focus on the football game, even though I was bored and had no idea what was going on. I'm sure Lucy would know since she's so smart. I bet she and Bryan have never gotten a C+ in math, and they probably get picked first in gym, too. Mom said dinner was ready and told us to wash up. Grandma came out of the bathroom and asked if we had some non-scented soap since she was allergic to the kind we had.

"Since when, Ma?" Dad asked. Mom just gritted her teeth and handed her a grubby bar of soap we kept next to the kitchen sink.

We sat down to eat, and Grandma asked how long we cooked the turkey. It was pretty obvious we had bought it, but she had to make mom come out and say it. Mom mentioned she got a new account at work and Dad said, "Great," while Grandma asked if the onion in the stuffing was fresh or dried. Mom sighed and told her to check the container. After dinner, Mom told me to sit with Grandma, who had an envelope full of pictures to show me.

First, there was the wedding shower of some girl I was related to but wouldn't know if she mugged me on the street. Then there were pictures of the amazing Lucy and Bryan. I looked over and my parents seemed to be getting along, so I guess I could put up with the slide show a little longer. Grandma asked about how modeling was going, and I showed her my portfolio. Mom had sent her the picture from the newspaper, but Grandma asked if I had a school picture for her. I wanted to lie and say I was sick on picture day, but Mom had put out my photo. My picture was so gross. My skin looked greasy, and my forehead showed through my bangs because my hair was so pale. The school should have hired a professional photographer who did retouching. I said I wasn't sure where they were, but Dad overheard and said he wanted one, too, so mom got them out. Note to self: remove stuff like school pictures from under the mattress next time mom offers to put clean sheets on my bed.

Dad put the football game on, and Grandma said it must be hard for Mom and me to live here on our own. Mom said we were doing fine, but she looked like she swallowed something sour. It went on until Dad said he had been looking to transfer to one of the clinics in town. I was shocked my mother hadn't told me. I couldn't wait to talk to her alone.

Devon called later while we were watching a Christmas movie and asked if I could come over tomorrow because her parents were going to a tailgate party. I didn't want to leave since Dad was here so I asked if she could come here instead. Devon's mother wanted to make sure it was okay with my mom since it was a holiday, so I put her on the phone. I went into the kitchen as soon as Mom was off the phone.

"Why didn't you tell me Dad was looking for a job here?"

"He only mentioned it recently, and I don't think he's done anything about it yet," she said.

"This is so great. He'll move here, and it'll be like old times."

She sucked in her bottom lip and let it roll off her teeth. "I don't want you to get your hopes up."

"What do you mean? Don't you want Dad to move here?" She didn't say anything, and I got mad. "I can't believe you. You made me move away from him and now he wants to—"

"It's not — I'm not keeping your dad from moving here. He can come here anytime he wants. I wanted him to move here in the first place," she said.

My eyes were burning as I went to my room, which now smelled like Grandma's perfume. I came back out and sat on the couch. Dad asked if I wanted another cherry cola, but Mom said I didn't need any more soda.

"Laine, I was asking her. You want another soda, kiddo?" I nodded just to annoy her, and he refilled my glass. Around midnight, Mom said I should go to sleep since Devon was coming over tomorrow.

"But I want to watch the end of the movie," I said.

Dad said it was almost over, which I knew wasn't true because I had seen it before.

"Do whatever you want," Mom said as she went into the kitchen. Every once in a while I'd hear her slam something down on the counter. Dad leaned over and whispered we had to "stick together." It was just like when I was little and he used to let me stay up to watch TV on Friday nights. It was only until eleven o'clock, but it was a big deal back then. He'd make white cheddar popcorn, and we'd all sit on the couch and eat. Until we got the new couch and then mom wouldn't let us eat on it anymore.

The movie ended, and I got up before Mom could say anything. I couldn't sleep (Mom would say it was because of the soda), and I went to go to the bathroom. I overheard Mom doing the loud whisper fighting they used to do back in Chicago when they thought I couldn't hear them. I went up to Mom's bedroom door.

"You come around and all of a sudden you're overriding me — it's easy to play Dad five times a year," she said.

"Hey, I'm not the one who moved four hours away—"

"It always comes back to my job. I had to leave grad school to raise her while you got to go to medical school. Well, maybe I wanted to do something for me."

So I ruined my mother's life. Wonderful. Dad argued/whispered back she was the one who had wanted to start a family right away. Great, so he didn't want me either. He said something about "unfair" and "roadblocks," but he was better at lowering his voice than she was so I missed a bit. I went back to the den and cried into my pillow. My chest felt hot and tight like it did whenever they fought. Why couldn't I have normal parents who liked each other?

When I was in the second grade, my friend, Sadie Goodacre, found out her parents were getting divorced. I felt so bad for her, and I thought I'd die if my parents ever split up. I never thought I would have to go through it. Why couldn't they just work it out? Didn't they still love each other? Or did they regret the whole thing — including having me?

Sadie's dad got remarried the next year, and he and his new wife had a baby. Sadie never got to go to his new house, and her dad never came over to do stuff with her. What if my dad got remarried and had another kid and he wanted to be with his new family? Or what if Mom married Ronald and they had a kid and I was just a loser tagging along?

I woke up when I heard someone in the shower. I went into the kitchen where Grandma was making breakfast. She was making oatmeal, which isn't my favorite, but I mashed up some bananas with milk and sugar to make it taste better. Grandma asked me how school was going, and I said everything was fine because I didn't want her to know she had a dummy for a granddaughter. It would be such a shock after Lucy.

"Must be hard not having your dad around," she said.

I was going to say we were doing okay, but I was always making excuses and saying everything was fine. No, I didn't mind not getting to see my dad, and no, I didn't mind if Tori ate the last slice of pizza or if Ericka bought the sweater I wanted. I was sick of being the one who always gave in. Ericka always said, "Landry won't mind," because everyone thought I didn't care. I was sick of hiding what I was feeling. Of course, if I had said anything to Ericka or Tori they would have gotten mad at me, and if I told Grandma anything, then she'd tell my parents and they'd get into it again.

Dad came into the kitchen and poured a cup of coffee. He ruffled my hair as he walked past me. "Sleep okay, kiddo?"

Actually, no. Your fighting kept me awake, and I spent most of the night crying and feeling sick.

"Yeah."

"Devon's going to be here in a half hour," Mom said coming into the room. She grabbed a piece of toast and started buttering it like she wanted to hurt it. I got up and noticed Dad was mashing up bananas in his oatmeal, too. I washed my hair, since it smelled like a wet dog from crying on it. My eyes started to fill up again while I was blow drying. My eyes looked red, and my skin was puffy. Normally, I wouldn't have cared since I felt like crap, but I didn't want Devon to see me like this so I put on some of Mom's mascara.

Devon brought over stuff to make cookies. We had a gingerbread man cookie cutter so I made a Colin cookie.

Devon tried to make a Blake Alderson one, but she had to make his hair blue because we had no gray icing. I started to make pink icing to make an outfit for my Cadia doll cookie when she stopped me.

"No, make purple instead. Then I can make purple hip huggers for Blake," she said.

"Since when does Blake Alderson wear hip huggers?" Dad asked.

"All the time," she said.

"I must have missed it somehow. Landry, is this you?" he asked.

"It's her Cadia doll cookie," Devon said. "Landry, you should do one of you for the Colin cookie."

I rolled out more dough and started mixing the purple icing.

"How long are your dad and Grandma staying?" Devon asked. I said they were driving back Sunday morning. "I always thought you looked exactly like your mom, but you look like your dad, too," she said. "Same eyes and chin."

"Yup, but I don't have the butt chin."

"The what?" she asked, and I pointed to the line my dad had in his chin. "Oh yeah. He looks kinda like the guy who played Blake's brother in *Vengeance of Fire*," she said.

"I dunno. I guess."

After Devon left, Dad asked me about my other friends.

"How's the soccer player?"

"Tori? We don't hang out much anymore," I said.

"Why not? She seemed nice. She's an honor roll student, isn't she?" he asked.

"I've been hanging out with Devon and her friends. Devon's smart, and she got second place in poetry in the writing contest."

"She seems nice, but you shouldn't neglect your old friends just because you meet someone new," Dad said.

My grandma came in to say goodnight, and I asked Dad when he thought he might be able to transfer here. He started shifting in his chair.

"Well, it's not easy to find another clinic." He stopped and looked at me. "You'd like it if I moved here? You and your mom wouldn't get sick of having me around?" He tried to make a joke out of it.

"Don't you want to live with us anymore?" Crap, my voice broke, and you could tell I was about to start blubbering.

Dad leaned his head against mine. "I know it's hard. It's hard for me, too, and I hate being apart from you guys, but—"

Tears were spilling down my face now. But what? Either he wanted to live with us or he didn't.

"Your mom and I need to work some stuff out," he said.

I figured it meant one day they'd take me out separately and tell me while they both loved me, they were going to take some time away from one another and oh, won't the space do us all a lot of good? Well no, it sucked, and I was sick of this. I didn't want to scream, "Make a decision," and have them say, "Okay, let's get a divorce," but this waiting and wondering stunk, too. Everything had been fine, and now it was all messed up again. I went to get ready for bed, but when I came out to say "goodnight," I overheard Dad saying this was getting to me.

"Do we have to get into this right now?" Mom asked.

"Laine, I hate being separated from you guys," he said. "I don't like leaving the clinic, but if I have to… but where would I live? I don't want to live in the same town and have to get an apartment somewhere."

Something touched my arm, and I almost screamed. I whirled around and saw Grandma standing there with a finger to her lips. She led me back to the den.

"Let them try and work things out, honey," she said, sitting next to me.

"I thought everything was back to normal after Dad was here last time. Mom was sad when he left and they talked on the phone all the time, but I guess she's mad because she had to quit school to take care of me."

Grandma said my mom had wanted to take care of me. It didn't make me feel any better, but I told her it did. She gave me a kiss on the forehead and told me to go to sleep.

In the morning, I went into the kitchen to grab a bowl of cereal before Dad got up because I felt stupid for crying in front of him. No such luck. He was already at the table and asked if I wanted to go to a movie today. I shrugged.

"We could go to the museum," he said, and I made a face. "No takers. Okay, how about... the mall?"

"For real?"

"Yeah." He looked less than thrilled.

"I'll go get dressed." I tore out of the room before he could change his mind. I came back when he was asking Mom to go.

"Have you ever shopped with her?" she asked. "She's got a mind of her own."

"I wonder where she gets it from?" he said. She put her hand up to protest, and he walked up and put his hand around hers. "Kidding. We can go out for lunch, too," he said.

Mom said she'd go, and Grandma and I piled into the backseat of Dad's car. I noticed my parents were going out of their way to be polite to one another, and I got the feeling Grandma had said something to them. Dad even dropped us off at the door. After we ate, Mom wanted to look at couches at Jordan's furniture store. While she was looking, Dad found some bookcases he liked. His old bookcase was in our den. Great, let's buy more furniture for his apartment so he'll never leave Chicago.

"What do you think of this couch?" Mom asked.

"It's kind of formal, but if you like it," he said.

"I thought we could move the other one in the living room downstairs," she said.

"What are you guys talking about?" I asked.

"We're thinking about finishing the basement and making a family room and an office down there," she said.

"Why? Is Dad moving in?" I asked.

"Well, he's going to see about transferring," she said. I wasn't getting the answer I wanted so I went to Dad.

"Hopefully, I'll find some place I like. I don't want to go into private practice—"

"But will you live with us?" I asked.

"Of course," he said. "Now I think a new flat TV would look nice in the basement, but your mom wants some frou-frou thing to hold the TV you guys already have. I think you should decide."

Mom cleared her throat. "Fine, we'll get another TV. I could never stand all the sports you watched anyway."

We ended up leaving the store because Mom said we should pick out a carpet before we got any furniture. We stopped at the bookstore, and I found a copy of *Jane Eyre*. Mom usually makes me pay half, but Dad bought it for me. He and I stood in line at the café, and I asked if I could get a latte. I read in *Young and Fun* Talisa always requested a latte on the set when she had to work. Of course she also asked for lavender candles, fresh peonies, and organic chicken salads. If I could request something, I'd ask for a hamburger to be flown in from my favorite burger place no matter what part of the country I was in. I had been in love with those olive burgers ever since I ate one when I was on a road trip to Flint with Mom.

"Do you drink coffee?" he asked.

I wasn't crazy about it, but it seemed like something I should like. I ordered a white chocolate mocha latte.

"If your mom asks, you're drinking hot chocolate, okay?" he said as we walked to the table. "She always accuses me of giving into you and this is just one more—" he cut off as Mom came over.

"You and your whipped cream," she said as Dad and I exchanged a look. I thought something with two kinds of chocolate in it would be a little sweeter, but it wasn't bad.

Tori called when I got home and asked if I could sleep over next Friday for her birthday. I hadn't been to Tori's house in a long time, and I wondered if it would be weird spending the night with Tori and Ericka again. Then Tori said Ericka's mom wouldn't let her sleep over because they were going up north on Saturday. Maybe it wouldn't be too bad with just Tori there.

My dad seemed happy I was going over to the soccer player/brain's house, so I pointed out I needed to buy her a birthday gift. Mom said he didn't need to give me any money, but he took out his wallet anyway.

"Hey, remember this picture?" Dad asked pulling out a photo of me with the Easter Bunny.

"I remember buying the dress," Mom said. "You'd only try on the ones with hats."

"I was four," I said, not wanting to bring up the fact if I had been born with better hair, then I wouldn't have needed a hat.

Nineteen

I didn't know how Yasmin McCarty had time to do her hair every day. It seemed like all the girls either already knew how to style it or had naturally perfect hair like Arianna and Devon. My hair didn't curl well, and it fell flat after two minutes. I curled it on the first day of school, but Ericka said curly hair "wasn't me." She was probably right.

Peyton was also having hair problems in class.

"I hate my hair," she said.

"Are you kidding? I'd kill for your hair. I'd love to have dark red hair, and it's so thick—"

"It's like wire." She wrapped a strand around a pencil, and it was curled when she unrolled it. "See? I wish I had blonde hair like yours. It's always silky like the conditioner commercial where the girl keeps whirling around."

"Please, it's albino blonde. I'd much rather have your hair," I said.

She gave me a funny look. "Albino blonde? What are you talking about? It's so pretty." I told her what Ericka said.

"She's just jealous, Landry. Who wouldn't be with the frizz ball on her head?"

"Poor Kyle," India said as she sat down.

161

"What? Why?" I asked.

"Arianna just broke up with him. She told him she just wants to be friends, but everybody knows she likes Stuart." India got quiet when Kyle walked into the room.

Arianna and Kyle hadn't talked in class last hour, but we did have a test. I couldn't focus on the chapter questions, and I spent the whole class wondering whom Kyle might like next.

Ericka was already at Tori's house when I got there for the party. I bought Tori a Crazytones CD, but I think she only pretends to like the band because all the girls on the soccer team listen to them. She put on the CD as Ericka went through her soccer pictures.

"Who's this?" Ericka asked. "He's hot."

"Dave. He helps our coach out. Everybody has a huge crush on him," Tori said.

"Let me see," I said peering over the top. "Hana told me about him."

"He's no Kyle," Ericka said staring at me. When was she going to leave?

Ericka started talking about all the people she couldn't stand at school. She was ripping Thalia apart, and when I stood up for her, she gave me the look where her pale green eyes go right through you. Then she said Hana had gained weight.

"Hana's not fat," I said. Ericka gave me a look, and I swear I wanted to run after those words as soon as they were out of my mouth. "Um, I like your hair, Ericka. Where did you get it done?" I asked.

"Tambylyn's," she said fluffing it with her fingers.

Her hair was too curly to wear it short, and it looked like a bushy triangle on her head.

"Landry, your hair looked good braided last week," she said.

"Thanks. Peyton did it on the bus," I said.

"It was so much prettier than just lying there like usual," she said.

I hated how she insulted me, but she did it in a fake sweet voice so I couldn't get mad at her. Well, at least to her face. Sometimes she said mean things I didn't even catch until I get home, and then it was too late to do anything about it. Ericka has always gone after my hair since last summer when we played this dumb game called "I Wish." The three of us all had to say stuff we wanted, and I wished my hair wasn't so light and straight. I said I wanted dark, thick, wavy hair, and ever since then she's attacked my hair. Why had I been sad when she stopped talking to me again?

Tori said Ericka's hair always looked good, and Ericka got a stupid smirk on her face. Tori's told me a million times she hates Ericka's hair. Mrs. Robins brought in a cookies n' cream ice cream cake, which I always hate because it tastes like dirt in ice cream. I kept looking at the clock and wondering when Ericka's mom would pick her up. Tori wanted to play a card game, but Ericka wanted to play truth or dare. Ericka got her way, and she went first.

"Okay, um... truth," she said.

I wanted to ask, "How do you get your hair so bushy?" but instead I asked if there was anybody she liked.

"Stuart Graham, but don't tell anyone," she said.

Stuart would laugh in her face, but I swore to keep it a secret. I thought she was stupid for telling me about Stuart seeing as she told him about my liking Kyle. I still can't believe Tori told her my secret. I went next, and Tori asked who I had a crush on. I wasn't about to say Kyle again, so I said Cristian and explained I met him at the mall. They both looked impressed. Then we dared Ericka to go knock on Tori's older brother's door. Matthew was a senior and Ericka always got nervous around him, so it was kind of funny.

Tori grabbed my arm, and we hid in the laundry room when she went upstairs. Ericka couldn't find us and I could hear her padding around in her bare feet going, "You guys?" I started to feel bad so I walked out, but

Tori didn't come out right away. Ericka's feelings were hurt and I should have felt bad, but I hated the way her lower lip pouted when she became "Victim Girl."

Ericka's dad finally came to pick her up, and Tori and I rolled out our sleeping bags.

"Ericka threw up last time we had a sleepover, and we had to sleep with all the windows open," Tori said. "It was so cold."

"She threw up and didn't go home?" I asked.

"No, because it was at her birthday party," Tori said looking embarrassed. Well, it wasn't like Ericka had been speaking to me then, but it still hurt to know I hadn't been invited.

"My mom thought it was dumb she didn't invite you, but you know how Ericka gets," she said, playing with a string on her sleeping bag.

"Yeah," I said. Way to stick up for me, Tor. She flipped over on her stomach and started telling me about how Ericka had been driving her crazy. I snuggled down in my sleeping bag as I listened. It was just like old times with us laying on the dark carpeting in Tori's family room and complaining about our friends. At first I was into it, but then it was, like, enough. I wondered if I was going to have to spend the rest of my weekends listening to her complain about Ericka, but never having the guts to do anything about it. I guess I must have fallen asleep while she was talking because the next morning she said something about "boring me." Well, how much complaining can a person take? I couldn't say I had been listening because sometimes I snore a little when I sleep. Ericka thoughtfully told me last summer.

Tori's dad made pancakes for breakfast, which I hated. He covered it in syrup, and the maple smell made my stomach do flip-flops. I managed to get one pancake down without throwing up, and Mr. Robins offered me another one. I shook my head, and Mrs. Robins poured me a big glass of soy milk, which is the only thing which

makes me feel sicker than pancakes. To make matters
worse, Mrs. Robins had gotten syrup on the outside of
the glass and I go nuts when my hands get sticky. It's
just the grossest feeling in the world. Tori was chowing
down like she hadn't eaten in days, while Mrs. Robins
was eating a delicious looking donut.

Tori's brother came downstairs wearing sweatpants.
Matthew's hair was all messed up, but it made him look
even cuter. He gave us this head jerk like "Hey," and
stuffed a donut in his mouth.

"Anybody want the last one?" he asked. Please, give
it to me. For the love of all which is good, give me the
donut. I was starving for something not syrup-covered.

"Landry? Wanna split it?" he asked.

"Huh? Oh yeah, yes. Please." He broke it in half and
handed it to me. I took a bite and tried to keep the pow-
dered sugar from giving me a mustache. I was surprised he
offered it to me since I always felt invisible around him.

Tori and I went upstairs to get dressed, and I put on
some lip gloss in case Matthew was roaming the hall.
Tori wanted to see if her parents would drive us to the
movies, but I just wanted to go home and take a shower.
I told her I had to get home, and her dad dropped me off.
I called Devon as soon as I had finished my shower.

"How was the party?" she asked.

"Okay, so what's up?" I asked.

"Nothing," she said, sounding bored. "I went to the
movies last night with India. Oh, my mom needs to use
the phone so I gotta get off."

She hung up without saying goodbye. I sat on the
floor and twisted my hair into little bunches. The phone
rang, and I thought it was Devon calling back.

"Landry? What are you doing today?" Peyton asked.

"Nothing. Why?"

"My mom's on a cleaning kick, and I gotta get out of
here. Do you want to go to the mall? My dad will drive if
your mom can pick up," she said.

I threw on some jeans and didn't feel like doing my hair, so I just put it in a ponytail. Peyton came to the door wearing jeans and a ponytail, too.

"Where do you want to eat?" she asked. "Tacos?" I didn't feel like a taco, but I said it was fine. "Do you want pizza instead?" she asked, looking around the food court.

I shrugged. "If you do." The pizza smelled so good I was almost drooling.

"You pick," she said.

"Well, you said tacos."

"We could eat at different places," she said. "But I think I'll get a slice of pizza."

"Pizza sounds good," I said, following her in line.

"They have cheesecake," she said. I loved cheesecake, and we decided to get a piece. We inhaled the pizza, but we both felt stuffed halfway through the cheesecake.

"I'm going to burst," she said leaning her head back on the booth. "But remind me to buy some of those gummy fish things before we leave."

"How can you think about eating again?" I asked. "But I might get one of those suckers dipped in chocolate," I said. I wiped the cheesecake off my mouth, but I didn't bother to put on any more gloss.

We bought some candy, and she suggested we go to a furniture store. We sat in the sale section in the back where they shove all of the ugly chairs no one will buy. No one paid any attention to us back there in the corner and we ate our candy before going to the toy store. I was looking at the video games when she kicked a big beach ball down the aisle at me. We were laughing so hard people were staring.

"What do you wanna do next?" she asked.

"I don't know. What do you wanna do?" I asked. I wanted to go to the bookstore, but I wasn't going to bring it up in case she'd think I was a nerd or something.

"Do you want to go to the bookstore?" she asked.

We grabbed some books and magazines and went to sit on the ladybug seats in the children's section. There was only one little girl there, but she was too busy wiping her runny nose all over her sleeve to bother us.

"There's Yasmin," Peyton said.

I looked up, and there she was looking like a model with her dark hair in a sleek ponytail wearing jeans and an expensive looking angora sweater. We were basically wearing the same type of outfit, but Yasmin looked like a cover model and I looked like a kid going to playgroup. I started to go back to my magazine when I heard a familiar voice. Kyle came around the corner, and reached over to take Yasmin's hand. Oh crap.

"They got back together?" Peyton asked. "I didn't think Kyle would get a new girlfriend so fast after Arianna."

I nodded and hoped she couldn't see how upset I was, but my face gave me away. Peyton suggested we get something to drink. I was going to get a white chocolate mocha, but she ordered a hot chocolate with extra whipped cream and it sounded better. We sat in the café, and I told her I didn't want anyone to know I liked Kyle — especially Devon. She swore she wouldn't say anything.

"Kyle's a jerk. He keeps dating girls who are all friends. It's just weird," she said, licking whipped cream off her upper lip.

"He's too short for me anyway," I said.

"And he has girl hands," she said. She looked past me. "How does Yasmin move in those jeans? They cost a fortune, too."

I looked over to where Yasmin was leaning against the magazine rack. Her super straight ponytail made her look at least seventeen, while mine was more like a flattened broom. We sat looking at magazines for an hour.

Mom picked us up at six o'clock and took us out for dinner after Peyton had checked in with her parents. Mom even let us order dessert.

"Did you have fun?" Mom asked when we dropped Peyton off. I nodded. "She seems like such a nice girl," she said.

When I got home I checked my e-mail, and Tori had written me about how she was glad we were friends again. She said Ericka had said the *American Ingénue* thing had changed me, but Tori told her it hadn't. As I logged off, it felt weird to know Ericka had been saying stuff about me. I wondered what else she thought about me.

Twenty

~~~~~~

On Monday, Tori told me she ended up going to the movies with her dad after they dropped me off.

"My dad sat on something and had chocolate all over his pants when he walked out of the theater," Tori said. "What did you do?"

Devon was watching me, so I shrugged as I got on the bus.

"I ate the rest of the candy last night," Peyton said, moving her bag so I could sit next to her.

"Didn't you buy a pound of it?" I asked, and she made a face.

"Kinda, but we didn't have any good candy at my house. My dad only buys chocolate covered cherries, and those taste like cough syrup," she said.

"I don't like fruit in my candy," I said.

India agreed, but Devon pulled out her poetry journal and started writing. I leaned over the seat and asked what she was writing, but she made a noise and scrunched down in the seat. Devon got up as soon as the bus stopped, and I had to run to catch up with her. I slowed down when I got inside so Ms. Ashcroft wouldn't have a fit. I went to Devon's locker, but the first bell rang and she started walking to her class.

"Are you mad at me?" I asked.

"I gotta get to class," she said.

"Okay, see you at lunch," I said. The second bell rang, and everyone disappeared into the classrooms. I was left in the hall with my coat and backpack still on.

"Why are you wearing your jacket?" Thalia asked when I sat down. "Did you miss the bus again?"

"No, I'm cold," I said. It was hard to write with puffy sleeves, and I was getting hot.

Devon didn't wait for me at lunch, and I had to walk to the cafeteria by myself. I saw her sitting at Hana's table, but there weren't any empty chairs. Ashanti wasn't there either, so I sat at Ericka and Tori's table. My tater tots were soggy and usually there was at least one chicken nugget with real chicken in it, but today they were all fatty. Then my straw broke in my juice box, and I had to drink out of the little hole. The juice dribbled down my chin and got on my white sweater.

"Are you ready to go outside?" I looked up, and Devon was standing there.

I wasn't finished eating, but I was so happy she was talking to me I got up and dumped my tray in the garbage. Devon said Doug wanted us to go to the Cougars basketball game on Friday.

"We have to go," she said. "And my mom said she'd drive us."

I actually had an audition for a fashion show on Saturday morning, so I knew my mom wouldn't want me to stay out late. I called my mom at work as soon as I got home, and she just sighed.

"Landry, you've got to be responsible and look at this like a career," she said.

"I know, but we won't be out too late, and I'll go to bed as soon as I get home. Promise," I said. "Nobody's ever going to invite me to do stuff again if I always have to say no," I said.

Mom gave in, so I called Devon to tell her I could go.

On Friday, Devon and her mom came to pick me up for the game. Devon wore a jean skirt and had even put on eyeliner. It made her brown eyes look huge. The public school gym was much bigger than ours with tons of banners hanging from the ceiling. There were a lot of older kids sitting in groups, and I shrank back. Even Devon looked freaked out for a minute, but then she saw Doug and Jeremy sitting in the bleachers. She sat next to Doug, and I sat between her and Jeremy. She and Doug were talking, and she elbowed me and whispered to me to talk to Jeremy. I couldn't think of anything to say so I asked him about the cute blond guy who was playing.

"Oh, Vladi Yagudin," he said.

Okay, now what? "He's good," I said.

"Yeah."

"Doug and I are going to get some candy. Do you want anything?" Devon asked.

"I'll go with you." I got up so she couldn't leave without me.

Doug bought her a box of candy, and he talked to Devon like I wasn't even there. I just stared at the team pictures on the wall.

"I've got to go to the bathroom. Be right back," he said.

"Isn't he cute?" she asked.

"Because he has to go to the toilet?"

She sighed. "No, because he bought me candy."

"I guess," I said. She was staring over at Doug, who was standing at the end of the hall with his arm around another girl. Devon's shoulders tensed up.

"Let's go sit down. He knows where to find us," she said.

We went back to the top where Jeremy was talking to some guys he knew. He introduced us as "Devon and what's-your-name-again?" Devon started talking to one of the guys, but Jeremy kept interrupting them. It was pretty obvious Jeremy liked her. Nobody seemed to notice I was alive, so I just sat there eating Devon's candy and watching the game. The varsity players came out to warm up when the J.V. game ended. Doug hadn't come back yet, but Cristian came and sat in front of me.

"Hey guys," he said.

He started talking to me about school, and I ended up telling him I had a modeling audition tomorrow.

"You model?" he asked. I nodded. "Cool. I'll be able to say, 'I know her,' when you're famous. Hey, can I have some?" he asked pointing to my candy. I passed him the box as Doug came over to sit down.

"Did you get lost?" Devon asked him. She leaned toward the guy she was flirting with and put her hand on his arm. Doug reached for the candy box, and Cristian said they were mine. Doug stared at me like he forgot I was even there. I told Cristian Doug had bought the candy, but no one heard me since they were all watching Vladi, the basketball player, walking up to us. I had never seen anyone so hot in my life. He was tall with blond bangs, and he looked like an adult. Vladi sat sideways on the bleacher in front of me, and Doug passed him the candy box. Note to self: always have food. It gave guys a reason to talk to you. Vladi looked at me and nodded.

"What's up?" he asked.

"Hi," I said. Oh yeah, he'll fall in love with me now.

"This is Landry and Devon," Cristian said.

Vladi stretched out his legs as Doug started kissing his butt and telling him how great he played. Even Devon had gotten quiet. Vladi asked what school we went to, and Devon said we went to Hillcrest. Vladi looked at me.

"How old are you," he said.

"I'll be fourteen soon." Great, I must have looked twelve.

"Hey, Vladi, we're leaving."

I looked down, and some guy was waving at Vladi to join them.

Vladi winked at me as he walked down the stairs. Oh wow, an older guy had winked at me. I could die now.

I picked up a program off the floor on the way out. It was torn, but I could kind of make out Vladi's face underneath a dirty shoe print. All it said under his name was he was six-two. I felt like I was floating as we walked out of the gym.

"Do you guys want to go out for ice cream with us?" Doug asked.

The guy Devon had been flirting with had left without asking for her number, so Devon had started talking to Doug again. We walked up to the counter to order, and Jeremy said he'd pay for Devon. She ordered a caramel sundae, and the guy behind the counter asked what I wanted so Jeremy ended up paying for my ice cream cone, too. It was pretty obvious he wasn't thrilled about having to pay for me. I offered him some money, but I don't think he wanted to look cheap in front of Devon.

I slid into the booth next to Cristian, and he offered me one of the little brownies from his sundae. I didn't finish my ice cream because I couldn't figure out how to eat the cone without making a fool of myself. Doug had to meet up with his older sister for a ride, but Cristian and Jeremy walked us back to the school where Devon's dad was picking us up. Jeremy looked nervous and asked Devon if he could talk to her alone, so they went around the corner by the gym door.

"Gloves — you're smart," Cristian said as he shoved his hands deep into his pockets. Jeremy and Devon came back just as her dad drove up. Cristian asked me for my e-mail address and I figured he was just being nice, but I searched my coat pockets for a pen and paper. Nothing. Not even a gum wrapper.

"I'll remember it," he said. I told him my e-mail address, and he walked backward down the sidewalk reciting it. Devon asked her dad if I could come over. I knew I needed to get home, but I didn't want to make her mad by saying I had to get up early to model. So I went to her house and she waited until we were in her bedroom before she told me Jeremy had tried to kiss her.

"It was so gross. He was nervous, and his mouth was open," she said pulling a pillow to her face.

"What'd you do?" I asked.

"I backed away and told him I had a cold," she cracked up. "I didn't even know he liked me."

"Please, if looks could kill then the other guy you were talking to would have caught on fire," I said.

She screwed up her face.

"Can you believe Vladi Yagudin winked at me?" I asked.

"Who?"

"The cute basketball player," I said. How many guys did she know named Vladi?

"Oh, him. Did he?" she picked up a bottle of nail polish and started fixing her nails.

I started to tell her how Cristian had asked for my e-mail address when the phone rang. It was for her mom, but I decided not to tell her about Cristian because he probably wouldn't write to me anyway and then I'd look stupid. Devon and I made plans to go to the movies tomorrow night, and I checked my e-mail as soon as I got home. I noticed an address I didn't recognize.

To: Albright@alphamail.com
From: Cris996@alphamail.com
Re: Hey
Did you have fun tonight? I can't believe they lost. What are you doing tomorrow?
-Cristian

I hadn't even noticed who won the last game. I thought about waiting to write back like I had such a busy life, but then I decided to e-mail him in case he was still on-line and we could Instant Message each other. I told him Devon and I were going to the movies tomorrow and I waited online for ten minutes, but he didn't write me back.

Twenty-One

I loved sleeping in on Saturday mornings, but today was the fashion show audition so I had to get up and get ready. Plus, I wanted to check my e-mail to see if Cristian wrote me back. I got an e-mail from him saying he and Doug were thinking about going to a movie and wanted to know which one we were going to see. He made it sound like they might go see a movie, or play football, or go mountain climbing, but I wrote back and told him which movie we were planning to see and at what time, just in case they did go.

Mom drove me to my audition in Rockford for the fashion show. I knew it was just a little store, but Delilah said they did a show every year before Christmas. Mom wanted to stay, but I told her to wait for me some place else because I knew she'd make me nervous.

"What's the address again?" Mom asked.

"Two-twenty-four," I said. "Wait, it's a store for little kids?"

"Well, what did you think a store named Wee Fashions would be, genius?" she asked.

I actually hadn't seen the name of the store, and I thought Delilah meant *Oui Fashions*, like the French word for "yes." I guess I had just been excited to get the chance to be in a fashion show. Once I got inside there

were about twenty girls there, but they were all younger
— much younger. I was the oldest one there — and the
tallest. The storeowner, Kasia, gave us numbers and had
us each walk across the store and then gave us clothes to
try on. I was surprised anything in the store would fit
me, but there were a couple of ugly flowered dresses and
some weird teddy bear sweat suit outfit for me to wear.
One of the dresses had a big white collar, and the waist
was past my hips. They were the kind of dresses your
grandmother would buy you. And they all cost over two
hundred dollars.

Kasia made her decision and called out our numbers.
She called my number, but probably just because she
wanted at least one older kid in the show. She had us
line up, and the store workers gave us accessories for
each outfit. I was wearing four outfits, and they had to
mark down everything we were wearing and then put
the accessories in little bags attached to the hangers. I
was supposed to provide my own black shoes — flats, no
heels, and tights. I asked if I needed to bring my own
makeup, and Kasia stared at me.

"Just keep it natural," she said. "But no nail polish
or perfume. I don't want the scent on the clothes. There's
a ten percent discount on the clothes for the models."

I nodded, but there was no way I'd ever want any of
those clothes. Afterward, I went to find my mom at the
coffee shop across the street.

"I'm in the show," I said. "But everyone else is way
younger than me."

She seemed happy for me and asked if we were supposed to call Delilah. I shook my head. Kasia had already
said she'd contact our agents. I didn't realize how late it
was until Mom pointed out we had to get home to pick up
Devon for the five o'clock movie. I was starving since I
skipped lunch because I was nervous and didn't want to
get sick during the audition. Mom went through the
drive-thru and got me a burger and fries.

"Stop eating so fast, Landry," Mom said. "You're going to make yourself sick. Just call Devon and see if she can go to a later movie."

I called Devon and she checked the newspaper for the movie times. "There's one at seven-fifteen," she said.

"Okay, good. I'm just eating now since I missed lunch. Guess what? I'm going to be in this fashion show—"

"Landry? My dad has to use the phone. I'll see you about seven, 'kay?"

When my mom dropped us off at the movies, we saw Cristian and Doug leaving the theater. They walked over, and Cristian said I told him we were going to the five o'clock show. Oops.

"It sucks we missed seeing the guys because of your dumb audition," Devon said. I didn't say anything, but it wasn't like she even knew they were going to be at the theater. I hadn't even told her about Cris asking for my e-mail address. The movie was okay, but I was kind of mad at Devon for acting like it was my fault we didn't get to hang out with the guys. After the movie, we went to a café in the mall to get Italian sodas.

"When did you tell Cristian we were going to the movies?" she asked leaning over. Her hair smelled like Bouncy Hair shampoo.

"He asked me for my e-mail address last night, and I told him when I wrote back."

"You didn't tell me he asked you," she said. "Do you think he likes you?"

"Nah. They were probably gonna see a movie anyway," I said.

"Yeah, probably." She pulled out her straw and licked the end. "Let's walk around before we call my mom."

Even though Perry Mall was smaller than Harper Hills Mall, which was the one we usually went to, I liked the Perry one better. I mean, I had kinda been discovered here. Of course, it was also the reason Ericka and Tori had stopped talking to me. I asked Devon if we could stop at the bookstore, and she went to look at the journals. She showed me a butterfly journal just like the one she carries in her backpack. I was going to get the blue one, but she told me to get it in bright pink so we'd match. When I got home I called Peyton to tell her about Vladi and Cristian.

"Oh wow, I want to go to the next home game so I can see him," she said. "And make sure to tell your other boyfriend, Cristian, to meet us there."

"Yeah, I wish. I was so nervous yesterday. Going to a public school game was big, but having Vladi talk to me was like... wow," I said. "You're going to think I'm a loser, but I saved the candy box he touched."

"So not stupid. I saved a cigarette butt the bass player from Playing Dead dropped outside an airport until my mom made me throw it out," she said.

"You saw Adonis at the airport? I used to like him, but then he married a swimsuit model," I said.

"I stopped liking him, too, but I think he and Freesia split up," she said. "You know, his real name is Bert Ferdinand."

My mom came into the kitchen later and pointed to her watch. I looked at the clock above the stove and was surprised it had gotten so late. We had been on the phone for almost two hours. I went to write in my new journal and used my stuffed mouse as a pillow. I tried to write in my best handwriting, but I wrote faster when I started to write about getting chosen for the fashion show and about Vladi and Cristian and it looked sloppy.

I almost missed the bus on Monday. Mrs. Jackson had started to drive off, but she stopped when she saw me running like a lunatic. I got on panting and sat next to Devon.

"Did you bring your journal?" she asked, holding hers up.

I had written personal stuff in it I didn't want her to see, so I said I left it at home. I had also left my best friend bracelet at home, and she noticed. Her window was open a crack, and she rolled her bracelet off her wrist and held it up to the opening.

"I might as well throw mine out since it means nothing to you," she said. "This is the first time I've ever taken it off."

I wanted to ask if she wore it to bed and in the shower and didn't it get all gross? Instead, I said I was sorry and I'd start wearing mine all the time, too. I made up some stupid story about taking it off to clean my room so it wouldn't get ruined.

"I was in a hurry today — I mean, look at my hair," I said.

"Yeah, I guess. Here, borrow my brush," she said. I thought it was cool she'd share her brush with me because Ericka never let anybody borrow hers.

"Landry, your hair looks fine," Peyton said.

My hair got even flatter when I brushed it and I didn't have a rubber band, but Peyton took the clip out of her hair for me. India started brushing her hair with Devon's brush next, and her hair was like silk. It almost reached the back of her pants. It was a perfect honey color and looked amazing with her aqua eyes. She, Devon, and Peyton always looked so good without even trying, and I felt like such a blob next to them. Peyton had amazing dark red hair and matching reddish-brown eyes, but she always managed to make me feel good about myself, even if I was having an ugly day.

Later, when we were heading to our lockers, I saw Stuart walk up behind Thalia and trip her. Her bag was open and stuff went flying all over the hall. He moved away from her, and it looked like she had tripped over her own feet. Devon rolled her eyes.

"What a klutz," she said.

India sidestepped Thalia's math book, and Peyton bent down to pull out some papers stuck under Devon's foot.

"Devon, watch it. You almost ripped her homework," Peyton said. Thalia was scrambling to grab her pens and pencils as they rolled down the hall. Kyle picked up a math test and announced she had gotten a sixty-eight percent on it. He held it up like he was going to play keep-away with it but then handed it to her.

"Loser," Thalia said as she pulled the paper away from him.

I knew Thalia had said it because it was what Arianna called him right before they broke up. I handed Thalia the stuff I picked up, and Kyle looked at me.

"Landry, did you get the math homework done? Can I borrow it?" he asked, flashing me a smile.

I usually let him copy a problem or two, but I lied and said I didn't finish it. Let Yasmin do his homework for him. Thalia went on about what a jerk Kyle was as we walked to class.

"No wonder Arianna dumped his butt. He's so immature and short," she said. "Like he did any better on the test."

"He's got girl hands, too," I said. She smirked as Ms. Ashcroft walked in. Thalia passed me a note saying she hoped Yasmin would break up with him. I wrote back I didn't care. Why did guys always go for the Yasmins and Ariannas of the world? I mean, just because they were cute, super athletic, got good grades in math, had perfect hair and—

"Landry?" asked Ms. Ashcroft.

Thalia elbowed me. "Number fifteen," she whispered. Oops, I didn't have an answer down.

"Cumbersome," Thalia said under her breath.

I repeated it and shot her a grateful look. Stupid Kyle. We had computer class this week, and Ashanti, Thalia, and I sat at the same computer station. We were supposed to do typing drills where we type sentences over and over until the stopwatch goes off to see how many words we can type in a minute. We're supposed to type with a piece of paper over our hands so we can't look at the keyboard, but I sit far enough in the back so I can peek.

"Landry, Tad's staring at you," Thalia said. "He was looking at you in homeroom, but I thought it was because you zoned out."

"Maybe he likes you," Ashanti said. "Too bad you already have a man."

At first, I thought she was making fun of me for liking Kyle, but then I realized she was talking about Cristian.

"So what do you wanna do for your birthday?" Ashanti asked.

"Not sure yet."

I hadn't even thought about it since Mom had been busy picking out a new carpet for the basement for the last week.

Mom was in a bad mood when I got home because the carpet guys had come late and she had taken time off from work to be there for them.

When I got home, I went downstairs and the basement had an overpowering new carpet smell. It seemed a lot bluer than the little square mom had showed me, but it looked okay. I asked my mom what we were going to do for my birthday.

"Do you want to go out to dinner with some of your friends?" she asked.

"Okay, so Devon, Peyton, India, Ashanti, Thalia, Tori, and Ericka," I said.

"It might be cheaper to have them come over for pizza and cake," she said.

"A sleepover?" I said.

"Well…I guess," she sighed. I said we could sleep in the basement, but she said it was too cold, but we could use the living room. I called Devon first. Pretty soon

Devon, Peyton, Ashanti, Thalia, Ericka, and India were all coming, but Tori couldn't make it. She said she had to stay home and watch her little cousins, but we could get together next weekend at her house. Ashanti was surprised Tori wasn't coming.

"Couldn't her brother watch them or something? It's your fourteenth birthday and she's, like, one of your best friends," she said.

"I dunno."

"Well, what do you want for your birthday?"

"I don't know. Colin to ask me out?" I said.

"What if he has plans?"

"He'd change 'em for me."

Dad called and said he was going to take the train in for my birthday. I wanted to ask if he had found any jobs here yet, but he was busy and got off the phone pretty quick. Mom wanted to know what I wanted for my birthday. The only thing I could think of was the new TV Dad wanted. I figured it was too expensive and she raised her eyebrows, but she didn't say no right away.

It was so hard to pay attention in class that week. All I could think about was my party and Dad coming over. I was in my own world and even Yasmin hanging all over Kyle in the hall couldn't upset me. Well, as much anyway. While I was counting down to my party, Arianna had broken up with Stuart twice and Cristian had written me once. Devon said I should tell him my birthday was on Saturday, but I didn't want to act like I wanted him to buy me something. His e-mails seemed more like a friend thing, so I forwarded it to Ashanti and she called me after she read them.

"Okay, it seems like he doesn't want to say too much... maybe he wants to see how you feel first," she said.

"I knew it. He just wants to be friends," I said. I was disappointed, but a little relieved.

"Maybe not. He does say maybe he'll see you at another game. And Landry, the fact he wrote you at all is pretty good. Halle used to e-mail Stuart all the time, and he didn't write back too often," she said.

"How often does Jay write you?" I asked.

"Well, I read in this book of my mom's you shouldn't write the guy right back. You sort of make him hang for a while, and he should e-mail you three times more than you e-mail him," she said.

"Oh wow. Do you wait before you write back?" I asked.

She said she waited a little bit, but not too long.

"Maggie e-mails guys right back and they like it, but Yasmin makes 'em wait and they like her, too, so I don't know," she said. "Do you like Cristian?"

I made her promise not to make fun of me and told her I was a little freaked out by him.

"He's cute... maybe too cute. I dunno. I like him, but I don't know what to say to him. He's nice, but he makes my stomach hurt," I said.

"What do you mean?" she asked.

"Sometimes I get so nervous it feels like I'm going to throw up. You know, like butterflies and stuff. Plus, I still have a huge crush on the basketball player. I know there's no way anything could ever happen with him, but... he's so hot," I said.

"He did look cute in the program you showed me," she said. "You're not far apart age-wise. And maybe he'll flunk a grade, but would you want him if he was held back?"

"I wouldn't care if he couldn't count. All he has to do is sit there and look cute," I said.

"My mom says the same thing about my Bradley. Did you watch today's show?" she asked.

"Yeah, I bet you died when he walked out of the shower," I said.

"Best. Episode. Ever."

Twenty-Two

Devon asked me to go to the away game on Friday. Her dad was willing to drive India, Peyton, and me to Bentley High, but my mother said she didn't want me to go out the night before the fashion show.

"Mom, it's just a stupid kids' fashion show. Nobody's going to be there. The store is, like, the size of our living room," I said.

"No. End of discussion."

I told Devon I couldn't go, and she wasn't happy. "Well, can you go shopping with India and me tomorrow?"

"What time? The show starts at noon," I said.

She said they were leaving at noon. She was starting to sound bored, so I said maybe I could meet her at the mall after the fashion show. I told her to leave her cell phone on, and I'd call her when I was done.

"If my phone has any battery left," she said. I thought it was weird to say since she could just charge her phone overnight. I told her I'd probably be done by two o'clock.

"Call me, I guess. *If* we're still there."

Devon always stayed at the mall forever, but all of a sudden, now she wants to shop for just two hours?

I got up early on Saturday morning. I checked my e-mail before I got in the shower, but nobody had bothered to e-mail me about the game. I washed my hair and put on my makeup while it air dried. Delilah had told me to hold off on using heated hair appliances since they can wreck your hair. I put on some navy shadow liner around my eyes like I had seen in *Young and Fun* and used some of my mom's bronzing powder. I thought I looked hot, but when I got to the show, Kasia, the owner, asked me to wipe off some of the eye makeup.

We had to change in the backroom, and I felt weird being the only girl there who wore a bra. One of the assistants came over to help me with my outfit. I had to wear the ugliest dress first, but it wasn't like some major talent scout was sitting in the Wee Fashions audience. I felt more confident since, because they were all kids, for once I was the hottest girl there. I didn't even worry about tripping because there were only thirty people there, so what did it matter if I fell? It wasn't like I was going to get discovered today anyway. It was mostly for experience and for my modeling resume. My hair got staticky after I pulled the sweatshirt on for the last outfit, so one of the assistants ran over and twisted my hair up in a bun. It looked cute, so I left it up after the show. Kasia came back afterward and thanked us all for being in the show.

"You were all wonderful," she said. "Help yourself to some refreshments after you change."

I wanted to leave right away to meet Devon and India at the mall, but mom said I couldn't be rude and she made me stay. I drank some watered down fruit punch and ate a lemon bar while my mom talked to some of the parents. I knew it would take a half hour to get from here to the mall, but my mom said it would be "unprofessional" to just take off when the show was over. I tried talking to one of the ten-year-old models and got depressed after finding out she had been working since she was six and had already done a ton of commercials. All the girls had been working way longer than I had. Mom said we could go, but when I called Devon her phone wasn't on. I left a message for her to call me back.

"What do you want to do?" Mom asked.

I told her to take me to the mall, and maybe I could find them.

"You'll never—"

"I gotta go. Devon will get mad if I don't show up."

Mom took me to the mall, and I went to all the stores I thought she could possibly be in. It wasn't a huge mall, but it felt enormous as I ran around trying to find them. I tried calling Devon again, but there was no answer, so we went home.

Devon called me fifteen minutes later and said she and India had left the mall early to get their hair done together.

"We both just got an inch taken off, but they straightened my hair and did it in these cool loose waves. It looks hot," she said.

I had never gone to get my hair done with one of my friends before. It seemed like a best friend thing to do, and I felt incredibly left out. She asked how my fashion show went, and we talked for a while. She didn't seem mad I hadn't met her, but she seemed... different somehow. I tried not to worry about it as we talked about my upcoming birthday party.

On Friday, everyone came over for the party. Ashanti had brought a magazine and wanted us to do a quiz in it on how well you knew your friend. Since it was my birthday, she had me fill out the answers and they all had to guess. I thought Devon would know me the best, but she got the second lowest score and India got the lowest. Peyton and Ashanti had perfect scores, and Ericka only had one wrong. Devon sat with her arms folded.

I opened my presents after we finished dessert. Thalia had tied a chocolate rose to her gift bag and inside was a designer makeup bag with a picture of New York City on it. It came with a set of makeup brushes inside, and she had bought a Little Rose lip gloss to put inside the bag. It was perfect to take on my modeling jobs. India gave me a University of Michigan sweatshirt, but it had the new clothes smell, which always gave me a headache.

Ericka gave me a bunch of hair things, and Peyton gave me a book on writing and a journal. I wanted to save Devon's present for last, so I opened Ashanti's gift next. Ashanti had made my card out of a collage of Colin pictures, and she gave me a blue shiny purse, which matched her pink one, but was in my favorite color. She told me to look inside and there was a DVD of *A Moment to Die*, which was an independent film the actor who played Colin had done a year ago. I thought it was weird she didn't remember our machine wasn't working, but then she looked at my mom.

"Whoops," Ashanti covered her mouth with her hand.

Mom was laughing. "I told Ashanti I got a new one to replace the broken one when she called to find out what you wanted for your birthday. You're going to have to act surprised in front of Dad when you open it and see the new TV."

I was shocked my mom had actually bought it. Did this mean my dad would be moving in soon? I couldn't ask her then, so I went back to opening gifts. I thought Devon's present would be some cool best friend thing, but it was a plain pink scrapbook. I told her I loved it and flipped through the blank pages. We all decided to spread out our sleeping bags and have more cake, but India said she felt sick from all the soda she drank. She sprawled out on the couch, and I hoped she wouldn't puke on it.

Peyton asked if she could look through my photo album. Thalia leaned over and said my cousin Bryan was hot.

"Devon, are you going to leave my dad for him?" Peyton asked. Devon threw my stuffed mouse at her, but Peyton caught him before he hit the floor. I stuck my mouse in the closet and then pointed out the pictures of Brad's sister, Lucy. I told them how my grandma thought they were both perfect.

"Look on the bright side, maybe your cousins hate your guts because they hear about what a brilliant writer and model you are," Thalia said. We all cracked up.

Devon wanted to call Doug and Cristian, but I felt stupid calling them. Ashanti could tell I didn't want to call them and suggested we play truth or dare instead.

"Truth or dare's for kids," Devon said.

Ashanti didn't get upset, but you could tell she wasn't happy. I tried to change the subject and asked Peyton to French braid my hair. India kept saying her stomach hurt, and Devon told her to move her sleeping bag next to hers when we went back into the living room.

"Let's watch videos," Ashanti said.

Devon rolled her eyes, but I said it sounded okay. Devon and India moved behind me, and I started to feel uncomfortable because they were sitting so far away from the rest of us. My favorite video, "Kick Me When I'm Down," came on, but I kept wondering if India and Devon were whispering stuff about me. Then Devon said she and India were going to sleep in my room if we were just going to watch videos all night. Ashanti sighed, and I suggested we see what else was on because I didn't want Devon to get mad at me. We found a horror movie about a toxic waste spill in a cemetery, and the chemicals made dead people come back to life. It was almost too stupid to be scary — almost.

"Landry, I've got to go to the bathroom super bad. Will you come with me?" Ericka asked.

"You know where it is," Devon said.

"Uh, zombies," Ericka said.

"They don't exist," India said rolling her eyes.

"Fine, I'll just go right here on the floor," Ericka said. I had to go to the bathroom anyway and had been waiting for someone else to go first. Ashanti and Peyton went with us, and we took turns going while the rest of us stood outside the door. Ashanti made us talk to her through the door so she'd know we were still there. Devon came over and said we should hide in the basement to freak her out, but I said I didn't want to leave Ashanti by herself. Devon gave me a funny look so I said I was afraid to go in the basement at night.

"You guys, I don't hear talking," Ashanti said through the door. Peyton whispered we were all there, and she better hurry up if she didn't want a flood.

We went back to the movie, and all of the girls fell asleep except for Peyton and me. We decided to watch another movie to calm us down and tried to ignore the fact there was a cemetery not too far from my house. Peyton said the cemetery around the corner was super old so even if those people did come alive, they probably wouldn't be able to run after us like the ones in the movie. Then we started to picture what they might look like and freaked ourselves out. She stopped talking after a while, and I couldn't tell if she was asleep or not so I switched the TV off.

I woke up around four in the morning, and Devon was sleeping with her mouth open. My sleeping bag was twisted around, and it was uncomfortable lying on the rough zipper. I got up to straighten it out, and Peyton looked up. I moved my sleeping bag sideways so it was next to hers.

"Happy birthday," she whispered. "Do you feel any different?"

I shook my head, and she flipped over on her back. "I know. I never do either on my birthdays," she said.

We went back to sleep, and Mom had donuts for us when we woke up. It was kind of strange seeing what everybody looked like first thing in the morning. Thalia's dark hair was sticking out of her braid, and Ericka's bushy hair was smashed flat on one side. Ashanti's mom came after breakfast and offered to drop Devon off since she lives down the street, but Devon told her she was going to stay.

After everyone had left, Devon and I poured bowls of cereal and watched cartoons until Mom began vacuuming around us. Devon took the hint and said she'd walk home.

"We should have a sleepover at my house sometime," she said as we walked down the driveway. "Maybe next weekend."

I thought I had told her I was doing something with Tori next weekend, but maybe she forgot. I didn't want to bring it up, so I told her I didn't think I could.

"Why not—"

"Hey, I gotta get back to clean up for my dad," I said.

"Okay. Well, happy birthday. Have fun with your dad." She gave me a hug, and I thanked her for her present. "Was it your favorite?" she asked.

She was smiling so I wasn't sure if she was joking or not. I didn't want to say "yes" and have the other girls find out and hurt somebody's feelings. I just laughed and handed her the sleeping bag. Mom was vacuuming potato chips off the living room floor when I walked in.

"You got some cute stuff," she said. "I was looking through the writing book Peyton gave you. I've never seen one written for kids — sorry, teens, before." She stopped to pull a piece of wrapping paper out of the vacuum hose.

"And Ashanti's purse was even cuter than she described on the phone... and the makeup stuff." She unplugged the vacuum. "Your friends know what you like."

"The scrapbook was nice, huh?"

"Did you want one?" she asked.

I didn't, but I said Devon and I would work on it together. "Wasn't it cute?"

"Yeah." She wiped her forehead.

"Too bad Tori couldn't come," I said.

"I didn't get why she couldn't come," she said.

I shrugged. I thought it was weird she didn't ask her parents if she could come over later. I mean, she didn't have to watch her cousins overnight.

"Well, she's gonna have me spend the night next weekend," I said.

"Can you plug the vacuum back in?" she asked. "There's something stuck under the couch."

"I'm just glad India didn't get sick on the couch last night," I said.

"India didn't feel good? Strange. She ate more do-nuts for breakfast than anybody," she said.

"I guess she did. Well, she should feel better because Devon sure kissed her butt enough," I said. "Hey, do you like my hair? Peyton did it."

"Cute. You better get dressed. Dad will be here soon."

I went back to my room and threw on my jeans. I put on the sweatshirt India had given me and smoothed the little hairs popping out of my braid. I heard Dad pull up and ran to give me a big hug as soon as he walked through the door.

"Happy birthday," he said.

"I wanna show you what I got for my birthday." He followed me to my room where I had spread my gifts out on my dresser.

"Hey, a book on writing. Have you written any more stories?" he asked.

"No. Devon thought I should try to write poetry, but I wasn't good at it."

"I liked your short story," he said.

"Ashanti wants me to write a story with her and this soap opera guy she likes and one with me and Colin in it." I pointed to the card she made me.

"You still like this clown?" Dad asked. "Well, at least he's not all pierced and tattooed."

"Actually he has two tattoos," I said. "There's one of the sun on his shoulder and something in Latin on his lower back. It says, 'You are what you believe' or something."

"Uh-huh. You don't have any tattoos I should know about, do you?" he asked.

I rolled my eyes, but I had this fantasy of me marrying Colin and we'd both get each other's names tattooed on our inner wrists. I read Talisa Milan's boyfriend had her name on his wrist.

"Of course, I'm not allowed to get a tattoo while I'm under contract with the modeling agency, but I might get one when I'm done modeling," I said.

"This from a girl who wouldn't even get a flu shot because she doesn't like needles," he said.

"I'm sure they'll have a new way to do tattoos by then," I said.

I asked if he'd ever get a tattoo of Mom's name. He pretended to think about it and stuck his head out the door.

"Hon? Do you want me to get your name tattooed on my arm?" he asked.

"Please, you cry over a paper cut," she said.

"Lucy has one," Dad said. "But don't tell Grandma."

Perfect Lucy had a tattoo? He said Uncle Martin found out she had gotten one on her lower back, and he made my dad check her out to make sure she didn't get hepatitis from it.

"What does it look like?" I asked. I was hoping it was some guy's name or something else Grandma would freak out over.

"A flower design," he said.

I asked if he'd care if I got one when I was older, and he said I had to wait until he was dead. Mom came in and said I couldn't even get one after she was dead. Dad slipped his arm around her waist and said I should open my presents. I would have asked by now, but I didn't care as much since I already knew what I was getting. I could tell which one was the DVD player, and I opened it first. I pretended to be surprised, and I think Dad bought it. Mom had the TV set up in the basement already. They also got me some new movies. I opened Grandma's gift next, which was a gift certificate for a bookstore. I had gotten some cards in the mail from my aunts and uncles, but there was no money in the envelopes. I know because I shook them out just in case. Cheap-os.

Dad set up the DVD player, and we finished up my birthday cake and watched the *A Moment to Die* DVD. Dad said the movie would sound better when we got the sound system he wanted.

"It's coming out of your paycheck, buddy boy," she said.

Dad left on Sunday afternoon. I wouldn't get to see him again until Mom and I went to Chicago for Christmas. He said he'd put up a tree in his apartment because last year he forgot to get one and it was a big letdown opening presents around the heating vent.

On Monday, Devon asked me to spend the night at her house this weekend. I told her I had already promised Tori I would sleep over, and she got an attitude.

"You said you would when you walked me home," she said.

"I told you I didn't think I could," I said.

"So Tori's your best friend again?"

"Devon, I already promised her, but maybe—"

"She dumped your butt when you got picked for the modeling thing, and she didn't even come to your party," she said as she walked away.

Twenty-Three

On Thursday, I found out Devon had asked India to spend the night instead. I was hurt and wanted to tell Tori I couldn't sleep over, but I didn't want her to get mad at me again, so I tried to act like it didn't bother me. I couldn't even get excited about going over to Tori's. I used to love spending the night at her house. I always felt comfortable there because her parents left us alone. Now all I could think about was if Devon would be speaking to me on Monday and if she and India would be best friends when the weekend was over.

On Friday, Devon walked down to the cafeteria without me. She didn't ignore me when I sat down, but she spent the whole lunch hour joking around with Hana. We didn't even go outside to walk around because they were having so much fun together. Later, when I was at my locker, Devon yelled to India to hurry up because her mom was waiting for them. I felt like crap until Hana came over and gave me a birthday card with a movie gift card in it.

"I forgot to give this to you at lunch," she said. "Sorry I missed your party, but maybe we could get together next weekend or something."

Tori was excited about having me over, and her dad dropped us off to pick out movies while he went to get the pizza. We were looking at the new releases when I heard Devon's laugh. She and India were in the comedy section with their heads bent down together. I should have known better than to go to the movie store around the corner. Tori looked over and asked if we were fighting. I shook my head and hoped she couldn't see how sick I felt. I tried to lead Tori over to the horror movie section, but she walked over to the action side and bumped into India.

"Hey," India said. "What are you guys renting?"

Devon came over and said they had to go and told us to "have fun." They walked up to the counter with their arms linked.

We went back to Tori's house, and she and her mom had baked brownies for my birthday. They were good and even Matthew ate a brownie with us. He got up from the table to get a glass of soy milk.

"Landry, you want some?" he asked holding up the carton.

I hated soy milk, but I was not about to turn him down. We went into the living room to watch the movie, and Tori gave me my presents. I got a long sleeved pink T-shirt with glittery strawberries on it and a book called *Murder at the Chocolate Shop* because we had been into mysteries last summer.

"Is Devon mad at you because you're spending the night here?" she asked.

I shrugged. "She just wanted me to come over this weekend."

"It's like you can't have any other friends," she said. "Ericka said she got all possessive of you at your party."

I said it was no big deal and we went back to watching the movie. It was sort of like old times except I kept wondering what Devon and India were doing and if she was having more fun with India. After all, Devon had been right. Tori had dumped my butt when Ericka got mad at me.

When I got home the next morning, Mom told me Devon had called twice. I called her back, and she said she and India were meeting Peyton at the movies. I was super tired, but I said I'd go. Mom told me to ask if I could get a ride with them since Devon lived up the street. I felt stupid asking since she didn't offer, but Devon said they could pick me up. Devon and India came up to the door together, and India was wearing Devon's red sweater and her favorite jeans. I had to sit in the front with Mrs. Abrams because the two of them were in the back. Devon reached over the seat to turn up the radio.

"I love this song," she said as she and India sang along.

Mrs. Abrams dropped us off, and India jokingly said, "Thanks, Mom" to her. I tried to smile as I followed them into the theater. Peyton was already there, and I ended up sitting on the end next to Devon. It wouldn't have been so bad if Devon hadn't kept turning away from me to talk to India. Just as the previews started, these two guys starting throwing popcorn at Devon. She pretended to be annoyed, but you could tell she liked it.

"Let's move to the top row," India said. We got up, and Peyton decided to get some popcorn. I went with her, and she asked me if I wanted to share popcorn so we could buy some candy, too. I wasn't hungry, in fact my stomach hurt, but I would have to sit next to her if we shared popcorn, so I agreed. We bought a bag of candy, a large bucket of popcorn, and two sodas. I offered India and Devon some candy, but they never ate when boys were around. Peyton leaned back and put her feet up on the seat in front of her. She stuck the popcorn between us and gave me some napkins.

"I can't watch a movie without snacks," she said as the previews started. I nodded and started to relax.

After the movie, we stood outside waiting for Peyton's dad to pick her up. Devon hadn't called her mom yet because she and India were still talking to the guys who had been throwing popcorn at her. Mr. Urich pulled up, and Peyton looked over at India and Devon and asked if I wanted to come over. I didn't want to stand around waiting for them, so I nodded and ran over to tell Devon.

"You're going home with her?" she asked.

"I'm tired so her dad's gonna drop me off," I said.

"Oh, okay. Call me," she said.

We got to Peyton's house and her mom was curled up on the couch with their dog, Truffles.

"Hi Landry. How was the movie?" she asked. Her mom was always so sweet.

We went up to Peyton's bedroom, which had lots of white furniture and a furry white rug you could sink your feet into. I took off my shoes and dug my toes into the carpet. She had tons of photos up on her memo board, and I noticed she had put my school picture up there, too.

"Do you think your mom would let you spend the night?" she asked.

I didn't know if mom would let me sleep over at someone's house two nights in a row, but her parents said it would be okay, so I called home.

"You're gonna feel awful tomorrow. You couldn't have slept much at Tori's," Mom said.

"Puh-lease?"

"Do you have a lot of homework, or can you take a nap tomorrow afternoon?" she asked.

"Finished my math in class," I said. Like I ever took a nap when I stayed up late.

"Do you want me to bring your stuff over?" she said sighing.

I started to say she could just bring the overnight bag I took to Tori's, but Mrs. Urich said I could borrow some of Peyton's sweats and she had an extra toothbrush, too.

"No need to put your mom out," she said.

We went back to Peyton's room, and she took her stuffed animals off her daybed so I could sleep on it. I don't mind sleeping on the floor when I stay overnight at someone's house, but it was nice to have a soft mattress to sleep on. We started talking, and she told me she had a crush on Stuart, but swore me to secrecy.

"I never tell anyone who I like. And I don't want India to know because she liked him first and she freaked out when I said he was cute the other day. It was like she owned him or something," she said. "Anyway, he's been kind of a jerk lately."

My best friend bracelet was bothering me so I took it off. She asked if she could see it.

"Devon, India, and I used to have best friend earrings, and it was so annoying. Devon would get mad at one of us and say she was going to throw hers away or she lost it," she said.

I didn't know Devon had any best friend jewelry with India and Peyton. It made me feel weird even though I knew they had been best friends before I came along. I asked her what happened to the earring.

"It fell off in my aunt's pool, but I didn't care. They both got, like, super possessive about it. It was a huge thing if one of us forgot to wear it. India kept getting mad at me for not wearing it and then she'd hold a grudge, like, forever," she said.

We started talking about our families, and I told her I was worried about my parents separating. Ashanti knew it bothered me Dad was still living back in Chicago, but we had never talked about it too much. I told Peyton about the fight I overheard them having, and I was afraid they might get divorced. She didn't say anything, and I was afraid she fell asleep or she felt weird since I had told her something so personal.

Then she propped herself up on her elbow. "It sounds like they're trying to work things out. Have you talked to your mom about it?"

I was surprised she sounded interested at all. I said my mom got weird on me when I tried to bring it up and how I started to cry when I talked to my dad about it.

"I can't believe I'm telling you all of this. You must be so bored," I said.

"No. I wanna help. You'd help me if I had a problem," she said.

She told me to talk to my mom when we were in the car so she couldn't walk away or say she was too busy. I had never talked to any of my other friends about my parents because I didn't want them to know I *had* any problems. I know lots of people's parents get divorced, but I felt like it would make me look weird or something, so I just pretended everything was okay with us living apart. Peyton and I ended up talking until three in the morning.

Twenty-Four

On Monday, I noticed Devon didn't have her bracelet on. I didn't say anything and thought about taking mine off, but I didn't want her to get mad. I asked her about the boys outside the movie theater. She said they had called her house at night, and she and India talked to them until midnight. I wondered if India had slept over two nights in a row, but she didn't ask me what I did at night, so I kept my mouth shut. I asked Peyton not to say anything about me spending the night at her house.

"Devon gets kind of weird about stuff sometimes," I said, and she nodded.

I waited for Devon at lunchtime, and she came over with Hana. She told Hana about the guys at the movies while we stood in line. I got stuck with the broccoli soup, but it didn't matter because my stomach kind of hurt anyway. She and Hana walked to our usual table, but Ashanti called me over. Devon barely noticed when I walked over to Ashanti's table.

"What's wrong?" Ashanti asked. I looked over at Halle and Maggie who were busy looking a magazine. I shrugged, and Ashanti told me to sit down. I started to say I had to sit with Devon, but I looked up and realized Devon hadn't saved me a seat. Ashanti looked at my soup and gave me half of her ham sandwich and moved her potato chip bag toward me. I didn't feel like talking, but she un-

201

derstood. Devon got up to go outside, and she raised her eyebrows at me and tilted her head toward the door for me to get up and join her. It reminded me of the look Peyton's mom gave Truffles when she wanted her to go to the bathroom outside. I held up a chip to show her I was still eating, and she shrugged and left without me. Ashanti walked me back to class and asked if I wanted to come over to watch Brad and Colin after school.

I wasn't sure where to sit when I got on the bus. Devon would think I was ignoring her if I sat with Ashanti, but Ashanti might get weird on me if I sat with Devon. I waited until the last minute to get on the bus, and by then, they were both sitting with other people. I ended up having to sit behind the bus driver. I probably would have tossed myself out the window if Ashanti hadn't asked me to come over. Of course, I could never get the bus windows to slide down so I was probably safe.

Ashanti helped me with my math homework after we watched *As the Days Roll On*. I told her my dad would pay her since he had been bugging me to get a tutor, but she said it was no big deal.

"Unless your dad wants to pay me to be friends with you," she said laughing. She asked me what was going on with Devon, and I lied and said everything was fine.

"Remember how she and India used to fight all the time last year?" she asked.

"I guess," I said.

"I could have hit her at your party. I mean, come on, 'If you guys are gonna watch TV all night then we're gonna sleep in the other room,'" Ashanti said in a whiny voice. "It's like, if I don't get my way, I'm gonna take my ball and go home."

I didn't say anything.

"I know you're friends with her, but she bugs me sometimes," she said.

Ashanti showed me the new sweaters her mom had bought her for school. School clothes are almost always boring because we have a dress code, but these sweaters were soft and pretty. She had a light blue one, and it was fuzzy and beautiful. I held it in front of me, and she said it looked good.

"Light colors don't look good on me." I put it back on the bed, but she held it again.

"No, it looks pretty with your hair and eyes," she said. "See?"

I looked in the mirror, and the color did make my blue eyes stand out. I used to have a baby blue sweater my grandma had bought me, but Ericka told me I looked pale in it, so I never wore it again even though Mom said Grandma had spent a lot of money on it. I wasn't even sure where it was anymore.

"You can borrow it if you want," she said.

"You should wear it first," I said.

She shook her head. "Don't worry about it. I was planning on wearing the white one tomorrow. Just don't order the spaghetti."

"I'll get a sloppy joe instead," I said, and she stuck her tongue out. "My hair looks so blah today," I said.

"It looks fine. I have matching hair for it," she said digging through her drawer. "Want me to put it in your hair?"

I sat on her bed, and she kneeled behind me and pulled the top section of my hair back, while leaving the rest down. It looked cute the way she had styled it, but I wanted my hair to look like hers — with the top part of her hair pulled back.

When I went home, Mom thought my hair looked cute.

"Just like Ashanti's," she said.

I went to my room and put the sweater in front of me. I liked the way my hair looked, but the barrette kept sliding down because my hair wasn't as thick as Ashanti's. I put it back the way Ashanti had done it the first time, and it did look better.

Twenty-Five

The next day I got up early to do my hair. I put the bracelet in my pocket so I could decide if I wanted to wear it after I saw Devon's arm. Tori said I looked cute at the bus stop. I told her I was wearing Ashanti's sweater. She said I should try pulling my hair up like Ashanti's, but I said it wouldn't hold.

Devon didn't say much. She just talked about how cold it was, and she had her hands pulled inside her sleeves so I couldn't see her wrists. Ashanti wasn't on the bus, so I sat with Peyton.

"Oh, I love your sweater. The color looks so good on you," Peyton said.

"It's Ashanti's."

"Super cute," Peyton said.

Thalia told me I looked good in homeroom, and Kyle rubbed my shoulders in math class and said, "Fuzzy."

Thankfully Yasmin wasn't in our class or she would have had me killed. Ashanti looked gorgeous in the white turtleneck sweater. It set off her dark hair and eyes and made her look like she should be at some rich ski resort or something. Even Jay told her she looked "hot." On the way to class Peyton passed me a note.

Landry-
Do you have to work, or can you do something on Friday? We could go to the J.V. game and see Vladi or hang out at my house. I won't say anything to Devon if you don't want me to.
Got-to-go, Peyton

At lunch, Devon said we should all go to the game on Friday. I thought Peyton had meant for just the two of us to do something because she had written she wouldn't say anything to Devon. I wasn't sure what was going on, but I told Peyton how Devon wanted us to go to the game.

"Oh, you told her?" she asked.

"No, I thought you did," I said.

She shook her head. "No, but if you wanna go in a group..."

India walked in so we changed the subject and started talking about the assignment on the board. Peyton and I didn't bring up the plans for Friday night, but on the ride home, Devon said her mom could drive us to the game. I asked Mom if I could go to the game, but she wanted to know who I was going with.

"Devon, India, and Peyton," I said. "Devon said her mom could drop us off."

Mom thought for a moment. "I can take you guys and pick you up. I'll let you go to the J.V. game, but I don't like the idea of you guys staying there later with the older kids," she said.

"But everybody goes to the varsity game," I said.

"I get nervous with you guys going over to the public high school. Besides, Devon is a little more, um, advanced than you," she said.

"What do you mean?"

"She's... more into boys," she said.

"I'm into boys," I said.

She sighed. "She's more likely to give a guy her number."

I went into the kitchen to call Devon, and she said she wanted everybody to come over to her house after the game. I told her my mom would only let me go to the J.V. game, but she said they were staying for the varsity game. I can't believe Devon's overprotective mother would let her go to the varsity game, while my mom wouldn't. I went back in my mom's room and flopped on her bed.

"I don't want to leave by myself," I said.

"And I don't want you coming out of the gym alone at night. See if Peyton will go with you," she said, handing me the cell phone.

Peyton was fine with my mom driving us. She said her parents weren't crazy about her staying for the varsity game either.

"I have no idea what to wear to this thing. Can I wear jeans?" she asked. "Because Devon said something about a skirt."

"I'll wear jeans if you do so at least if we look dumb then we'll look dumb together," I said. "I'm going to see if Ashanti wants to come with us, too."

Ashanti said she was in and she was fine with leaving early. I hung up the phone and wondered if going to this game was such a good idea after all. I wanted to see Vladi again, but did I want my friends around when he ignored me?

Twenty-Six

Peyton came over after school to get ready. She did my hair with a big barrel curling iron. Peyton put on the lip gloss she had gotten from Thalia's party, and I started to put on the gloss I bought with Devon when Peyton asked if I still had the one I got from the party. She said the color Thalia picked out for me looked better so I put it on instead.

We picked Ashanti up, and Mom made us promise not to talk to strange boys or drink anything we hadn't bought ourselves. She wanted us to call her right after the J.V. game, and we had to wait inside until we saw her flash her lights three times. She was so embarrassing sometimes. I'm surprised she didn't want me to sit in a car seat and color on the way to the game.

"Did you e-mail Cristian?" Devon asked as soon as she saw us.

I said he never wrote me back. I knew there were a lot of fourteen-year-olds there from the public school because we sometimes got together and had city-wide tournaments and meets, but I still felt like a little kid. For some reason, students from the public school looked way older than the ones from Hillcrest.

Devon made us wait over by the concession stand for Doug. Peyton and I bought some candy, but I wanted to go into the gym to watch Vladi play. Ashanti was getting

bored since we were just standing around, so she told
Devon we were going to watch the game.

"Whatever. India and I are gonna wait for the guys,"
Devon said.

We sat in the front since there were a bunch of loud
older guys sitting on the top of the bleachers. The J.V.
team won their game, and more people started to come
into the gym for the varsity game. I said I wanted to stay
until Vladi came out of the locker room.

"Won't your mom get mad?" Peyton asked.

"I'm texting her, but it'll take her a while to get here,
so we'll be okay," I said.

Vladi came out, and he seemed sort of shy as he
ducked his head whenever somebody yelled out his name.
He made his way through the crowd, and Ashanti pushed
me right into his path. I almost died as he stopped and
looked at me.

"Hey, what's up?" he asked.

"Hi." I felt someone poking me so I said, "You were
great." Seriously, could I get any dumber?

"Thanks," he said. "Are you staying for the varsity
game?" he asked.

Mother, you're ruining my life. Why, why, why are
you so overprotective?

"Because, we're heading over to Ignatowski's Ice
Cream Palace now. You should come," he said as he
walked away to join his friends.

"Oh my. Oh my. Oh. My," Ashanti said.

"Hottest guy I've ever seen," Peyton said.

"Oh, we are so going for ice cream," I said.

We went to tell Devon and India, but they wanted to
stay since Doug had finally shown up. We ran out to the
car before mom even flashed her lights once.

"We've gotta go to Ignatowski's Ice Cream Palace," I
said.

"Why?" she asked as we all piled into the car.

"I never ask for anything, but—"

"Seriously?" Mom said.

"Mo-om. The hottest guy on the planet basically asked us to go," I said.

"Asked *her*," Peyton said. "The rest of us were invisible."

Mom wanted to know how old he was, and we all acted like we had no idea.

"He's tall so it's hard to tell," Ashanti said.

Mom sighed. "So some strange guy—"

"No, I know him. He's a friend," I said, and the girls nodded.

Mom said they had to check with their parents. Peyton's parents were fine with it, and Ashanti's dad said she could go as long as she was home by eleven.

"Eleven? I thought he'd say ten. The old man's getting soft," Ashanti said.

Mom gave me money for all of us and said she'd sit somewhere else. Vladi and his friends were sitting at a table in the center of the restaurant. There weren't many people in the restaurant since the varsity game was still going on. We got our ice cream, and Peyton asked where we should sit. I wasn't sure if we should walk near his table and then act surprised to see him there, but Ashanti pointed out he did tell me I should go there. We didn't have to decide because he waved us over.

I figured Vladi wouldn't remember my name so I tried to think of a way I could work it into the conversation without looking like a total dork. I couldn't come up with any way to bring my name up, but I was surprised how easy he was to talk to. He asked me about my favorite movies, and he was telling me about his dog when his friend said they had to leave.

"I guess I gotta go. See ya, Landry," he said as he got up.

I waited until he had cleared the doorway before I screamed, "He remembered my name!" Ashanti said Vladi and his friends were still standing outside so I should try to control my happy dance a little.

"You should go out there," she said.

"Why?" I asked.

"Remember what I said about guys being freaked out by groups? If you want him to ask for your e-mail, you need to be alone. Just pretend you have to go get something out of the car."

"Get my jacket," Peyton said. "I left it in your mom's car. Get her keys."

I don't know if it was all the sugar I had eaten or if I had just gone insane, but I got the keys and went to get Peyton's coat.

"Hey," Vladi said as I walked over to our car. My nose was starting to run from the cold, and I had to sniff loudly to keep it from running down my face.

"Hi," I said.

"Can I get your e-mail address?" he asked.

I was going to have to buy a whole new journal to record this moment. I found a pen in the glove compartment but no paper. He pulled out the paper ring which had been around his ice cream cone, and I wrote on it. His friends yelled at him to hurry up.

"I gotta go. See ya around," he said as he jogged back to his friends.

"What happened?" Ashanti asked the second I came back.

"First, you are the smartest person in the universe and I'm naming my first born after you," I said.

"Ashanti Yagudin Jr. I like it, but I might change my name if I become famous," she said.

"Ashanti Peyton Yagudin Jr. because it was her jacket that gave me the reason to go out there, which gave him the reason to come over and ask me for my e-mail address," I said.

They freaked out, and Peyton pointed out I had forgotten to bring her jacket inside and she was freezing after eating ice cream. I gave her my coat, and they pumped me for details.

"He asked for my e-mail address, I gave it, and he'll probably never write me," I said.

"Did you get his, too?" Peyton asked.

"No, but I wouldn't write to him first even if he gave it to me."

"He's adorbs. This is major," Ashanti said.

I told Mom when we got in the car. She said he looked cute from where she was sitting and asked how old he was again.

"It won't matter when we're in college," I said.

"Is he eighteen?" she asked. "Because so help me—"

Ashanti said he was definitely not eighteen because they put all the eighteen-year-olds on the varsity team.

"You know, he speaks English well so he's probably lived here for a while," Peyton said.

"I'm going with him if he goes back to Russia," I said.

"I'll go with you. Maybe it's a country full of hot men," Ashanti said.

"I think Mr. Ivanov is from there," Peyton said.

"Maybe he'll grow up and look like the janitor. Mr. Ivanov's pretty hot for an older guy," Ashanti said.

"Mr. Ivanov is cool. He got my locker open when it had gum stuck in it," I said.

"How did you get gum stuck in your locker?" Mom asked.

I shrugged. I figured either Tori or Ericka shoved it in there when they were mad at me, but I never told anybody about it even though I got a tardy in science because it made me late.

I started thinking about what Devon was doing, and I wondered if she and India went somewhere with Doug and Jeremy after the game. They'd probably start double dating and every weekend the four of them would go out and they'd introduce Cristian to Peyton and then they'd be one big happy family. Meanwhile, I'd still be waiting by the computer for Vladi to e-mail me.

I snuggled up with my mouse when I got home. So what if some hot older guy had talked to me? He was never going to ask me out. Mom came in to tell me Devon was on the phone.

"Hey," Devon said.

"I have something to tell—"

"India, shut up! Hold on a sec," she said putting the phone down. "Sorry, she's so hyper. She had two Super Slushies tonight. We just got back. What time did you get home?" she asked.

"I dunno," I said.

"Did you go anywhere afterward?" she asked.

"We stopped at Ignatowski's and—"

"All of you? India — shush," she said. I could hear India laughing in the background.

"Yeah, Vladi said he was going so—"

"The older guy? He asked you to go with him?" she asked.

"Well, he mentioned he was going—"

"So you followed him?" she asked.

"Well, no—"

She put me on hold while she answered her other line. "Gotta let ya go. It's Doug. I'll call you back."

Devon didn't call me until Saturday afternoon, and then she was in a bad mood.

"I can't believe India. She was flirting with Doug on the phone last night," she said.

"India?" I asked.

Devon said India had even let Doug have a sip of her soda at the game. I didn't think it sounded too bad, but I wasn't going to start anything.

"I tried to ignore the drink thing yesterday, but then he called again this morning and asked me for her phone number. What a jerk."

"What did you do?" I asked.

"I said I had to ask her. He's such a loser."

"Does India like him?" I asked.

"She says she doesn't, but you wouldn't know it by the way she acted. Hey, can you come over? Maybe you could spend the night," she said.

Part of me wanted to go, but I didn't feel like spending another weekend sleeping over at someone else's house. I told her my mom wouldn't let me stay overnight, but maybe I could come over for a little while.

"Why won't she let you sleep over?" she asked.

I didn't want to her to know I had slept over at both Tori's and Peyton's houses last weekend, so I made up some excuse about Mom wanting me home tonight. It sounded pretty weak even to me.

"Whatever, hold on, my mom's calling me." She came back to the phone and said her mom had to go to Kalamazoo to pick something up. "I guess I'll go with her since you can't sleep over. E-mail me tomorrow, okay?"

I e-mailed her about Vladi, and the only thing she said when she wrote back was she didn't think he would be interested in a fourteen-year-old.

Twenty-Seven

I made sure to put my bracelet on Monday morning, and Devon had hers on, too. She sat next to Peyton on the bus and I started to sit with India, but Devon gave me a look, so I sat by myself. Thalia asked me what was going on between Devon and India when I got to homeroom.

"It's just like Yasmin and Arianna. One minute they're best friends, but then they hate each other," she said.

At lunch, Devon told me India said I thought I was so cool because Vladi had talked to me. India had also said I thought I was hot because I had been on TV and I was a model, but she thought there were way prettier girls in our class. I didn't know what to say, and Hana looked uncomfortable. It didn't help I was already feeling self-conscious about the fact I hadn't gotten any calls from the modeling agency. India waved to me when I walked into social studies. I had felt bad for her this morning, but now I didn't care what happened to her. She said Peyton had a dentist appointment and wasn't going to be in class.

Mrs. Hearst passed out maps, and we had to color the different countries. There weren't enough colored pencils, so I went over to Tori and Ericka's table. India followed me over. Ericka, Tori, and I joked around, but India didn't say much. India was taking up the colored pencils when Kyle bumped into her, and they went all over the floor. Everybody just walked around her, but I stopped to help her pick the pencils up.

"Thanks," she said.

India sat by herself on the bus, and Devon gave her the silent treatment until Thursday. India told Devon she thought Doug was the world's biggest jerk, and they agreed they were both too good for him. They sat together on the bus and talked the whole way home from school.

However, Devon was mad at her again on Friday because she found out Doug had gotten India's e-mail address. India was whispering something to Peyton when I walked into social studies. You could see India was upset, and she stopped talking as soon as I sat down. Fabulous. I thought about sitting with Tori and Ericka, but then Peyton would think I was mad at her. So I sat with them and tried to ignore India. Peyton called me after school, and I asked if India and Devon were speaking to each other yet.

"I don't know. I'm so sick of it. Anyway, do you want to see a movie tonight?" she asked.

I started to answer when my other line beeped. I put her on hold, and it was Devon asking why I wasn't on the bus. I told her I got a ride from Ashanti's dad, and she asked if I wanted to come over. I pretended I got another call and clicked back over to Peyton.

"It's Devon and she wants me to come over," I said.

"Tell her you're going to the movies. Wait, no. Then she'll want to come, and I need a break from her," she said. "Say you can't, but don't tell her what you're doing."

I went back to Devon and said I had to call her back, but I didn't think I could come over. I didn't want to lie, but I didn't want her to get mad at me either. Peyton was reading off movie times when she got another call.

"Now Devon wants *me* to come over," she said.

I didn't even tell Devon I couldn't come over for sure and she had already invited somebody else over. Why did I have to lie just because I wanted to hang out with Peyton?

"Maybe we should just invite her to go with us," I said.

"Do you want to?" she asked.

No, I wanted some time away from Devon's drama. I was just in a bad mood, period. I was mad at India for talking about me. Plus, I was sick of acting like nothing had ever happened between Ericka, Tori, and me. I wanted to tell them all where to go, but I couldn't because then everybody would get mad at me and I'd be alone again.

I needed a Devon-free night. The only reason Devon had wanted me to come over was because she was mad at India, and now I knew it didn't even have to be me. Anyone would do.

"I don't know what to do," I said. I should have told Devon the truth from the start. Now I'd have to lie to get myself out of it.

"I guess we have to invite her now or we'll hear about it," Peyton said. "And then India will get mad if we don't invite her."

"And she'll hold it against you," I said. "But they'll ignore each other if we invite them both…"

Mom came home and needed to use the phone. I told Peyton I'd call her back, and I asked Mom if she'd drop us off at the theater.

"Do you have money for a movie?" she asked. "Because I didn't get a chance to stop at the bank."

All I had was five bucks. Crap, I couldn't even go to the movies, but mom said Peyton could come over to watch one.

"Can Devon come, too?" I asked.

"I suppose, but make sure it's after dinner because I don't feel like cooking and I have no cash for pizza."

"Any chance I could ask Ashanti?"

"Fine, but no more. I need to finish up some work tonight so I don't want it too loud," she said.

Peyton said her dad could drive her, and Ashanti was going to bring the movie. Devon still wanted me to come over, but she said she'd come. Ashanti brought over *The Hidden Sorority Diaries*, which we had both been dying to see, and Peyton brought some caramel corn her dad made with chocolate chips in it.

"*Terror at the Outlet Mall* is on channel seventy-eight tonight. We have to watch it," Devon said as she walked in.

"Is it super scary? You know how easily I get upset," I said. "I still can't look at the cemetery on Knapp after the movie we watched on my birthday."

"You'll be fine," she said. "It wasn't even scary."

Ashanti raised her eyebrows at me, and I didn't know what to say. We put the movie on, and Devon curled up on the couch while the rest of us sat on the floor. Devon started choking on a piece of caramel corn so I got up to get everybody something to drink, and Ashanti followed me into the kitchen.

"I'm going to lose it. You better keep me away from sharp objects," she said as she filled a glass with ice.

"I'll take the cube with the pointy edges then," I said. I could hear Devon saying something about India in the living room. Peyton crossed her eyes at me when we came back with the sodas.

"Do you have any cherry cola?" Devon asked.

"It's not a restaurant," Ashanti said. Devon raised her eyebrows at me. I shook my head, and she took the glass from me.

The movie was gory, and there was a scene where some dead guy was laying on the taco stand with the color drained out of his face. It reminded me of when my dad told me he had to work on cadavers in medical school. I didn't know what a cadaver was, and he said it was a dead person. I couldn't get the picture out of my mind, and I had to sleep in my parents' room. I remembered I kept poking my mom and dad when they were asleep so they would make a sound or move just so I'd know they were still alive. I just knew this stupid movie was going to give me nightmares.

Ashanti's parents came to pick her up. As soon as I shut the door, Devon started in on her.

"Have you ever noticed how Ashanti thinks she's better than everyone?"

"No she doesn't," I said, and Devon gave me a look. Peyton calls it the "how dare you defy me" look.

"Maybe I should give her my bracelet so you two can be best friends since you like her better than me," Devon said.

She was always hanging the stupid bracelet over me. It was more like a handcuff these days. Of course, I said it wasn't true, and she backed off after I kissed her rear enough. Devon called me the next day, but I didn't answer when I saw her dad's name pop up on the caller ID. I even took off my chat option on my social media page so she couldn't Instant Message me.

I froze my butt off at the bus stop on Monday. It had snowed the night before and the streets were covered, but we still had school. The bus was late, and it crawled up the street. We had to sit in front because our bus driver had picked up some kids from the public school since their bus was stuck in the snow. Ashanti was sitting behind us with some guy, and I had to sit on the end of the seat next to Devon and India. I slid off the seat every time the bus hit a bump. Devon started going through my bag for some gum when she spotted my journal.

"Hey, you finally brought it," she said. I tried to grab it, but she pulled it away from me.

"Why don't you want me to see it? Did you write stuff about me in here?" she asked, narrowing her eyes.

"No, I just... it's private."

"We're best friends," she said. "We're supposed to tell each other everything."

She opened it and I tried to grab it, but India blocked my arm and it was two against one. Ashanti reached over and pulled it away from Devon.

"It's Landry's," she said.

"What's your problem?" Devon said glaring at her. "It's none of your business."

"It *is* my business."

Just then one of the public school kids shot a huge wad of paper at the back of the bus driver's head.

"All right," Mrs. Jackson said. "I want complete silence. Do you hear me? I don't want to see an arm or leg move into the aisle or else I will stop this bus and we will sit here all day if we have to."

I had never heard Mrs. Jackson raise her voice, and I heard some kid swear at her. If anyone from Hillcrest ever said anything like that we'd get suspended. Ashanti and Devon didn't say another word.

We arrived at school, and the hallways were gray and slimy from the snow. Ms. Ashcroft kept yelling, "Wipe your feet, people. Haven't you kids ever heard of boots?"

Mom made me wear my stupid rubber duckies since my cute boots were still wet from the night before. I tugged my pant legs down hoping Mrs. Hearst wouldn't say what a little trouper I was to wear my boots, and everyone would think I was a giant loser. Kyle said, "Nice boots," in math, and I couldn't tell if he was making fun of me so I pretended not to hear him.

Arianna glanced down at my feet and said she used to have a pair like mine. I was glad she didn't say, "Until I got a life and stopped letting my mommy dress me."

We were going to have indoor lunch period because of the snowstorm. I thought it would be okay because I would be in the science room with Devon, Ericka, and

Tori after lunch, but Mrs. Lacey said we had to come back up to her room after we ate. At least Ericka was in this class. Arianna started going on about how hard it would be being apart from Stuart, which was complete crap since they broke up every other day.

"This sucks. I hate having indoor lunch," Devon said on the way to the cafeteria. I nodded, but I used to like hiding out in the library during lunch back when no one was talking to me. Plus, I didn't feel like freezing my butt off outside in the courtyard.

The cafeteria only had cold stuff for lunch, like peanut butter and jelly sandwiches, because the roads were icy. I took a sandwich, but when I unwrapped the foil, I found my sandwich had been made with the last two pieces in the loaf, so it was basically just peanut butter on end pieces with no jelly. I never ate the crust and now I was stuck with an all crust sandwich. Plus, the peanut butter was loose and runny because the cafeteria workers had added milk to it to make more sandwiches.

After lunch, I stopped in the bathroom where Peyton was putting her hair in a ponytail.

"Doesn't this suck? During my lunch hour, the boys tried to throw Thalia's books out the window when Mrs. Tamar wasn't looking," she said. "Hey, what's the matter?"

I told her Devon tried to read my journal on the bus.

"She's PMS-ing so bad today," she said. "What did you do?"

"Ashanti got it back, but Devon acted kinda weird at lunch."

"Silent treatment?" she asked.

"No, but... I dunno. She was just different."

"Did Mr. Hotness e-mail you yet?" she asked. I shook my head. "I'd stay, but Mrs. Tamar will get her panties in a knot if I don't get back to class," she said.

I washed the peanut butter off my hands, and I saw a flash off silver when I went to turn on the hand dryer.

My best friend bracelet had fallen off and gone into the vent. There was no way I could reach into the vent to get it. Ericka came into the bathroom and said I better get back to the room or Mrs. Lacey would get mad.

"My bracelet fell down the vent," I said, and she came over to see.

"Go tell Mr. Ivanov. Maybe he can get it out for you," she said. I started to head towards the janitor's closet, but she grabbed my arm. "We have to go back to the room. You can get it later."

We went back to class, and Mrs. Lacey was grading papers. I don't think she noticed or cared whether or not I was in the room. Ericka probably said that because she didn't want to be in there by herself. Devon asked me what happened to my bracelet when I got to science class. I told her it fell into the vent, and she asked what I was going to do about it.

"I'll talk to Mr. Ivanov after school."

"If it's still there," she said.

Not unless the vent fairy took it. Mrs. Tamar handed back our science quizzes and I tried to slip mine under my book, but Devon made me tell her what I got. I showed her my C.

"Ha, beat you. C+."

I would have thought she was kidding, but she acted like she thought she did a lot better on the quiz.

It was still snowing when I went to the bus line. Devon ran up and asked if I had gotten the bracelet back.

"I'll do it tomorrow," I said. "I don't want to miss the bus."

"You better get it today," she said.

"But my mom will be mad if I have to call her for a ride," I said.

She gave me an icy look, and I went to find Mr. Ivanov. I figured I might have enough time to tell him and still make it to the bus. I ended up having to run to the first and second grade hall to find him. He was finishing up a sandwich and wiped his hands on his overalls. I could hear the buses running outside, and I told him I had to catch the bus.

"We'll have to take this off the wall," he said, running his hand over the vent. "Don't have tools for it now, but I'll see what I can do."

I thanked him and ran to the bus line. The buses had started to pull away, but I could still see mine. I ran faster as my backpack thumped against my back.

"Wait," I yelled, pumping my legs harder. I chased it all the way to the corner, but it never stopped. I stood there panting and almost started to cry. My mom was in a meeting so I had to leave her a message. I felt stupid sitting in the office so I waited inside the double doors. She picked me up forty-five minutes later.

"Why did you miss the bus? You know I hate driving in this weather," she said glancing over at me. "What's the matter?"

"Nothing."

My throat was tight and hot, and I didn't want to start crying again. I went straight to my room, and I curled up on my bed until Mom called me for dinner. I called Devon after I ate, but her mom was on the other line. I tried calling Tori, but she was still eating so I went back to my room and fell asleep in my school clothes.

Twenty-Eight

School was canceled the next day because of the snow, and Mom decided to go into work late. We had chocolate chip waffles with whipped cream for breakfast, and I watched talk shows until Peyton called. She asked if I had talked to Mom about my dad yet. I told her what Mom said during breakfast about hoping he'd be able to move in before spring.

"Cool. Have you written any new stuff lately?" she asked.

I told her about a story I started in science class last week when Devon was ignoring me. It was about an alien, which was weird because I never wrote science fiction-y stuff.

"What happens?" she asked.

"It's about this alien who comes to earth and pretends to be human, but she can't fit in. It sounds stupid, I know," I said.

"No, I want to read it when you're done," she said.

I almost never let my friends read my stuff because I had read part of a story to Tori last summer. She had seemed bored and all she said when I got done was it didn't sound like it was finished. I reminded her it was just the beginning, but she acted like it wasn't any good. It hurt my feelings and I never showed her any more of my writing.

I was hoping for another snow day the next day, but some moron decided the roads were clear enough for us to go to school. However, they weren't decent enough for the bus to be on time. Tori and I were the only two idiots waiting for the bus, and I could see Mrs. Abrams's car running in their driveway. I could have walked over to see if she would give me a ride, but I was afraid to ask. I watched Mrs. Abrams back out of the driveway and hoped they would turn right and come pick Tori and me up, but they drove off without looking back. Tori and I got to school late, and I walked in with a bright red face and my hair sticking up because I had put my scarf around my head. I tried licking my hand to pat my hair down, but it didn't help.

Later, as I was going to lunch, Mr. Ivanov came up to me. "I got your bracelet back. It was stuck down there good," he said.

I followed him to the janitor's closet. I had never been in there before, and it was filled with all kinds of overhead machines and stuff. He picked up an envelope off the table.

"The clasp seemed loose so I tightened it. It shouldn't fall off your arm now," he said.

I slid it on.

"I can take off some of those links to make it tighter," he said. He took a pair of pliers, removed three of the links, and then put it back together.

"Thanks, Mr. Ivanov," I said. I went to the lunchroom and got a slice of pizza and a drink box. Devon was already sitting with Hana, and I showed her I got my bracelet back. She didn't say much. She just picked the pepperoni off her pizza.

"Guess what? I got an eighty-three percent on my math quiz," I said. "Ashanti's been helping me. Can you believe it?"

"Great," she said. She didn't sound too excited.

"What's wrong?" I asked. She shrugged and leaned on her arm.

Later, when I saw her in science class, Devon seemed interested in her paperback. She'd answer me if I asked her a question, but we didn't have a conversation. Still, she was talking to me, so I was happy. Mrs. Tamar wanted us to do the chapter questions, and Devon opened up her textbook.

"Did you see Halle's makeup today?" I asked. "It looks like her mascara smeared—"

"What did you get for number one?" she asked.

"Oh, I didn't do it yet. Anyway, Kyle was flirting with Arianna in math. I bet Yasmin will dump him again," I said.

"Don't care. Is it five?" she asked.

"Huh?"

She sighed and blew her bangs up. "Is five the answer to number one?" she asked.

"I guess. What's wrong?" I asked.

"Nothing. Can't you give it a rest?" she said.

"Are you mad at me?"

"No, but I'm gonna be if we don't finish this and I have to take it home," she said.

I couldn't focus on any of the questions. I just flipped back and forth in my book like I was trying to find the answers. I tried to pull my bracelet off because it was pinching me. I was used to it being loose, but now it was almost too tight since Mr. Ivanov had fixed it.

I called Peyton after school to see if she knew why Devon was acting weird.

"India told me Devon thought you were bragging about getting an A on your math quiz when she found out she's getting a D in math," she said.

"What? First of all, I haven't gotten an A in math since the third grade, and I didn't know she was getting a D. Why didn't she just tell me?" I stopped to catch my breath.

"Don't worry about it. Devon's always mad about something. And I don't think she's over not getting picked for the next round of the *American Ingénue* thing. Hey, did you see Vladi's picture in the paper? It's in tonight's sports section. He's moving to the varsity team," she said.

I told her we didn't get the paper delivered, so she said she'd bring it for me. I took my bracelet off and threw it toward my dresser. I missed, and it fell on the floor. I thought about calling Devon to apologize, but for what? Getting an eighty-three percent wasn't exactly bragging, and I didn't know she was getting a D in math. I just hope she didn't hold the *Ingénue* contest against me.

I missed the bus the next morning, and Mom had to drive me to school. I could tell my day was going to suck the second I saw India at Devon's locker. They were standing two inches apart and stared at me when I walked down the hall. I tried to smile, but I had no control over my facial muscles so I think I just twitched or something.

"Hi," I said.

"Hey," Devon said.

India stood up straighter like she was Devon's bodyguard and gave her a knowing look. That's the thanks I got for helping her pick up those stupid colored pencils she dropped. I should have stepped on her hand while she was down there.

"Oh, I'm so sorry. Did I get your hand with my shoe?" I'd say, and then I'd find a way to "accidentally" cut off about two feet of her hair. I hated the way India always wrote down her hair color as "honey." It was light brown, maybe dark blond. Honey. Maybe bees would attack her.

Peyton told me later Devon thought I was throwing my "Croatian boyfriend" in her face. First of all, he was Russian, and second, she always talked about Doug and I never got upset over it. Peyton said I shouldn't let it bother me, but it's easy to say when no one is mad at you. I decided to confront Devon when we got off the bus, so no one would see me grovel. I told Devon I was sorry, and I would never try to make her feel bad. I ended up saying Vladi would never like me and how I just got lucky on the quiz because I sucked at math. She said it was okay and gave me a hug. We were friends again, but I still felt like crap. Ashanti thought I was crazy for kissing Devon's butt.

"What did you do? Promise you'd never do better than her on a test as long as you lived?" she asked. "And did she expect you to walk away from the *American Ingénue* thing just because she didn't make it?"

"No, I'm just glad she's speaking to me again."

Peyton was also surprised when I told her I apologized to Devon.

"For what? You didn't do anything wrong," she said. "You've gotta stand up for yourself."

I'd rather have everybody like me than to prove something. Peyton asked if I wanted to do something this weekend, and we made plans to go to a movie on Friday. I was happy I had plans for the weekend, but it was kinda depressing knowing the modeling agency hadn't called with any jobs for me. At this rate, I'd never get famous.

Twenty-Nine

India was the only one sitting in the back of the bus the next morning. I sat behind her, and she slid around to talk to me.

"Hi," India said. "Did you read for class?"

I nodded. She was acting like nothing had happened, which annoyed me. Like I didn't know she and Devon had been talking about me. I'm sure she encouraged Devon to get mad at me so they could be best friends again.

"Want some gum?" she held out a pack. I took a piece and stuffed it into my mouth. "It's so cold today," she said. I didn't say anything. "Uh, it's weird it's so cold because it's all sunny outside."

"Yup," I said looking straight ahead.

She didn't say anything else until we got to school. I headed to my locker and pretended not to hear her say goodbye. Ashanti came over and asked if I would sit with her at lunch since Halle and Maggie were absent. I said she could sit at our table, and she made a face.

"No offense, but I don't want to sit with Devon," she said. "Is she going to get her panties in a bunch if you sit with me?" she asked.

I said it would be okay, but Devon started to get an attitude when I said I was sitting with Ashanti.

"I need to talk to her about a math test," I said. "My mom will kill me if I don't keep my grades up."

"Whatever. If you have to."

Later, Devon asked what we were doing this weekend, and I squirmed in my chair and said I was going to the movies with Peyton.

"I wonder why she didn't mention it to me," she said as she colored in the spleen on our worksheet. "I thought we'd all go to the mall."

I didn't say anything, but Peyton asked me why Devon suddenly thought we should all go to the mall instead of the movies.

"I told her I was going to a movie with you," I said. "And she sorta got the idea she was invited, too," I said. Peyton rolled her eyes. "What could I do?" I asked. "Say, 'Sorry, you can't come?'"

"Do you want her to?" she asked.

"No, I just wanted to go to the movies and not have drama."

"And I don't want to go shopping," she said. "All she ever wants to do is walk around and look for guys," Peyton cut off when India walked into class.

"So we're going to the mall tonight?" India asked. Peyton shrugged and later asked me what I wanted to do when we were walking out of class.

"I don't want anybody to get mad—"

"No, what do *you* want to do tonight?" she asked. I said I'd rather go to a movie.

Devon asked what time we were meeting at the mall when we got on the bus, and Peyton cleared her throat.

"Um, Landry and I kind of want to see a movie. So I guess we'll… sit this one out," she said.

Devon zeroed in on me. "You don't want to go with us?" she asked.

"Peyton asked me about going to a movie first, and I already said I'd go with her," I said.

"Fine, whatever," she said. She and India planned what they were going to wear. I felt a little left out, but at the same time I had stood up to her. Well, kinda.

Mom dropped us off at the theater, and we loaded up on popcorn, licorice, chocolate bars, and sodas. The best thing about going to a movie with Peyton was you could just pig out and have fun. I loved being able to relax and be myself. She didn't even get grossed out when I got popcorn stuck in my teeth. She took a piece of licorice and bit off each end to use as a straw and I tried it, too. When the movie ended, we went into the mall to check out the bookstore.

"Landry, they have the new Skylar Halston book. And they have number nine in the series. I don't have this one," she said.

"I'm missing number ten."

We took our books and went over to the magazine rack. She grabbed a bunch of magazines, and we went over to the café to get a soda and look through them.

"Those people over there are about to get off the couch," she said. "Grab your stuff." We flew over to the couch the second the couple got up. I had never gotten the couch at this bookstore. I was always stuck at the wobbly tables and uncomfortable chairs. Why someone would use spiky wood on a chair back was beyond me.

After we bought our books, she asked if I wanted to walk around before she called her mom. We went into Connick's Boutique, and she found a pair of earrings she wanted. I don't have my ears pierced because my dad says he gets a million people coming into the clinic with infections from piercings. The man knows how to scare a person when it comes to medical stuff.

I walked over to look at the rings, and they had a pretty one with red, yellow, and blue enamel in it. I slipped it on my finger, and it was a perfect fit. Usually rings slide right off me because I'm thin, which is why I lost my bracelet in the vent. I decided to get it, and Peyton said it was pretty. I said there was another one if Peyton wanted to try it on.

"I don't want to copy you," she said.

"It's okay, try it," I said.

She put it on, and the colors were different on her. She decided to buy the ring instead of the earrings, and we went to meet her mom.

"Your father's going to throw a fit," Mrs. Urich said pointing to the dog carrier on the front seat. "But look at her little face." We peered in and saw a brown puppy. "I went to the pound with your Aunt Rita, and I swear this puppy asked me to take her home with me," she said. "Her name is Bambi."

"She's so cute," I said.

"Landry, do you want to come over, or do you need to get home?" Mrs. Urich asked.

I went over to their house and Mr. Urich was okay with having another dog, but Truffles didn't seem to like her too much. We took Bambi up to Peyton's room, and she flew under the bed. Peyton had to get on her hands and knees to get the dog to come out. She pulled Bambi onto her lap and told me she thought she was getting a new tablet for Christmas.

"Are you going to Chicago for Christmas?" she asked.

"Yeah and we're going to go shopping before Christmas so I can pick out my presents," I said.

"See, I like to know what I'm getting, but I also want at least one surprise," she said.

Bambi tried to walk on the bed. I'm usually a little nervous around animals, but I picked her up. I could feel Bambi trembling so I held her close, and she seemed to relax.

"I love going to the big toy stores when I'm there," I said. "I know I'm too old to ask for toys, but sometimes I want them anyway."

"Oh, I know. I got a Cadia doll for my birthday last year and India thought it was weird I wanted a doll, but I love Cadia," she said.

"She is cute."

Truffles ran in the room, and Bambi shot out of my lap. Peyton grabbed her before she flew off the bed.

"Stop it. No, Truffles — stop! Mom! The dog's panicking."

Mrs. Urich came upstairs and picked up Truffles. "You don't like the competition, do ya?" Mrs. Urich said, nuzzling her.

"Do you want to exchange gifts?" she asked after her mom left.

I nodded. Last year I had bought books for Tori and Ericka, and I knew Ericka didn't like the one I gave her. I wondered if they were expecting gifts this year. We hadn't talked about it, but I'd probably at least get Tori something. Ashanti and I were exchanging gifts and Devon and I decided to get each other new journals, but we were calling them Christmukkah gifts since her family celebrated both Christmas and Hanukkah.

I checked my e-mail when I got home. Most of the messages were junk, but there was one which just said "Hi," in the subject line. I figured it was either a sneaky way to get you to open it and then it'd be the address to a porn link or something, but I opened it anyway.

To: Albright@ alphamail.com
From: VY0062@us.com
Re: Hi
Hi Landry,
How are you? Is school good? Are you coming to our game? I'm on varsity now, so it's the later game if you want to come.
See ya,
Vladi

He e-mailed me. About time. I didn't know what to write so I called Ashanti, and she told me to forward his message to her. She called back and said it sounded like he wanted to see me again.

"But what if he had to get a bunch of people to come to the game because the ticket money is going to feed starving puppies or something?" I asked.

"I doubt it, but even if it was true, he still thought of you," she said. "What are you going to say?"

"I have no clue. Any ideas?" I asked.

"I would wait a little bit before I wrote him back but not too long," she said.

She asked me about Cristian, and I told her he never e-mailed me back. Then she asked if Vladi made my stomach hurt.

"No, I can't stop smiling when I think about him," I said. "Will you go to the game with me?"

"Definitely," she said. "Ugh, my mom wants me to get off the phone, but let me know what you decide to write."

Thirty

Thursday was the last day of school before winter break. Tori and I exchanged gifts at the bus stop. We both got each other the new Skylar Halston book. I had brought a big chocolate Santa in case Ericka had something for me, but she didn't give me anything on the bus. I always bring a couple of extra cards and some candy canes to school just in case somebody has a gift or a card for me, which I wasn't expecting, but I always end up bringing them all back home.

Thalia gave me a Christmas card and a stuffed snowman in homeroom, so I gave her the chocolate Santa. Mrs. Lacey let us sit wherever we wanted in math class, and Kyle moved to our table. He gave Arianna and me root beer flavored candy canes. Arianna ate hers, but I wanted to keep mine. I thought Kyle was kind of a jerk, but part of me still liked him so I gave him one of my candy canes just as Ericka walked into the room.

"Um, we can sit wherever we want," I said.

"Move over by me," Ericka said.

I wanted to sit with Kyle, but I couldn't tell her, so I got up.

"Wait, I have something for you," Arianna said. "I almost forgot."

She handed me an envelope with my name in big curly red letters and a marshmallow candy cane taped to it. I opened it up, and inside she had written she hoped I had a great vacation. I gave her one of my cards and a candy cane before I moved to Ericka's table. Arianna hadn't given the marshmallow candy canes to everyone, so I felt kinda special.

Ashanti and I exchanged gifts at lunch. She gave me a DVD of *Jane Eyre,* and I gave her a subscription to *Soap Opera Hotties* magazine since I knew hers was expiring. Maggie and Halle brought their gifts for Ashanti to lunch, and I felt uncomfortable so I said I was going to talk to Devon and Hana. Maggie handed me a card with a cherry candy cane, so I gave her and Halle cards and candy canes before I went to see Devon and Hana. Hana and I had decided to exchange gifts, and she gave me a little stocking filled with different flavors of lip gloss and I had gotten her some cute notepads because she loves paper stuff. Devon unwrapped the purple journal I gave her, and she gave me one with a red and pink suede cover. I asked her if she wanted to go to the basketball game with Ashanti, Peyton, and me, but she and India were planning to go to the mall tonight.

"But we'll definitely get together when you get back from Chicago," she said. "Maybe you can spend the night."

I wrote out a card for India in history. I had already put her gift in the locker she shared with Devon. I realized I hadn't given Ericka a card yet, and I reached into my bag to get one. I pulled out the box, but it was empty. I've never run out of my backup cards before. Last year I only exchanged presents with Tori and Ericka, but this year I had gotten to know more people because of the fight. Ericka came over to my desk with a card for me.

"I kept forgetting to give this to you," she said. I felt stupid because I didn't have anything for her. "How come you got so much stuff?" she asked, looking at the gift bags next to me.

I shrugged and noticed she only had one gift bag by her seat. India came in wearing the pink and black star earrings I had given her.

"These are so cute," she said. "Open yours."

Ericka watched as I opened up a baby blue picture frame. India had put in a picture of the four of us. It was the one Peyton's dad had taken the night of the field trip. Ericka raised her eyebrow, but didn't say anything. She had only given me a card so I didn't owe her a gift, but I still felt uncomfortable. India asked if I was going to the mall with them, but I told her Peyton and I were going to the game with Ashanti.

"Sounds like fun. We're supposed to meet up with Doug and Jeremy at the mall. I'm probably not allowed to talk to Doug though," she said rolling her eyes. "Don't tell Devon what I said, okay?"

Mrs. Hearst put a movie on for us, but nobody paid attention to it. Normally, she'd bark at us for being "disorderly," but she didn't seem to care today. India leaned over and told us how Tad had given presents to all the teachers.

"How pathetic," she said, rolling her eyes.

I didn't say anything, but my mom had bought me some holiday towels to give to Mrs. Kharrazi since she had encouraged me with my writing. I left them in my locker when I went to her class earlier, but now I was glad I hadn't given them to her in front of everybody. I ended up dropping them off in her mailbox in the office after the final bell rang. As I was going out to the bus line, Thalia ran up to thank me again for the chocolate Santa.

"A bunch of us are going to the basketball game tomorrow night," I said. "Do you want to go with us?"

"Sounds great. I can meet you there," she said. "I'm dying to see what Vladi looks like."

Peyton came over after dinner to exchange presents. She gave me an enamel bracelet, which matched the ring we both had.

"I love the colors. It's perfect," I said.

I gave her a Skylar Halston biography and the earrings she liked from Connick's.

"I wanted this book, and you know I love the earrings. I'll wear them to the game," she said.

"I am so nervous about going," I said. "What if Vladi was just asking to be polite and when he sees me he's like, 'I didn't actually care if you came, stupid little girl'," I said.

"You do the accent quite well," she said, and I hit her with a pillow. "Landry, he won't. Did he e-mail you back when you told him you were coming?"

"No, because he doesn't care. He probably just needed someone to watch his girlfriend's purse while they go make out," I said.

"Nah, she could just take her purse with her," she said.

"Oh, thanks a lot."

"I'm kidding," she said.

She asked me what I was going to wear tomorrow, and I shrugged. She went to my closet and pulled out my yellow Franciszka T shirt, but I said there was a stain on it.

"Sick, what is it?" she asked.

"Chocolate... blood? I got it at the movie theater so I'm hoping it's chocolate," I said. "I keep hoping it'll come out because I spent a lot on it."

"Ew. How about this one?" she asked as she pulled out the light blue sweater my grandma had given me.

"I wondered what happened to it." I put it in front of me, and she said it would look good on me.

"But does it look like a Hillcrest sweater?" I asked. "I don't need to remind him I'm a sheltered private school girl."

"It's perfect," she said. "Is Tori coming with us tomorrow?"

"No, but Thalia's going to meet us there," I said. "When did going to the game seem like a good idea?"

"It'll be fun," she said. "I bet Vladi's counting down the minutes until he sees you again."

"Yeah, right. He probably found my e-mail address in his pocket and confused me with some hot girl who had given him her e-mail address," I said. "He's expecting some tall, gorgeous blonde to show up, and instead, he'll find me."

"You are a tall, gorgeous blonde," she said.

Thirty-One

I couldn't eat before the basketball game, and I went to the bathroom six times. Mr. Urich picked Ashanti and me up, but I wished my mom had driven us because I didn't want to puke in the Urich's car. Thalia met up with us, and the four of us stood in the doorway trying to find a place to sit.

"There's Tad's mom," Thalia said. "Let's sit in front of her."

Tad's mom started to ask us something, but I missed it because all I heard was the girl who was sitting in front of me say she couldn't wait to meet up with Vladi after the game. I couldn't get mad at him because, *A*, this girl was definitely an upperclassman; *B*, he never said he didn't have a girlfriend; and *C*, I hadn't asked the ticket people if the money was going for starving puppies. Why would I think Vladi might like me? I was just a stupid kid with bad hair. I said I was going to the bathroom, and Peyton came after me.

"I am so stupid," I said. "She's gorgeous. She could do a shampoo commercial."

"So what?" Peyton said. "You don't even know if she's his girlfriend."

She convinced me to go back to watch the game, and I found out the girl's name was Carey. It was so annoying the way she cheered every time Vladi touched the ball. She fluffed her wavy dark hair a million times, and it kept getting in my face. I wanted to call my mom when the game ended, but Ashanti said we should wait in the hall and let Vladi see I showed up.

"He's not going to care. I'll look like a groupie or something, and I don't want to see Carey all over him," I said.

"But then you'll know for sure," Thalia said.

"I could be happy not knowing," I said.

Vladi came out of the locker room, and Carey and her friend moved in on him. The three of them walked past us without even looking in our direction. I tried calling my mom, but the cell phone wasn't working, so I had to go outside to get a signal. Vladi was out there talking to Carey. Peyton said I should walk by and say, "Hi," but I just wanted to go home.

"Hey Landry, you came."

I saw Vladi was calling me over. "We're going for ice cream. You want to come?" he asked.

My brain and mouth weren't working together and I said, "We don't have a ride." How stupid, we could have walked. I am so dumb.

"We can give you a ride," he said.

My mother has lectured me about not getting into cars with strangers since I was four, yet I got into this guy Steve's car. Carey didn't go with us because her friend was able to drive there. Meanwhile, the four of us were so crammed into the tiny backseat that I lost all feeling in my right leg. Steve wasn't the worst driver I had ridden with if you counted the half-crazed taxi driver who almost killed Mom and me last summer. We got to Ignatowski's Ice Cream Palace alive, and I swore I would never drive with anyone I didn't know again.

I ordered a large caramel sundae and noticed Carey and her friend had only ordered diet sodas. You could tell Steve liked Carey, but she didn't seem to notice. Vladi and I talked about school, but Carey kept interrupting us. I felt so out of place next to her and her friend. I wanted to stay and talk to Vladi, but part of me just wanted to get out of there. I knew Carey was judging me, and it was pretty obvious she didn't think I was good enough for Vladi. As soon as she and her friend got up to go to the restroom, I got up, too.

"Are you leaving?" Vladi asked me.

"I should call my mom." Why couldn't I stop saying stupid stuff?

"We have to go, um... wash our hands," Ashanti said grabbing Thalia's arm. Peyton got up and followed them.

"I'm glad you came," he said.

"Oh, yeah. Me too," I said as I sat back down.

"I was kind of nervous playing in my first varsity game." He rolled his eyes.

"You were great," I said. Carey was now standing by the door. "I think she's waiting for you," I said.

"She's got a ride home," he said.

"Isn't she your girlfriend?" Even saying the word was like a knife through my gut.

"No, Steve likes her, but I don't think she likes him too much," he said.

"Vladi, we're going," Carey said.

"Okay. Bye," he said without turning around.

"Aren't you coming?" Carey sounded just like Ericka when she was annoyed.

"No, I'm going to hang out a while and finish my ice cream," he said. Steve offered to walk the girls to their car.

"Whatever," she said and Steve walked out behind them.

"What are you doing for Christmas?" he asked. I told him I was going to Chicago to see my dad, and he said his grandpa was coming to visit. Steve came back just as Peyton, Ashanti, and Thalia returned from the bathroom.

"Struck out," Steve said.

"She's not worth it," Vladi said.

"Easy for you to say," Steve said. "She likes you."

"Until she finds out I'm only fifteen and won't be able to drive anytime soon," Vladi said.

Thalia kicked me under the table.

"Landry, will you e-mail me from Chicago?" he asked.

"Yeah, I can use my dad's laptop," I said.

"Good. Can I get your number so we can text, too?"

Steve offered to take us home, but I wasn't going to risk it again so I called Mom and the guys waited with us until she showed up. I didn't think things could get any better, but then Vladi stopped me as we were walking out. He reminded me to e-mail him, and then he put his arms around my shoulders and gave me a hug. A hug. Like it was a normal thing to do. I managed to put my arms up and keep the screaming inside until I got in the car. Mom thought I was insane.

"He's fifteen," I said. "We're just a year apart, and Dad says I'm mature for my age."

"If only your father was," Mom said.

We took Thalia, Peyton, and Ashanti home. They were all happy for me, and Thalia wanted me to ask Vladi about Steve when I e-mailed him because she thought he was hot.

When we got home, Delilah had left a message on our answering machine about the stain removal commercial. It was supposed to air tomorrow morning on channel seventy-eight at nine o'clock. I couldn't wait to see it. Unfortunately, there was also a message from Grandma reminding us to bring a tape of the *Ingénue* competition with us when we came for Christmas.

"Lucy and Bryan will want to see it," Grandma said.

Not gonna happen. I would bring over my commercial tape though… unless the director used the footage where the sauce splattered in my face. I still e-mailed a bunch of my friends about the commercial, but not Devon, India, Ericka, or Tori. I didn't want to rub it in Dev-

on's face or have her hear about it from India, and I
didn't need Ericka and Tori to get mad again.

The next morning, I finished packing for Chicago
while my mom watched TV, looking for me. She was recording it on the DVR so we wouldn't miss the commercial, but I kept checking it to make sure we didn't have
too much stuff saved so it'd turn off or get deleted. I was
super paranoid I'd miss it. It came on, and there I was at
the picnic table looking all happy in my white Capri
pants. Then the jerk dumped the sauce on me. Mom said
I was "precious," which was exactly the problem. I ap-
peared about twelve years old. Still, at least I was in a
commercial. I didn't have any other jobs lined up, but
Delilah had said the spring fashion shows would be coming up soon. She said Kasia from Wee Fashions was interested in having me pose for some store advertise-
ments, which would be cool. It wasn't exactly
TeenDream, but what were ya gonna do?

Before we left I got a bunch of e-mails about the
commercial from Ashanti, Peyton, Hana, and Thalia. I
started to wonder if Vladi might have heard about the
competition and maybe that was the only reason he was
interested in me, so I wrote him a quick e-mail about the
commercial just to see what he'd say. He was online and
instant messaged me saying he didn't know I was doing
commercials and stuff. He seemed surprised, and I realized he had no clue I was ever on the show.

Mom and I boarded the train to Chicago at eleven. I
finished reading *Jane Eyre* while on the train, so I
leaned back in my seat and watched the houses roll by. I
asked Mom if we could drive to Chicago next time so we
could bring some of Dad's stuff back with us.

"I, uh, don't think your Dad's been actively looking
for a position—"

"So he's not moving in with us? Great." I slumped in
my seat. "Why are we even bothering to go there now? I
can't believe this."

She told me to calm down and said she had put Dad on hold because there was a chance she might be changing companies soon.

"So?"

"So your Dad would have to relocate twice then and—"

I sat up. "We'd move? What are you talking about? We can't move."

She said she had been talking to a company in Battle Creek. My mouth dropped open, and she said it was only about an hour and a half away.

"Then you can drive there and back every day," I said.

She gave me the "settle down" look and said nothing had been decided yet.

"It was just an offer."

"Yeah, an offer which could ruin my life. Do you know how hard it is to move right before high school? I have my friends here, and what about the modeling agency?"

This time I got the "end of discussion" look. "Nothing will probably even come from it, okay? I like where I am right now, so calm down. You're just like your father. Always overreacting like the sky's falling in."

I could have said telling someone their life was about to end was a pretty good reason to freak out, but I didn't want to start anything since we were going shopping for my presents tomorrow.

"Oh, your magazine came in the mail this morning," she said, pulling the new issue of *Young and Fun* out of her tote bag.

Talisa was on the cover with some other girls looking gorgeous as usual. I tried to relax as I read the article where she talked about her early days in modeling before the *American Ingénue* competition. She said she was taking online classes to get her business degree.

"I want to be able to read my own contracts and not rely on someone else telling me what they say," Talisa said. "You need to look at modeling as a business — a real career, and you always need a backup plan for the future. It looks like fun and glamour, but it's hard work. Even on my days off I'm always working toward a goal. I read all the time, too. Sometimes for fun and sometimes to learn. I don't want to be a stereotypical model. I worked hard to get where I am today."

She also talked about how many years she tried to get work in the industry. I didn't even realize she had struggled to get noticed as a model for so long. I thought her success had pretty much come overnight with the show. No wonder she had gone farther than the rest of the contestants.

"Before *Ingénue*, I was so happy to get any job," she said. "I did kiddie fashion shows where I was almost two feet taller than the other girls. You never know when your big break will come. But in the last month I've learned you can't neglect your family and friends for your career. I used to think I would get famous and leave all those girls who were mean to me in school behind, but you have to focus on the positive and not let all the other stuff bother you."

I was surprised to read even Talisa had problems. And she had issues with her forehead breaking out. I guess she was human after all. I put the magazine down and started to think about the competition. Maybe I would let Grandma see my commercial, but not the competition. No one would ever see it if I had my way.

"I won't make a decision until at least after New Year's," Mom said. "I do like that you seem settled at school. It's a big decision."

She looked unsure, and I relaxed. It didn't sound like she was leaning toward moving. I just had to convince her to stay in Grand Rapids. For now, all I wanted to do was to get to Chicago, see my dad, sleep in my old bedroom, and e-mail Peyton, Ashanti, Thalia, and Vladi.

I used to get nervous when I would go to Chicago for winter or spring break and I'd have to be away from Ericka and Tori for so long. I was always afraid I'd come back and they would have decided to be best friends without me or something. My biggest fear was getting back to school and being left out. But things were different now. I had other friends besides the two of them, and this time I felt like I had true friends I could count on. No matter what, Ashanti, Peyton, and Thalia would always be there for me. Plus, things were getting better between Devon and me. And now I had my modeling stuff to focus on, too. Maybe things weren't perfect, but for the first time in my life, I was looking forward to going back to school after vacation. I just had to convince my mom to stay in Grand Rapids, and my life would practically be perfect. Well, except for the fact the guy who played Colin on *As the Days Roll On* wasn't my boyfriend, but it seemed like I might have a guy in the running to be my real boyfriend. Sure, I didn't have any music video auditions lined up, but I could work on it. The future was looking bright right now.

About the Author

~~~~~~

Krysten Lindsay Hager is a writer and journalist from Michigan and has lived in South Dakota and Portugal. She currently resides in the Dayton, Ohio area with her husband. You can find her at:

http://krystenlindsay.blogspot.com/